11|07
SS

MEANS TO
AN END

Other books by Michael Hachey:

A Matter of Motive

MEANS TO
AN END

•

Michael Hachey

AVALON BOOKS
NEW YORK

Published by Thomas Bouregy & Co., Inc.
160 Madison Avenue, New York, NY 10016

Library of Congress Cataloging-in-Publication Data

Hachey, Michael.
    Means to an end / Michael Hachey.
        p. cm.
    ISBN 978-0-8034-9868-6 (acid-free paper)
    1. Police—Wisconsin—Fiction. 2. Wisconsin—Fiction. I. Title.

    PS3608.A246M43 2007
    813'.6—dc22

                                                            2007024156

PRINTED IN THE UNITED STATES OF AMERICA
ON ACID-FREE PAPER
BY HADDON CRAFTSMEN, BLOOMSBURG, PENNSYLVANIA

For Pat Chapman

Special thanks to: Tony and Sally Manzara, Lori Meyer, Jessica Rapbbeke, Leroy Buck, Bob Klanderman, my editor, Cynthia Chapin, and most of all Kathie Hachey.

Chapter One

Friday

The Doberman was a silent missile sprinting smoothly over the dark grass. Muscles working, head steady, it disappeared and reappeared in the patches of moonlight that filtered down through the trees dotting the manicured grounds of the Wallace Pearle estate. Veering neither left nor right, the animal homed in on the man standing just outside the eight-foot steel fence, three hundred feet away. The only sounds disturbing the 2:00 A.M. calm were the dog's rhythmic, athletic breathing and the soft, urgent cadence of its paws on the grass. The professionally trained dog didn't waste its energy barking; barking was for show. When it reached the fence, it pulled up short and froze, staring. A few feet away, on the other side of the steel barrier and partially obscured by lilac bushes in full, fragrant bloom, the man stared back. The Doberman was patient; it could wait all night if it had to. But it didn't have to.

In the moonlight, the man could tell that the dog was a female. "You look hungry, girl." The Doberman's ears pricked up at the soothing sound of the man's voice. "You look like you could use a good meal."

1

The T-bone steak landed on the grass with a soft thud two feet in front of the dog. The dog looked at it for a second and then returned its gaze to its quarry. After a few seconds its nose twitched, and it glanced down at the steak again and then away. The man waited, motionless, while the dog repeated the gesture several times, its head bobbing in homage to the aroma. Finally it stepped forward and reached down, grabbing the steak in its jaws. It backed away several feet, where it settled to the ground and began eating the meat, its eyes locked on the man outside the fence.

In three minutes it devoured the one-pound steak and began gnawing on the bone. Ten minutes later its large head began to droop. Only when the Doberman was completely still and had been snoring lightly for several minutes did the man emerge from behind the bushes. He was of average height and solidly built, with close-cropped, silver gray hair and a mole, prominently placed, high on his left cheek—what the police would refer to as an identifying characteristic.

He put on a black watch cap and black gloves to match the black pants and shirt he wore, then tossed a rope ladder over the steel fence. In a matter of seconds he was standing next to the dog. He produced a leather muzzle from his clothing and placed it on the dog's head, gently cinching it tight. He wasn't interested in punishing the dog, but he had to take into account possible variations in the effects of the barbiturates in the meat; the dog could wake up before he was safely back over the fence. After a lifetime in the business, the man understood that it was all about the details.

He began walking quickly toward the northeast corner of the house, where a gray metal box was mounted to the cedar siding five feet above the ground. He used a screwdriver to open the box and a pair of wire cutters to sever the thick main phone line coming into the house. When he did this, phone service to the entire estate was cut, which also disarmed the burglar alarm that shared the phone line.

The man took his time and walked completely around the large house, studying the exterior and looking for any sign of activity within. Anybody could invade an empty home, but going into an occupied one required stealth and well-considered precautions applied with careful patience. Burglars who engaged in such a delicate activity were a dying breed among the gangbanger, machine-gun mentality of the modern community of criminals.

When he had examined every door and window in the two-story home, which he judged to contain as many as twenty-five rooms, the man selected the service door that led into the attached, four-car garage. He knew that typical homeowners didn't spend money on quality garage door locks. It never occurred to them that once an intruder was inside the garage and safely out of sight, he could take his time getting through the door that led into the house. He examined the lock for a minute, using a small flashlight, then withdrew a slim leather case from his pocket, from which he selected a pick and a tensioner. He inserted the tensioner and held the cylinder in place while he used the pick to finesse the spring-loaded pins into place one by one. In three minutes the lock was open. The man stepped inside, taking care to close the door behind him.

He paused and ran his flashlight around the space. There were three cars, a workbench, now used for storage, and the usual dusty stacks of discarded remnants of forgotten interests. He walked around the cars until he arrived at the door that led into the house. He studied the lock and realized it was going to take a few minutes to get through the door silently. Unless . . . He tried the knob. It turned easily, and he gently pushed the unlocked door open. Typical, he thought, and his regard for the intelligence of the occupants dropped another notch. He knew from his research that there were no in-house pets, but he listened carefully for any sound as he walked through the back hall. He passed the laundry room and gently opened the door at the end of the hall. He was standing at the entrance to a long room with a fireplace at the far end. He waited, letting his eyes adjust to the dark, while he listened to the sounds of the house. Assisted by the white moonlight filtering in through the windows, he studied the mementos that covered the rustic brick walls of the family room. If money was any indication of success, then Wallace Pearle was one of the most successful painters in America.

After a decent interval the man toured the first-floor rooms, taking care to move silently, alert for squeaking floorboards. There was a spacious kitchen featuring a large center island with an array of copper pots hanging above. On his way through he plucked an apple from the large fruit bowl on the counter for later. He walked through a formal dining room, which led to the great room with a high ceiling and another, much larger fireplace. The room contained three separate groupings of overstuffed furniture and perhaps a dozen paintings.

He paused, using his flashlight to examine one painting in particular. It was positioned directly above the fireplace and depicted a beautiful young woman with long blond hair braided delicately at the sides. She was sitting on a window seat and gazing at something through the panes, out of the painting's view. She wore a necklace with a sapphire pendant. The man pulled an ottoman over to the fireplace, stepped up onto it, and examined the girl's face more closely. Her expression was absolutely luminous and almost seemed to tell him what held her interest so keenly—almost.

He was familiar with the painting; it was called *Girl on a Window Seat,* and he knew who the girl in the painting was. At the time Wallace Pearle had painted it, in 1984, she was his mistress. When the work was originally completed, the unsurpassed radiance of the girl's expression had generated speculation in art circles as to exactly what it was she was supposed to be gazing at. At the time Wallace Pearle had demonstrated wise restraint and kept his mouth shut, thereby increasing the painting's value by a considerable sum. Later, of course, the painting's value shot up again, but for a completely different reason.

The man indulged himself for another minute and then turned off the flashlight and stepped off the ottoman, deciding that it was time to go to work. He left the great room, walking past the large staircase and into a back hallway that led to a pair of rooms that appeared to be offices. This was probably where the safe would be if they had one on the premises, but tonight wasn't that kind of night; the man had something simpler and quicker in mind.

After completing his survey of the first floor by giving the offices a brief look, he returned to the staircase and went up to the second floor, which consisted largely of bedrooms, lots of bedrooms. He crept along the hallway, silently opening doors, glancing inside, and closing them. He counted one sitting room and five empty guest rooms before he found the first occupied bedroom. The light snoring that came from the bed was music to his ears. He kept moving until he had surveyed every second-floor room. There was a man in one room, probably Wallace Pearle himself, and a woman in each of two other rooms. That's interesting, he thought; the wife apparently sleeps in a separate bedroom. He knew that the Pearles didn't have any children, so he speculated that the second woman was probably a relative or a guest, or possibly even a maid or housekeeper. He selected one of the two women's rooms and entered. He moved silently to the bedside and stood over the sleeping figure, pausing to study her breathing. It was deep and regular. As long as he didn't bump into the furniture, he was as safe as in his mother's arms.

The room was quite large, but then, they all were. There were two dressers, one next to the bed and one on the wall opposite the foot of the bed. The room was so spacious that when he walked to the farther dresser, he was a good twenty feet from the bed's footboard. A vaguely Oriental-looking jewelry box rested on the top of the dresser. Holding his tiny flashlight in his teeth, the man opened the box, placed a jeweler's loupe in his eye, and examined the contents. At first glance some of the pieces looked impressive, but his excitement quickly subsided when he took a closer look. They were pretty and ornamental but not worth taking. Then he went through the drawers, beginning with the top one. His search was methodical and thorough.

In the third drawer he found a second jewelry box. The contents of this one consisted of a larger selection and showed more promise. Again using the loupe, he sorted through the pieces, slipping almost all of them into his black bag.

When he was done, he silently let himself out and entered the second woman's room, where he repeated the routine. This room was smaller, and he was disappointed to find only paste jewelry in a black lacquered box on top of the dresser. His hopes climbed when in the bottom drawer, buried under clothing, he found a second, wooden box. The box, however, held only a single photograph. His interest piqued, he pulled it out and examined it under the glow from his flashlight. It was a photo of a man, a woman, and a child. The photo was old and yellowed and distinguished only by the slightly unusual facial characteristics of the man. Though his chin was clean-shaven, his black sideburns extended down and then forward until they united with his thick mustache. He placed the photo back into the box and returned it to the drawer, then collected his bag and left the bedroom and its sleeping occupant.

On his way out of the house, he couldn't resist stopping in the great room again. He stood in front of the fireplace, staring up at *Girl on a Window Seat*. It was definitely worth some serious money, but was it too famous to fence? His experience in handling hot art had taught him that art collectors were fanatics, and no matter how famous a painting was, a buyer could always be found; it was simply a matter of how many cents on the dollar you were willing to settle for. He stood there for a full minute weighing his options, then suddenly stepped up onto the ottoman and lifted the painting from the wall. He placed it on the floor, took a small knife from his pocket, and with four precise movements cut the painting out of the frame. He rolled up the canvas, and the same obsessive attention to detail that made him a highly successful thief compelled him to hang the empty frame back on the wall.

He exited the house using the same garage door through which he had entered. When he stepped outside, the Doberman was waiting for him. With the muzzle in place it could neither bark nor bite but only thrash its head from side to side in frustration. The man took his time locking the door.

The dog followed him all the way to the edge of the estate, where the man climbed back over the fence using the rope ladder. After he'd removed the ladder, he lured the dog closer to the fence. When it was close enough, he thrust his arm through the bars and grabbed its head by the muzzle strap. He pulled it up against the fence, reached through, and unbuckled and removed the muzzle, careful to take his hands away quickly. As he put the muzzle into his black bag, pent up frustration got the better of the Doberman's training, and it began barking. The man took a second steak from a plastic bag he had left concealed in the bushes and tossed it over the fence. The Doberman abandoned its barking and was already tearing at the meat as the man tossed his watch cap and gloves into his bag and walked casually away.

Chapter Two

May 1983

W hen Ellie Myers read in the Sunday classified section of the *St. Paul Pioneer Press* that the painter, Wallace Pearle, intended to hire a personal secretary, she was able to sum up her prospects for the job in two words: *fat* and *chance*. She'd never worked as a private secretary, and she didn't know anything about the art world, though Wallace Pearle was so well known that even she'd heard of him. His name seemed to surface whenever classy artists were discussed. She'd even seen a thing on *60 Minutes* once about how he'd painted a portrait of President Ronald Reagan. According to the show, the painting still hung in the White House, despite Nancy Reagan's attempt to take it with them when her husband left office. Ellie suspected that an artist as famous and successful as Pearle would have dozens of applicants, maybe hundreds, clamoring to be his personal secretary.

It was going on two months since Ellie had been laid off from Anderson Windows in Bayport, not that the job had been anything to shout about. In spite of her precious bachelor's degree in business administration, her entire time there had been spent working as a glorified secretary. The only things her degree had done for her was saddle her with a student loan to repay and get her a more formal termination notice than the plant workers had received. Still, after queuing up in the unemployment line for a couple of months, her old job was starting to look remarkably appealing.

On this particular Sunday, Ellie was sifting through the growing pile of bills choking her kitchen table, trying to decide which one would have the honor of administering the *coup de grâce* to her pathetic bank account. As morning dragged into afternoon, she glanced again at the Pearle ad, beginning to view the job differently. So what if Wallace Pearle was rich and famous and educated in England? Ellie had accomplishments of her own that she could point to. Besides, her mother had a pen pal in England, Kathleen Withington, whom Ellie had actually visited once with her parents several years back. In the end her mind was finally decided by the nagging vision of returning, broke and out of work at the age of twenty-nine, to her old bedroom in her parents' home. At two o'clock, careful to keep the desperation out of her voice, she picked up the phone and called the number in the paper. To her surprise, she was rewarded with an interview scheduled for the following day.

On Monday morning, Ellie stood in front of her bedroom mirror and subjected herself to a frank examination of her appearance. Her blue eyes, luminously pale skin, and finely textured blond hair were hand-me-downs from her Norwegian ancestors. The delicate wrinkles just beginning to form around her eyes attested to the fact that she would turn thirty this year and was, as her mother would be quick to point out, still single. Her hair was straight, moderately long, and held in place by a thin braid on each side that swept down and back, meeting in the middle. She'd considered putting her hair up in a more businesslike style for the interview but decided against it, feeling uncomfortable with a look she thought might be too severe.

Satisfied that her white blouse, black pants, and charcoal gray jacket presented a sufficiently businesslike appearance, she grabbed her briefcase and car keys off the dresser and walked out the door.

Everybody knew that Wallace Pearle lived in Higgins Point, but as far as Ellie could tell, nobody had any idea why, though the town certainly did have its charms. With a population under five hundred, there was an actual Main Street and a modest business district with a hardware store, dry cleaner, bakery, and other practical enterprises that hadn't yet been displaced by antique stores and art galleries. The residential streets were lined with full-grown trees and modest one-of-a-kind homes, not the ticky-tacky rows of identical boxes that were becoming the norm in modern suburbs. And the St. Croix River, a national scenic waterway, flowed only two blocks west of Main Street. Higgins Point was small enough that the drive from Ellie's apartment on Andrews Street to the painter's home took less than five minutes.

In spite of their proximity, Ellie had never met the man nor had occasion to venture up the private drive to his house, so when she got there she wasn't ready for what she saw. Looking out the open window of her '77 Chevy Nova at the grounds of his estate, she wondered if she was still in Higgins Point. There were large stands of trees breaking up expanses of sun-dappled lawn that looked vast enough to accommodate a football game. There were rock gardens with stone benches, and she saw two fountains. There were even Greek statues that reminded her of that famous mansion in California that she'd seen on a TV special, San something or other. Then she emerged from the trees and saw the house. It was so large that she thought, *there's been a mistake; that's a hotel.* The facade was mainly white stucco broken up by dark brown beams in a Tudor style. It was two stories with handsome carved woodwork framing the many windows. A section of the facade was distressed brick for the full height, and sculpted shrubs ran intermittently across the front of the house.

Ellie parked on the curved drive near the front door, got out of her car, and then froze. She stood looking at the house, holding her briefcase across her chest and wishing she had put her hair up in the more businesslike style. Finally, forcing her legs into movement, she walked across the immaculate asphalt driveway and stepped up onto the low porch. She rang the bell, and when she didn't hear anything, she pushed it again before it occurred to her that maybe the bell rang at a discreet volume inside the home.

Finally a woman wearing a maid's uniform opened the door. When Ellie explained that she had an appointment with Mr. Pearle, the woman bowed her head slightly and invited Ellie to enter by stepping aside and opening the door wider. The foyer was two stories high with a curved marble stairway sweeping up to the second floor. A large crystal chandelier hung directly overhead. The maid indicated that Ellie should follow and proceeded to lead her through the house, which contained an amazing collection of art objects.

Eventually they arrived at a door that opened to the backyard, though Ellie seriously doubted it was referred to as a backyard. It was probably called the west lawn, she thought.

The maid pointed at a group of buildings perhaps fifty yards away and said, "You will find Señor Pearle in the studio."

Ellie thought it was a little odd that Mr. Pearle wasn't here at the main house to meet her. After all, her interview was presumably on his schedule. *Well,* she thought, *he is Wallace Pearle. If he wants to interview me in his studio, so be it.* She thanked the maid and began walking across the grounds toward the buildings. As she drew nearer, she realized that the grouping consisted of several small cottages and one larger, single-story structure with a high roof. This, she assumed, must be the studio.

A young man was standing outside the large building, having a cigarette. As she got closer, Ellie saw that he was wearing paint-spattered jeans and a sweatshirt, and the cigarette that dangled from his lips was unlit. When she finally reached him, the young man took the cigarette out of his mouth.

"I don't suppose you have a match," he said.

"Sure." Ellie reached into her jacket pocket, fished out a book of matches with GRAND CANYON NATIONAL PARK printed on the cover, and handed it to him.

"Thanks." He lit his cigarette and then held the pack out to her. "Want one?"

"No thanks. I don't smoke."

The young man grinned around the cigarette. "If you don't smoke, why do you carry matches?"

"You never know when you're going to need them," Ellie replied. "Like now, for example. Do you work for Wallace Pearle?"

He shook his head and took a long, indulgent drag off the cigarette, blowing the smoke off to one side. "Student. My name's Carl." He studied the matches for a second, turning them over in his fingers, and then handed them back to her. "Ever been to the Grand Canyon?"

Ellie shook her head.

"I didn't think so."

"Is this his studio?"

The man nodded. "He's inside." When Ellie hesitated, he said, "It's okay, he won't bite. Just don't call him Wally."

Ellie smiled in acknowledgment of the humor, straightened her suit jacket, and took a deep breath. When she pushed the door open, she was almost overcome by the acrid fumes of oil paint and thinner. The interior of the studio was one large open space with a vaulted ceiling, filled with the rich strains of softly playing classical music. Windows on three walls let in a tremendous amount of sunlight, and the fourth wall was covered with unframed paintings and charcoal sketches. A hodgepodge of paint palettes, jars of brushes, bottles of fluid, rags, tubes of paint, white plaster models, and spotlights seemed to be thrown about with no rhyme or reason. Unframed oil paintings leaned against the walls and were stacked a dozen deep in the corners. It all made the room feel both open and cluttered at the same time. There were five easels spread around the room, some holding paintings, others holding what looked like large black-and-white photographs. An artist stood before each easel, dividing his attention between his model and his canvas. One student appeared to be dangling some sort of plumb bob on a string.

Across the room a tall, slender man, whom Ellie recognized from photos in *TIME Magazine* as Wallace Pearle, stood beside one of the students, speaking in a low voice. He was apparently explaining something to the young man and, using a thin brush, was punctuating his remarks with gestures at various sections of the student's painting. Ellie was hesitant to barge in on Mr. Pearle in the middle of his instruction, so she stood just inside the door and took the opportunity to study him while she waited. He was perhaps six feet tall, dressed in dark, loose-fitting trousers, a baggy sweatshirt, and tennis shoes. His thick brown hair was a bit long and combed straight back, revealing a high forehead, which lent him an air of aristocratic intelligence. An impeccably trimmed mustache and goatee completed the overall effect. The students all seemed to be covered in paint specks from head to toe, but while Pearle's clothes were, likewise, dappled with a rainbow of paint spatters, she noted that his hair and face were clean. Her impression was of a man accustomed to imposing control on chaos.

Wallace Pearle stepped back from the canvas, glanced around, and finally noticed her. He immediately walked over and smiled as he offered his hand. "You must be—"

"Ellie Myers." Banishing the fear from her voice, Ellie thrust her hand forward, determined to make a strong, positive first impression. *Remember,* she told herself, *you don't need this job—you can always eat cat food.*

"Here about the secretarial position," he said, as he shook her hand gently and then held it.

"Yes, sir. It's an honor to meet you."

Wallace paused at this and looked at her. "You have remarkable eyes. Are you an organized individual?"

Ellie barely had time to decide whether the compliment on her eyes was appropriate before being blindsided by the question, but she welcomed any topic that wasn't on the subject of art. "Yes," she was able to say with firm conviction. "Yes, I'm very organized. That is, I'm an organized—"

"Are you educated?" He released her hand.

"Uh, yes, of course." She suddenly remembered the briefcase she was carrying and opened it, withdrawing her resume. "I have a degree in—"

"How about hobbies?" Wallace ignored the offered resume and gently traded her hand for her elbow, leading her toward the nearest easel. "I find that hobbies are an excellent indicator of character. They speak volumes about an individual's industriousness and curiosity and perseverance. Don't you agree?"

"I suppose they do. I never really thought about it." *Don't tell him you never thought about it, stupid!* "I have hobbies." *Oh, God, why did I say that? Now he's going to ask me what my hobbies are.*

"Splendid. Tell me about your hobbies."

Ellie's mind went into lockdown. *Is watching reruns of* I Love Lucy *while I paint my toenails a hobby,* she wondered frantically. *How about shopping? Wait, I keep a small garden.* "I enjoy gardening," she declared in what she thought was a reasonably calm voice, considering.

"Ah, gardening. We actually maintain a modest green-house here. I find that it can be a very calming, a very . . . pastoral diversion."

Ellie thought about dumping chemicals onto her tomato plants to assassinate the aphids, scratching her hands raw in the losing battle with weeds, and sweating over butternut squash that always seemed to wind up looking like anemic avocados.

"Yes, it's very relaxing," she assured him.

Wallace paused beside a student whose easel held one of the photographs she had noticed earlier. Looking more closely, Ellie now realized that it was actually a charcoal sketch, but it was done with such a high degree of precision that it looked like a black-and-white photo. Ten feet away on a wooden pedestal sat a white plaster cast of what was apparently a giant eye. There was a spotlight trained on it, creating a dramatic shadow.

"Jensen, here, is doing a study in charcoal of *David*'s eye."

"David?"

"Michelangelo's *David,* of course."

"Of course."

"Casts of various parts of that statue's anatomy are very popular studies for developing an eye for proportion. Stand just here, please. You have to place your head exactly where Jensen's is when he's working." Wallace guided Ellie to the spot where the student had been standing. "Okay, look at the cast."

Ellie studied the model of the eye.

"Now look at the sketch."

She turned her head slightly to the easel. "They're the same," she said. She looked back and forth several times, wondering how he could draw the eye so perfectly. "They're identical."

"I wish," the student said, grinning.

"Actually, they're far from identical," Wallace explained. "But Jensen, here, is definitely developing a talent for capturing proportion."

"Yes!" Jensen said, performing a tiny arm pump.

Wallace ignored Jensen's gesture and addressed himself to Ellie. "Can you say anything insightful about this sketch?"

Ellie opened her mouth before realizing that she had no idea what to say. She closed her mouth and smiled at Wallace weakly.

"I see," he said, and he led her toward another easel. "When drawing, one works with lines. When painting, one works with mass. Learning to create the feeling of the mass of a three-dimensional object on a two-dimensional surface using charcoal helps teach the student how to create a convincing three-dimensional effect with paint on canvas. At any rate, that is the expectation."

The impromptu lecture sent a wave of realization and then nausea through Ellie. Once, right after graduation, she had miscalculated badly and interviewed with Dayton's Department Store for a marketing management position. Within five minutes it had become obvious to everyone concerned that, barring having an uncle at the executive vice president level, Ellie was wildly unqualified for the position. The remaining twenty-five minutes of the interview had been pure hell. But the upset stomach she had experienced on that occasion was only a close second to what she was feeling now. She gamely accepted the role of art neophyte and attempted to gather her wits and ask a question—any question—to hurry things along and get the inevitable rejection over with. She'd noticed that virtually all of the dozens of casts sitting around the room on tables and shelves were pure white plaster.

"Why are the models all white?" she asked.

"To achieve the purest gradations of shadow," Wallace explained. "Also, when studying form, it helps the student to eliminate any distractions. Dealing with color and hue can be not only distracting but totally engrossing. Consider Phillip, here."

They arrived at another student, who was wearing a set of headphones. He paused and stepped back from his canvas when he saw his instructor approach.

"Phillip is working on a still life in oil."

Ellie felt a small relief when Wallace turned his gaze from her to the painting. It portrayed a glass of red wine next to a breadboard with a large piece of cheese, a loaf of bread, and a knife resting on it. The painting was an exact, full-color rendering of the actual objects arranged on the table in front of the student.

"It looks so realistic," Ellie said, "it's amazing."

"It's realistic because it's a study in classical realism," Wallace explained. "Phillip is developing the ability to paint exactly what he sees. If his artistic tastes eventually guide him into other styles—and, given his abysmal taste in music, I'm sure they will—he'll have a sound grounding in the fundamentals of his craft, regardless of what sort of questionable things he might attempt. Very good, Phillip."

Phillip removed his headphones. "What?"

"I said your cheese looks like a block of wood. Miss Myers—it is Miss, is it not?"

"Oh, yes, it is."

"Miss Myers, what is your opinion of Phillip's use of negative space?"

"Negative space?"

"Certainly you understand that 'negative space' is the impact on the overall composition in a painting achieved by the effective use of the areas between the objects. Or perhaps you simply have no opinion?"

In those old fifties comedies that Ellie loved to watch, this is where Judy Holliday would have come up with just the right wisecrack to melt the boss's heart and get the job. *The way things are going,* she thought, *what have I got to lose?* She looked Wallace Pearle squarely in the eye and said, "I think that negative space is overrated, don't you?"

Wallace Pearle paused at this and studied Ellie for a second. "What I think, Miss Myers, is that you must be a very talented personal secretary, because it's clear you're not depending upon your encyclopedic knowledge of art to secure this position."

Ouch! There was no way Ellie could put a positive spin on that. Her hopes sank even lower, and she began thinking how attractive a cashier's position at the Maplewood Target store would be.

Wallace led her away from the students and toward the corner storage shelves, where, presumably, he would put a mercifully private end to this waste of his precious time.

"You have a resume with you," he said. "Perhaps it's time to take a look at it."

Ellie produced the resume and waited while Wallace read it. It was a brief wait.

"One job since graduating, and no experience as a personal secretary."

"I was an assistant office manager during my last year at Anderson Windows." Despite her efforts to the contrary, Ellie's voice faded a bit at the end.

Wallace handed the resume back. "And you enjoy gardening."

"I also play the clarinet." Where did *that* come from, she wondered. She hadn't touched her clarinet in four years. "That is, I *played* the clarinet—in the UW concert band."

Wallace smiled. "The UW concert band?"

"University of Wisconsin at Madison," she clarified. Oh, my God, she thought, was that a look of interest? If it was, she was on thin ice.

"Do you play classical?"

"Sure." The ice was getting thinner. "That is, I used to."

"I dabble at the piano, myself." He paused and looked at her. "Perhaps sometime we could indulge ourselves with a bit of a duet."

"I'd love that." Dangerously thin ice. Wait. Does that mean I'm hired? He must have meant, *if I hire you.* Though Ellie still possessed enough of her wits to avoid actually blurting it out, the question expanded in her mind until it pushed everything else out of the way. Then he reached out and touched—actually touched—her hair, all the time staring into her eyes.

"I apologize for my forwardness, but I was thinking that it might be interesting to paint you."

Ellie's mind was a swirl of conflicting emotions, torn between concerns over appropriate business behavior and visions of paid-off student loans. Wallace took her by one elbow and led her back to the center of the room, where they were more or less surrounded by the five students, each still diligently focused on his project.

He raised his voice and said, "Excuse me, may I have your attention, please?"

Everyone but Phillip turned to him.

Wallace frowned and waved a hand in Phillip's direction, and one of the students walked over and tapped his shoulder. As soon as Phillip had removed his headset, Wallace continued. "I would like all of you to meet Miss Ellie Myers. Please be lavish in your kindness toward her, as she will be our atelier's new Dragon Lady and will, no doubt, have a considerable impact on the kindness with which you are treated."

Wallace Pearle smiled and took her left hand in his, and when he placed his right hand over it, the welcoming warmth of acceptance washed over Ellie Myers.

Chapter Three

Saturday

Dexter Loomis used his damp towel to wipe the steam off the glass and then stared into the bathroom mirror. At six foot three, he had to stoop slightly to see anything above his chin. In the three years that he'd lived in this cottage since inheriting it from his Aunt Myra, he'd resisted the urge to change the bathroom fixtures because the low mirror and shower nozzle reminded him of her. Dexter's black hair was still wet from the shower and framed his thin face, clinging to his forehead, ears, and neck like sculpted shards of obsidian. He studied the thick shaving cream that covered his face, then positioned the safety razor below one sideburn and drew it down across his jaw, removing a swath of stubble.

"So, what's on your schedule for today?" He spoke into the mirror between razor strokes. "It's Saturday. Are you gonna hang around the yard and chase butterflies? Maybe take a nap? What's the matter, cat got your tongue?"

Asta, Dexter's wirehaired terrier, sat in the bathroom doorway, staring up at him, communicating her opinion of this one-sided conversation by tilting her head sideways.

"That's okay, sweetheart," Dexter cooed. "You can be coy if you want to."

Asta immediately stopped staring and resumed her previous activity, which was ignoring her lord and master and licking her paws.

Dexter finished shaving and combed his hair, and Asta followed him into the bedroom, where he put on his standard summertime police chief uniform, which consisted of blue jeans, light hiking boots, and a khaki shirt with the sleeves rolled up to the elbows. In November he would switch to his wintertime police chief uniform of blue jeans, heavy hiking boots, a khaki shirt, and a Carhartt jacket. And for those especially charming Wisconsin winter days, he would add a down vest under the jacket and a wool cap. Asta wheeled around suddenly, trotted out of the bedroom, and reappeared a minute later, dragging her leash in her mouth—a simple request, elegantly stated.

"Okay, my little Gromit, I'll take you out for walkies in just a minute."

Dexter reached for his badge on top of the dresser and happened to glance at the photograph of Ann Summer standing next to it. He just *happened* to glance at it, the way he'd just *happened* to glance at it every day for the past six months. Ann was a Special Agent with the homicide division of the Wisconsin Division of Criminal Investigation, but it wasn't her law enforcement resume that fascinated Dexter. Ann had piercing green eyes, looked great in a swimsuit, and was cuter than a capful of kittens. She also seemed to possess an amazing ability to short-circuit Dexter's electrical system with a single word or gesture. The problem was, she was stationed in Madison, three hundred miles away. Well, that was the immediate problem, but not the only one. Looking at the photo gave Dexter an all too familiar feeling in the pit of his stomach, like a mule kick followed by dry heaves. *Other men carry torches for women,* he thought. *I carry Tums.*

A ringing phone dragged him away from his trip down memory lane. It was Phyllis Beiderman, the secretary he shared with Mayor Dick Evenson, explaining that the county sheriff's office had called to report a burglary at the Wallace Pearle estate. Sheriff Bob Tilsen was already out there.

Dexter glanced down at Asta, who still had the leash in her mouth. "Tell them I'll be there as soon as I take Her Royal Highness out for her walk."

There was a brief pause at the other end. "Maybe I'll edit that a bit for you," Phyllis finally said.

"That's why you get the big office, Phyl."

Asta was mercifully quick, and fifteen minutes later Dexter was driving slowly up the long, curved driveway, past the manicured lawn and professionally sculpted topiary, of the Pearle estate. The main house was a giant, two-story Tudor that reminded him of old British movies. It was a good hundred yards from the gate that fronted on Pearle Lane, a road that began at County Road A and ended at the estate. Pearle Lane had, of course, been renamed in honor of its illustrious occupant.

Wallace Pearle was easily Higgins Point's most famous citizen. Not to put too fine a point on it, he was Higgins Point's only famous citizen. His standing among critics in the art world had been secured in the eighties, when he'd been commissioned to paint President Ronald Reagan's portrait. Though Dexter dabbled in watercolors as a hobby, he didn't know very much about Pearle's art, other than the fact that it was in a classic-looking style and reportedly sold for large sums of money. Wallace Pearle had been successful for so long now that Dexter was sure the man could never spend what he'd earned and was probably banking money for his descendants. His choice to live in a tiny Wisconsin town rather than in, for example, a plush beach house on Maui was obviously a function of personal taste, not lack of funds, and was generally accepted with few raised eyebrows. After all, weren't the man's predilections born in the lofty and mysterious realms of artistic temperament and thus beyond the understanding of mere mortals?

Dexter was driving slowly because he wasn't all that eager to get there. He knew that Sheriff Tilsen was inside, undoubtedly doing all sorts of impressive cop things, and Dexter didn't really have much of a plan as to how he was going to proceed when he finally did arrive. When he stepped out of his Jeep and began walking across the drive, he reasoned that if he covered half of the remaining distance to the front door each minute, then theoretically he'd never arrive. But he was forced to abandon this plan as impractical when he stepped up onto the low porch.

According to Phyllis, the call was a simple burglary. The problem was that the ten months Dexter Loomis had spent as police chief represented the sum total of his law enforcement experience to date, and he hadn't handled too many burglaries. In fact, the actual running count was . . . none. Riding herd on a town as small as Higgins Point, tucked away in rural western Wisconsin, hadn't provided him with the opportunity to encounter a great deal of conventional crime. The one glaring exception had occurred shortly after Dexter was hired the previous summer, and they'd discovered the dead body of Muriel Evenson, the mayor's daughter. By the time things had gotten sorted out, they'd uncovered embezzlement, blackmail, and a ring of meth labs, and four people were dead. And Dexter and Ann Summer, the DCI agent assigned to the case, had both come close to joining them. In the end, as with most murders, the whole thing had turned out to be a matter of motive.

Dexter stood in front of the large front door and pushed the bell. After a brief wait the door was opened by a woman with wavy, dark brown hair, dressed in black stretch pants and a turquoise sweater.

"Chief Loomis, Higgins Point Police," Dexter recited. "Are you Mrs. Pearle?"

She didn't speak, only shook her head, stepping aside to allow Dexter to enter. After he'd stepped in, she closed the door behind him. "Please follow me," she said. Her crisp, efficient movements and shyly averted gaze left Dexter with the impression of a quiet though somewhat intense woman.

As Dexter was led up the sweeping marble staircase that dominated the foyer, he wondered who his guide was. She wasn't Mrs. Pearle, but she didn't radiate what Dexter would have assumed were the vibes of a maid. At the top they turned left and walked past at least half a dozen closed doors before stopping at a room with the door open. Dexter was ushered in with a small hand gesture from the woman, who then departed. The room was a bedroom, though large enough that the expanse of gold carpet made the king-sized white antique bed appear rather lonely. *This is what money buys you,* thought Dexter. *Space.* Sheriff Bob Tilsen was at the other end of the room, in front of a matching white antique dresser, talking to Wallace Pearle. Dexter assumed that the woman standing with them was Mrs. Pearle.

Sheriff Tilsen paused for a moment when he saw Dexter in the doorway, and then continued. "As I was saying, you can rest assured that we'll do everything in our power to recover your property, including working closely with local law enforcement." He turned to Dexter. "Speaking of which, allow me to introduce Higgins Point's police chief, Dexter Loomis. Dexter, meet Wallace and Roberta Pearle."

Dexter nodded. "Hello, Bob. Mr. and Mrs. Pearle, glad to meet you. I'm sorry it had to be under these circumstances."

Wallace Pearle was a tall, thin man with a head of thick white hair and a snowy white goatee. His white shirt, gold watch chain, and pin-striped vest seemed to place him in a bygone era. He fixed his gaze intently on Dexter and leaned forward in a slightly formal fashion, offering his hand and managing to project a lifetime of accumulated culture in two words. "Honored, sir."

Dexter shook hands, fighting the impulse to bow. There was a subtle smile on Wallace's lips, and his handshake was exceedingly gentle. Dexter was conscious of using a light grip himself as he shook hands. *I can see the headlines now,* he thought: *Police Officer Breaks Wallace Pearle's Hand! Will He Ever Paint Again?*

Roberta Pearle's demeanor, on the other hand, seemed to be that of a weary attendee at a corporate board meeting. Clearly many years younger than her husband, she wore her auburn hair in a short, stylishly practical cut, and her skirt and jacket were businesslike gray. She nodded her head but didn't offer her hand. In fact, her impatience while she waited for her husband to complete his social niceties was almost palpable.

Dexter turned to Sheriff Tilsen. "So, what do we have here?"

"The problem," Tilsen explained, gesturing at the open dresser drawer, "is what we *don't* have here. We don't have Mrs. Pearle's jewelry."

"Do you have a description of the pieces taken," Dexter asked, "and their value?"

Wallace answered Dexter's question before the sheriff was able to. "A sapphire necklace," he said, "along with several other necklaces, a tennis bracelet, a few pairs of earrings."

"Diamond earrings," Roberta added.

"We provided insurance photos of the pieces that were taken to the investigator earlier, but we'll have to get back to you on the value," Wallace explained.

"Was the jewelry the only thing taken?" Dexter asked.

"They didn't get into the safe," Roberta explained. "We don't keep large sums of money in the house, anyway, but whoever it was also took a painting."

"They took a painting? You mean one painted by Mr. Pearle?"

"Yes," Wallace said, "*Girl on a Window Seat.* It held a certain sentimental value for me, and if you could recover it, I would be very grateful. Its value is probably negligible," he explained, and then added, smiling, "at least while I'm still alive." This comment brought an alarmed and disapproving look from his wife.

"We'll do what we can," Dexter said. "You discovered the theft this morning?"

Wallace nodded. "Perhaps a half hour ago. When we saw the empty frame, we immediately checked my wife's jewelry box as well as the safe."

"But the jewelry was here when you went to bed?" Dexter asked, trying to judge if his questions sounded professional. He'd addressed the question to Mr. Pearle, but it was Mrs. Pearle who answered this time.

"This is my room. The dresser drawer was closed when I went to bed and closed when I woke up."

"What time did you go to bed?"

"I believe it was eleven o'clock."

"And Mr. Pearle doesn't sleep here?"

At this point Sheriff Tilsen cleared his throat. "Dex, Mr. and Mrs. Pearle have already given me a pretty complete statement. There's no point in making them run through everything again. I don't think we should keep them any longer than we have to." He turned to Roberta and, before Dexter could object, said, "Thank you for your time. I think we've got enough for now. We'll be in touch as things develop. If it's all right with you, I'll take a few minutes to bring Chief Loomis up to speed, and then we'll let ourselves out."

This speech restored the smile to Roberta Pearle's face. "Certainly, Sheriff. Please do keep us informed." She nodded at Dexter and said, "It was nice to meet you," and then placed a gentle hand on her husband's shoulder. Dexter watched her severe demeanor melt away when she addressed him.

"Wallace, we have to discuss the Stinson Gallery opening

in Los Angeles next month. They're pressing for a personal appearance."

Dexter could just make out Wallace Pearle mumbling to his wife as they left the room, "I despise Los Angeles." Then Dexter was left standing with Sheriff Tilsen in front of the dresser.

"Check the jewelry box and dresser for prints yet?" Dexter asked.

Tilsen nodded, and Dexter picked up the box and opened it. "Looks like the thief left a few items—pretty picky." He waited for the sheriff to offer more details, but Tilsen didn't say anything, so he set the box back on the dresser. "Did you find out how he got in?"

"We think probably the door to the garage." Tilsen said. "Look, Dexter, don't beat yourself up over this one. I've assigned a full-time investigator to it."

Dexter smiled. "I'm not beating myself up, Bob, but technically this is a town matter. It's within my jurisdiction."

"I understand the jurisdiction, and I don't have a problem with that. We can work together. All I'm saying is, let those of us who have the training take the lead."

"If you're waiting for an official invitation onto the case, you've got it," Dexter said. "You're welcome to contribute anything you can."

Tilsen's scowl told Dexter he was finding the sheriff's hot buttons. "County's got the manpower and the training, Dexter. I was just pointing that out, okay?"

"As I recall, the Pearles were healthy contributors to your election campaign last fall."

"Yeah, sure, they contributed, which is more than you did." Dexter grinned. "I didn't even vote for you."

Tilsen's voice was flat. "Collins dropped out. I ran unopposed, Dexter."

"Yeah, I know. I wrote in Wyatt Earp. But, getting back to my point, I get it that it's politically important for you to be as visible as possible solving this crime, and it wouldn't do you any good if some small-town cop came bumbling along and solved it for you."

"Please believe me, Dexter, when I say that the last thing I'm concerned about is your solving this crime. Why don't we walk out together?"

Dexter took a small notepad out of his shirt pocket. "Actually, I think I might take a look around the crime scene first." He glanced around the bedroom. "Which way is the garage, anyway?"

Tilsen just shook his head, turned, and walked away. Just as he got to the door, Dexter said, "If anything turns up, Bob, I'll be sure to keep you in the loop."

"Right back at ya, Dexter."

Dexter gave himself a brief tour of the upstairs—nothing but a lot of unoccupied bedrooms and sitting rooms—and then made his way back down to the foyer. Coming down the stairs, he felt like Rhett Butler in *Gone With the Wind.* One didn't simply walk down stairs like these, he thought. One *descended.*

He left the foyer area and passed through the kitchen, dining room, library, and the solarium, and the farther he walked, the lower his jaw dropped. There were objects of beauty on every side—vases, statues, paintings, and ornate furniture. Oriental rugs so beautiful they looked as if they should be hanging on the walls, and wall tapestries so delicate they looked as if they should be in museums under glass. Passing through the rooms, Dexter struggled to take it all in. He wondered how a thief would ever decide what to take.

He finally arrived at the entrance to an expansive room with a ceiling that he judged to be at least twenty feet high. In the center of one long wall, bracketed by ornate purple and gold tapestries, was a huge stone fireplace, unlit at the moment. *If this were a British mystery,* Dexter thought, that fireplace would be roaring, and I would be holding a snifter of brandy and a meerschaum pipe. He noticed a space above the fireplace where a rectangle of slightly darker paint indicated the recent location of a painting. In front of the fireplace, lying on a leather ottoman, was an empty frame. It was approximately two feet by three feet, and as he drew closer, he could clearly make out the severed edge of canvas along the inside of the frame. It was obviously the frame for the stolen painting. This was confirmed when he noticed traces of fingerprint powder residue still evident on the frame's lacquered surface.

He decided to take a look at the entrance from the garage and, after a couple of missteps, finally arrived at the back hallway. On his way by he happened to glance into the laundry room. Standing at a folding table, sorting clothes, was the same woman who had answered the door when he arrived.

Dexter cleared his throat. "Excuse me."

She turned when she heard his voice but said nothing.

"I'm sorry, but I didn't get your name earlier."

"Louise," she said.

"What's your last name?"

"Dahlman." She resumed sorting clothes.

Dexter wrote her name on his pad. "I'm Police Chief Loomis. I'm looking into last night's burglary. Do you live here?"

She nodded.

"Did you see or hear anything out of the ordinary last night, Louise?"

She shook her head.

He gestured at the pile of clothes waiting to be folded. "Do you work for the Pearles?"

She shook her head but offered nothing further.

The absence of an explanation left Dexter unsure what to ask next. "Are you related to the Pearles?"

"I'm a friend of Roberta's."

"So you're a houseguest."

"It's kind of complicated. I'm a close friend."

Dexter felt as if he was playing Twenty Questions. "Where do you stay? Where's your room?"

"At the north end of the hall on the second floor."

Louise Dahlman's face was plain and fortyish, not exactly beautiful but pretty in a very personal way. She had looks and coloring somewhat similar to Mrs. Pearle, though her hair was longer. She struck Dexter as painfully shy. He noted the lack of a wedding ring and envisioned a woman destined for spinsterhood, sequestering herself in this house, too introverted to take part in the mating dance required by today's society. He put the brakes on his thumbnail psychoanalysis when he recalled that, at forty-three, he himself was also unmarried and ate most of his meals in front of the television.

"You're sure you didn't hear anything or notice anything unusual last night? You know this guy might have even been in your room while you were sleeping."

The question brought only a shake of her head, so Dexter decided to stop imposing himself on her. "Thanks for talking to me, Louise. If anything does occur to you, be sure to let the police know, okay?"

She nodded, and when Dexter continued down the hall to examine the door that led to the garage, he heard Louise's voice behind him.

"We never lock that door." She was standing in the hall outside the laundry room. "We never bother. We keep the outside door locked."

Dexter thanked her and then opened the door and went through the garage to examine the outside door. He found no scratches around the lock that would indicate a forced entry, but he did notice more fingerprint powder residue left behind by the lab tech. Dexter stood and looked out over the grounds, beautifully maintained expanses of green broken up by groves of trees. The perimeter fence was at least a hundred yards away. The burglar could have come from any direction.

Dexter went back inside and walked through the house, rubbernecking at the art that surrounded him. When he reentered the great room, he paused by the discarded, empty frame and was looking at it, when he was suddenly addressed from behind.

"Excuse me, Officer?"

Dexter recognized the clipped, efficient speech pattern of Roberta Pearle before he turned around.

She was standing in the doorway, holding a sheaf of papers in her hands. "I didn't realize you were still here. What was your name again?"

"Chief Loomis, ma'am. And, I'm sorry, I guess I was stalling, admiring your art collection—especially your husband's art." Dexter felt that this white lie was justified.

"No need to apologize for that." She smiled. "We like that."

"Actually, I'm a bit of an art enthusiast myself. I do watercolors."

"Watercolors is a difficult medium. Do you show your work?"

"Sure," Dexter said, and then he smiled. "But you'd have to be in my living room to see it. It's just a hobby." He walked across the room to the doorway where she stood. "Since you're here, Mrs. Pearle, may I ask you a question?"

"Certainly."

"I spoke with"—Dexter glanced at his pad—"Louise Dahlman, your houseguest, and learned that she has a room upstairs, down the hall from you and your husband. Are the three of you the only ones who live here?"

"Year-round, yes. But of course there are the students."

"There are art students living here, in the house?"

"In the cottages. Wallace and I operate an atelier. Twice a

year he selects five gifted artists, whom he mentors for one semester. They're provided with room and board, and of course the instruction is also free."

"That's very generous."

"Wallace has always felt a sense of gratitude for the encouragement he received when he was young. He's had this program in place since the late seventies. In fact when I met him in—what was it?—1984, I was one of his students."

"You're an artist?" Dexter tried not to sound too surprised.

She smiled. "I'm Wallace's personal secretary and business manager."

"That must be quite a responsibility. I mean, given how famous your husband is, his art must generate as much income as, say, Thomas Kinkade."

Roberta's smile dimmed slightly while she composed her response. "It's not about the money," she explained, "or the fame. And I find it unfortunate that you would group my husband's work with that of a mall artist."

"Well, no, I didn't mean—"

"There's a difference between fame and eminence."

"Of course there—"

"Paris Hilton is famous; my husband is eminent. Do you see the difference?"

"Between Paris Hilton and your husband? I believe I do. So you were once a student here. Do you still paint?"

Roberta shook her head. "Not for many years. Even as a student I recognized almost immediately the depth of Wallace's talent and made the decision to dedicate my life to his gift. Over the past thirty years Wallace has built a towering reputation in the art world based on a brilliant body of work. I take it as my mission to guard that legacy and see that it remains intact, to see that his genius is recognized."

The way Roberta Pearle's gaze bored into him left Dexter in no doubt as to her sincerity. He got it: *Do not mess with the man's legacy.*

"I'm impressed by your dedication to your husband's art, Mrs. Pearle, but if I could go back to the students for a minute. You said they live in cottages on the grounds here?"

"That's correct, as does Mr. Silva, our summer grounds-keeper. There's a cluster of buildings in the northwest corner of the property that includes six cottages as well as Wallace's main studio." Dexter opened his mouth, and Roberta held up a hand. "I already know what you're going to ask. Did any of them hear anything last night?"

Dexter smiled. "Sounds like you know the drill."

"I was present earlier, when the sheriff questioned the students."

"Oh, I see. He talked to them already."

Roberta Pearle folded her arms. "Yes, before you arrived, and very thoroughly, I thought. None of them seems to have seen or heard anything unusual. I would have thought the sheriff would have told you that."

"Then I guess there's no point in bothering them again," Dexter said, brushing off her last little dig. "Well, thank you for your time, Mrs. Pearle. I'll just let myself out."

"Glad to be of help, Officer—I'm sorry, what was it again?"

"Loomis, ma'am. Chief Loomis."

Dexter turned to go and then stopped. "By the way, Mrs. Pearle."

She paused, her eyebrows raised. "Yes?"

"The stolen painting . . ." Dexter paused and waited for her to fill in the name.

"Girl on a Window Seat."

"Was it insured?"

"Of course. And in spite of what my husband told you upstairs—he doesn't concern himself with the business side of his art, I do—the current value of *Girl on a Window Seat* is close to a quarter of a million dollars."

Dexter found himself with very little to say in response. "Well, thanks. I appreciate your explaining that to me."

"Not at all."

Then an obvious thought occurred to Dexter. "In the interest of recovering your painting, do you happen to have a photograph of it? Something to help us identify what, exactly, we're looking for?"

"Certainly." She walked to a bookshelf built into one wall and selected a large photo album. "We keep photographs of every work." She leafed through the album for a minute and then handed it to Dexter. "This is the one. My husband painted it in 1984, the same year I came here."

Dexter accepted the weighty album and almost dropped it when he saw the eight-by-ten photo. He stared at the face of the blond woman, unable to think of a single thing to say. After an uncomfortably long time Mrs. Pearle gently pried the album out of Dexter's fingers and replaced it on the shelf. He didn't offer an explanation as to his unusual reaction, and she didn't ask for one. She excused herself and walked away, carrying her papers, leaving Dexter alone in the room. Before leaving he paused and looked up at the empty space above the fireplace again, this time with a bit more reverence.

Chapter Four

The silver-plated, snub-nosed .38 felt surprisingly heavy in Donald Berglund's hand, solid and substantial, like it would do the job. He drew back the hammer and pressed the business end of the gun into Eugene Otto's fleshy back. "You the scum sucker who iced Heavy Betty?" he growled.

"What are you doing?"

"Trying to say that line without laughing."

"I mean with the gun."

"Nothing. I cocked it."

Eugene Otto turned around and shook his head. He was much taller and rounder than his roommate. His light brown hair was thinning a bit prematurely for his age, and his skin had a pale, translucent quality that suggested a shut-in. His wire-rimmed glasses, magnifying overworked red eyes, suggested a well-read shut-in. "Don't cock the gun," he said. The strained condescension in his voice would have irritated anyone else but his roommate, who, after fifteen years of friendship, no longer noticed it.

"I thought I was supposed to be threatening to shoot you," Donald said.

"Don't cock the gun *yet*. It's too early."

"Too early?"

"Cocking the gun is all about raising the stakes, Don. What you want to do is wait and cock the gun later in the scene, to elevate the tension."

"Oh."

"See, that's the difference between fiction and nonfiction." Eugene took the unloaded gun from Donald's hand, showed him how to release the hammer without firing it, and then handed it back to him. "You nonfiction wonks spend all your time churning out reams of boring facts, whereas we—"

"Whereas you professional liars pump out implausible pulp prattle to foist onto a defenseless public."

"Now try to say that without spitting, and what do you mean by 'implausible'?"

Donald waved the gun as he spoke. "Heavy Betty? C'mon."

"That's why we put a fiction disclaimer in the front of every book."

"Oh, a fiction disclaimer. Oh, well, then. And I notice you didn't dispute my use of 'pulp prattle.' "

"Actually, I kind of like the phrase 'pulp prattle.' "

Donald Berglund set the gun on the coffee table on top of the manuscript of his roommate's work-in-progress, which was tentatively titled *Decaffeinated Death.* This would be the sixth book in Eugene's mystery series. Every title was alliterative—*Evil Encounter, Hothouse Homicide,* and so forth. Eugene acknowledged that he was borrowing the gimmick from Erle Stanley Gardner's *Perry Mason* series, but—what the heck?—everybody had to borrow from somebody. It never ceased to amaze Donald that Eugene could manage to write and publish five novels and make next to nothing from them. Ironically, of the two writers sharing a house in Higgins Point, it was he, the lowly *St. Paul Pioneer Press* reporter and would-be biographer, who was able to eke out a living at writing. Still, he envied his friend for his unflagging enthusiasm. Eugene never wavered; all he wanted to be was a pulp novelist.

Eugene slapped Donald on the back. "Right now, I think somebody needs a nap."

Donald looked at his friend for a second. "You know something? You're right, Eug. I've been beating my head against the deadline on the Wallace Pearle bio for weeks, and I'm still stuck on one last major issue."

"I thought it was going pretty good."

"It is, or was. The problem is, I'm supposed to be writing the story of the man's life, but for the past month I've been sidetracked by that thing in 1984."

"What thing? Oh, you mean that girl."

"Right. Pearle's secretary, Ellie Myers. Unsolved to this day, and after twenty years, the case has another victim."

"Another victim?" This got Eugene's attention. "What are you talking about?"

"Me. I'm the victim. I'm obsessed with her, and it's sabotaging my project. I wasted seven hours yesterday driving up to Superior to collect background info I'll probably never get a chance to use."

"So why'd you go?"

"What part of 'obsessed' don't you understand?"

"I was going to ask where you disappeared to," Eugene said. "Mrs. Kanick picked yesterday to stop by and nail us for getting spray paint on her driveway."

Donald gave him a dirty look. "You mean when *you* were painting your junkyard fender?"

Eugene grinned. "I told her you wouldn't do it again, but she's still going to add fifty bucks to next month's rent. It won't get rid of the paint—just her version of penance, I think. So really, what took you up to Superior?"

Donald shook his head. "I'm trying to follow up on a possible lead I found in Ellie Myers' personal effects."

"You aren't actually going to try to solve a twenty-year-old cold case, are you?"

"No, not exactly—it's kind of hard to explain."

"Ever think about checking with the Higgins Point police?" Eugene suggested. "They may have a police report on file."

"You know, that did occur to me, but I didn't think it was too likely." Donald sighed. "I guess if I can waste a day in Superior, I can spend a few minutes talking to the local cops. I'm going to hardball it with Wallace Pearle this afternoon. Maybe I'll stop by the station on my way."

"Hardball it? I thought you two were cozy."

"We're okay. He's being a little pigheaded is all, refusing to look at the practical side. But I found something that I'm pretty sure is going to convince him to see things my way."

"Oh, yeah? What's that?"

Donald shook his head. "Sorry, I'm going to play this hand a little close—at least for now."

Eugene looked at Donald over his glasses. "You're playing cute with me? *Moi?*"

Donald picked up the .38, doing his best to ignore Eugene's comment. "Let's go through your scene again. I promise not to cock the gun until you tell me, but I can't promise not to laugh."

"You just want to change the subject. I think the pizza's about ready, anyway." Eugene walked into the kitchen and continued talking. "Sometimes I don't think you appreciate how lucky you are to have a pizza connoisseur for a roommate."

"What I appreciate is the fact that as a pizza connoisseur, you have your imagination firmly grounded in pulp fiction. What's your latest concoction?"

"For my newest masterpiece we have a black bean and goat cheese creation featuring broccoli, leeks, and pineapple." Eugene opened the oven, allowing the aroma to waft out to Donald in the front room.

"Sounds like the blue plate, flatulence special, Eug. We'll open the windows while we eat."

There was a clatter of silverware and dishes in the kitchen. Eugene always insisted on providing silverware with pizza, which mystified Donald, who never used it but had long since stopped commenting on it. Donald walked into the kitchen, grabbed two Cokes out of the refrigerator, and tore two sections of paper toweling off the roll on the counter. He set them on the table and sat down.

"I've got an interview with Ray Danvers, the manager of the Two Bears Casino, on Monday," he announced.

Eugene slid a piece of pizza from his spatula onto Donald's plate. "I don't remember any mention of a casino manager in your first article."

"I've interviewed a couple of members of the tribal gaming commission but not the big guy. You actually read the article?"

Eugene slid another slice of pizza onto his own plate. "You may be a skinny, long-haired, fact-obsessed dweeb, Don, but I'm forced to admit that you're good at what you do. You must be on to something. What is it?"

"Your instincts are as sharp as ever." Donald reached for the salt shaker. "I do indeed have a rather pregnant question to ask Mr. Danvers."

"Don't put salt on your pizza."

Donald salted his pizza and took a bite. "Tastes great."

"You cretin." Eugene picked up the salt shaker, scowled at it as if it was a bug, and placed it out of Donald's reach. "So what's so pregnant about your question?"

"I'm going to show him a photo of a couple of his tribe's gaming commission members having a drink with some New Jersey hoods."

"Oh, yeah? Who?"

"Alfonse Manzara and one of his goons," Donald said, speaking around a mouthful of pizza.

Eugene set his knife and fork on the table and looked at his roommate. He cleared his throat. "Alfonse 'The Python' Manzara?"

"You've heard of him?"

"The guy who was on television last year walking out of the New Jersey courthouse with his coat over his head?"

Don grinned, still chewing.

"Let me ask you a question."

"Certainly," Don said.

"Are you crazy?"

Don swallowed and took a sip of his Coke. "I live with you, don't I?"

"Yeah, well, I may be looking for another roommate soon." Eugene cut off a piece of pizza, picked it up with his fork, and paused before putting it into his mouth. "How long do you think you're going to last, messing with a member in good standing of New Jersey's first family of crime?"

"I assume that was a rhetorical question."

"Don, you screw up, and what he'll do to you won't be rhetorical. He's got another nickname you know, 'Nine Fingers' Manzara."

"So I heard."

"Do you know why they call him that?"

Donald took a large bite of pizza but managed to say, "Nope."

"Nobody else does either. That's because everybody's afraid to ask him." Eugene shoveled the pizza in. "But I would point out that he has all ten of *his* fingers."

"I'd ask him, if he'd talk to me."

"Seriously, does this guy know you're investigating him?"

Donald shrugged. "I don't know. I did the one piece on the Two Bears Casino so far. Do you think he knows how to read?"

"But you didn't mention him in that first article."

"Of course not. I'm a responsible journalist, Eug. If I can't vet the facts, I don't put them in print. But now I have the photo, so I'm going to follow it up."

"A photo of Alfonse Manzara with a couple of tribal members?"

"Gaming commission members, yeah."

"I thought I read somewhere that he's never been photographed."

Donald grinned. "Pretty cool, huh?"

"And you think he's up to something?"

"I don't know, but my gut feeling is that Manzara's in Wisconsin to execute what I'd call a New Jersey–style hostile takeover of an Indian casino."

"Very funny. And you're putting yourself right in the middle. What's gonna happen when this casino manager tells Manzara that you have this photo?"

Donald shrugged. "They won't have to hear it from him. All they'll have to do is open the *Pioneer Press* to page one of the Wisconsin section and read my article. Eat your pizza. It's getting cold."

"I don't believe you."

Donald Berglund grinned. "Just gathering a few of those boring facts, Eug."

Chapter Five

It was Saturday afternoon when Donald Berglund parked his faded blue Volvo in front of the City Government Center. He grabbed a notepad off the seat as he got out of the car and walked in through the door next to the brass plaque that read: HIGGINS POINT POLICE DEPARTMENT.

Inside, two men were sitting across a desk from each other. One man was tall with longish black hair, dressed in blue jeans and a khaki shirt, and the other was an even taller black man who was wearing a brown uniform with an insignia identifying him as a medical technician for the city of New Richmond. They were staring at a chessboard that rested on the desk between them. When Donald opened the door, Khaki Shirt looked up, and a small dog lying in a corner jumped up and started barking.

Khaki Shirt rose from his seat. "Calm down, Asta," he said as he walked to the counter that separated them.

"May I help you?"

Donald looked for a badge but couldn't find one. "I'd like to speak to a police officer."

"Good luck," remarked the still-seated black man, his eyes never leaving the chessboard.

Khaki Shirt gave the black man a look and then pointed at his own shirt pocket for some reason. "I'm Chief Loomis. What can I do for you?"

Donald realized that Chief Loomis thought he was wearing his badge. *Oh, well,* he thought, *it is Saturday.* "My name's Donald Berglund, and I was wondering if you might be able to help me with something."

Dexter raised the hinged countertop. "Why don't you step into my office, Mr. Berglund, and have a seat. Can I get you some coffee?"

"Coffee would be great," Donald said. He rarely passed up a complimentary shot of caffeine. "And Don's good enough."

"Okay, Don, fair enough. We're pretty informal around here. You can call me Dexter."

Donald took a seat next to the black man and accepted the cup of coffee from Dexter.

"This is Grady Penz," Dexter said.

Donald nodded at Grady and took a tentative sip of his coffee. It tasted like weak tea. "Great coffee," he said, setting it down next to the chessboard. "I suppose I should start by explaining that I'm a writer."

"Really," Dexter said. "What kind of writer?"

"Reporting mostly. I do some investigative journalism. But my main project for the past eight months has been a biography of Wallace Pearle."

"Wallace Pearle. Our Wallace Pearle, the painter?"

"Right."

"Then you're here because of the burglary."

Donald was lost. "What burglary?"

"You mean that's not why you're here?"

"Was there a burglary at Wallace's house?"

Dexter cleared his throat. "What, exactly, is it I can help you with?"

Donald paused for a second to orient himself. "Like I

said, I'm working on Pearle's biography, and it's going pretty good, but there's one thing left that I really feel I need in order to complete the picture."

"And this is something I can supply?"

"Maybe. I'm looking for information on the events surrounding his involvement with a girl some twenty years ago."

"I get the impression you're not talking about his wife." Dexter smiled. "A mistress?"

Donald nodded. "It was before he married Roberta. Wallace's career had taken off big-time, and he decided he needed help, so he hired a personal secretary—a young woman named Ellie Myers."

Dexter stared at Donald for a minute and then picked up his cup and blew across it. "Ellie Myers." He said the name slowly. "Then that *was* her in the picture."

"What picture? Oh, you must have seen the portrait in the great room. Not bad, huh? That's her all right."

"She was Wallace Pearle's mistress?"

Donald was a little thrown by the sudden focus of Dexter's attention. "Uh, yeah, she was. I'm trying to—"

"In December of eighty-four I was a sophomore at UW Madison, studying Civil Engineering," Dexter explained, answering a question that Donald hadn't asked. "I was in the basement of my dorm, doing laundry, when they told me I had a call." Dexter didn't seem to address this comment to anyone. "It was my mom calling to tell me the news."

Grady and Donald stared at Dexter for a minute, and Donald finally cleared his throat and spoke. "Uh, that's right, she died in December," he said, trying to tread lightly until he could figure out this cop's angle. "So you knew about it."

Dexter seemed to come around suddenly. He looked at Donald and then at Grady and took a deep breath. "She was my babysitter."

"Your what?" Grady said.

"When I was six, she used to watch me." Dexter smiled.

"She was sixteen then, and I was madly in love with her." He looked at Donald. "You're looking for information about her affair with Pearle? I don't think that's something we—"

"No, not the affair," Donald hurried to clarify. "Wallace gave me enough on that. I'm trying to fill in some details about the way their affair ended—with her murder."

Dexter set his cup down but didn't speak, so Donald continued. "It happened right out at his estate, on December 17; to be exact." His intention had been to reveal this to the police chief in a way that might stimulate his interest in the case. But in light of Dexter's revelation, that hardly seemed necessary now.

"How can I help?" Dexter asked.

"You can let me have a look at the police report on the case."

Dexter leaned back in his chair and crossed his arms. "Well, let's see. The murder was never solved, which means the case was never closed, so the question becomes, should I allow you to have access to an open case file?"

"After twenty years, what's the harm? You didn't even remember the case until I brought it up," Donald pointed out.

"Oh, I remembered," Dexter said. "I just didn't realize that Ellie had been Pearle's mistress."

"Do you think a file still exists?" Donald asked.

"Lewis Coffers was the police chief in eighty-four. He just retired last year. He was pretty organized. If anyone would have kept a file that long, it'd be him." Dexter rotated his coffee cup on the table and glanced at Grady.

Grady shrugged.

"Sure," Dexter finally said. "Why not? If there's a file on the case, I don't suppose it's going to make any difference if you have a look at it."

Donald grinned. "That's great. I appreciate it."

Dexter got up from his desk and took a sip of coffee. "Sorry if the coffee's a little strong. Phyllis got in this morning and made it before I had a chance to."

Donald picked up his cup. "No, it's perfect," he said, and he set it back down without drinking.

"If it's still around, a file that old is going to be archived in the basement. I'll poke around down there and see what I can find. Can you come back in, say, an hour? If it's down there, I ought to be able to find it by then."

Donald's enthusiasm propelled him out of his chair. "Sure. I have a couple of errands I can run. I really appreciate this." Donald abandoned his untouched coffee and made his way out past the counter, pausing at the door. "I'll see you in about an hour." He closed the door behind himself, and as he walked to his car, he thought, *I love it when the pieces fall into place.*

Chapter Six

Donald Berglund's interview with Wallace Pearle was scheduled for four o'clock, and Donald had spent enough time with Pearle over the past eight months to know that that meant four o'clock. Pearle was an exacting man. Donald had come to learn that he liked things in his studio to remain in their proper places. He liked to smoke his briar pipe every night after dinner, which must be served at seven o'clock, in the formal dining room, with the good silver. During the months that his atelier seminars were in session, Wallace Pearle expected any students staying in his guest cottages to be present at dinner so they could discuss their day's work.

Over the course of several formal interviews and many more casual conversations, Donald had gleaned a fair amount of insight into what it was like for Pearle to grow up the only son in a family that had distinguished itself over the generations. His grandfather, Samuel Pearle, had begun as a lumberjack in northern Wisconsin. An iron man with saw-dust in his veins, he eventually owned his own mill and was still topping trees at the age of seventy-two when he suffered a heart attack and fell to his death. Wallace's father, William Alden Pearle, had spent his childhood toiling around the lumber camps but eventually managed to leave and educate himself. He entered government service, where he spent thirty years rising through the diplomatic ranks to the post of American ambassador to England. After Wallace finished prep school at the Northland Academy in Massachusetts in 1962, he'd been sent to England, where he attended Oxford. There he distinguished himself academically, even as he was awakening to, and being seduced by, his artistic nature. It was a testament to the understanding temperament of his parents, and especially his father, that when told by their son that he wanted to pursue a career in art, they respected and supported the decision. Once he was set on the course of serious art study, Wallace Pearle's life over the next thirty-five years was defined by one triumph after another.

Through conversations with Roberta, his wife of more than twenty years, and a few of his closer colleagues, Donald had come to understand that Pearle had been born and bred to be a private person. It had taken Donald a long time to even begin to know the man, but he had gradually come to realize a few things about his character. Wallace Pearle possessed a capacity to be absolutely charming and at the same time fiercely insistent. And in spite of a reluctance to demonstrate it publicly, he derived great enjoyment from his success and the monetary rewards it had secured for him.

It was this last aspect of his nature that Donald was counting on to help put the pitch he was planning to serve up this afternoon over the plate. The police report that Donald had obtained earlier that afternoon had been an eye-opener. After he managed to suppress his glee and thank Chief Loomis for the favor, he immediately began composing his speech to Wallace. Ellie Myers, the woman with whom Pearle had been in love more than twenty years ago, had been murdered, and the murder had gone unsolved. Pearle was already the star of his own biography. How would he like to be the star of the unsolved homicide? How would he like his bio to sell a million copies? If it worked, if Donald could make his point persuasively enough to Wallace, he might be able to avoid having to use the "nuclear option."

"Have you taken leave of your senses, dear boy?"

Donald Berglund knew he was in for an uphill struggle when Wallace Pearle adopted the British manner of speaking he'd picked up as a student at Oxford. It had been at least forty years since Pearle had crewed a rowing scull on the Thames, but he could still sound like an English squire when he wanted to. Crossing swords with an intellect like Pearle's could often range between frustrating and downright unnerving.

"The thing you have to keep in mind, sir, is that it's not going to do either one of us any good if we publish your biography and nobody reads it."

They were sitting in Pearle's study. There was a broad mahogany desk between them with an antique brass sextant on it. The painter was studying Donald as though he were an Escher print—an optical illusion, not to be believed.

"I fail to see how incriminating myself in the death of my—of Ellie Myers—is necessary to sell your book. I've been reviewing sections of your manuscript as you have completed them and am satisfied that your writing is of a very high quality. The book should certainly fetch excellent reviews."

"I hope you're right, sir. Good reviews would make my ego very happy, but with all due respect, what do good reviews have to do with selling lots of books?"

Pearle's face betrayed his confusion, clearly an expression he wasn't used to exhibiting. "Well, certainly good reviews are necessary," he said.

Donald paused, trying to decide how he was going to put this. "Let me ask you this, sir. What makes you want to buy a book?"

Both men glanced up at the hundreds of expensive-looking hardcover editions that surrounded them on the shelves that lined Pearle's study. Wallace remained silent.

"What I'm getting at, sir, is that there are only two real reasons anybody buys an expensive book: either they've read that author before and liked him, or someone they trust recommended the book."

"But surely all the advertising—"

"The advertising's great as far as it will take us, but have you walked into a bookstore lately? It's a blizzard of titles. We need something that'll make us stand out in the snowstorm. We need to get people talking."

Donald could see that Wallace Pearle was beginning to grow a little uncomfortable in his current role of student. He cautioned himself to keep the lecture as brief as possible.

"If this thing was some uplifting literary tome about a woman overcoming insurmountable odds in her quest for some sort of deliverance, we might have a shot at getting it on Oprah. One word from her and we wouldn't need to do anything else except cash the royalty checks. But it's not going to be on Oprah, so we have to look for another way to attract attention to the book. Call me crazy, but I think delving into the story of your relationship with a woman who was murdered in this very house some twenty years ago will get people talking. The fact that it was never solved adds mystery, and when it's revealed that you were originally a suspect in the investigation, we'll leave Oprah in the dust."

Wallace Pearle leaned back in his leather chair and stared at Donald. "You began this unseemly conversation by informing me that I was once considered a suspect in Ellie Myers' death. How did you come to find out that I was a suspect?"

"It was in the police report, but it was never leaked to the public. Coffers didn't act on it because he didn't have any evidence. It never amounted to more than a hunch."

"Of course he didn't have any evidence," Pearle pointed out rather forcefully. "There wouldn't have been any, would there—since I was innocent."

"Of course you're innocent," Donald agreed emphatically. "Coffers couldn't even get a judge to sign a search warrant. I'm not trying to convict you of a twenty-year-old murder, sir. I just want to sell some books. We've got a sensational piece of news that's landed right in our laps. Maybe it'll make a little money for both of us—maybe it'll make a lot."

Wallace Pearle looked directly into Donald's eyes. "After all our talks together, I thought you had come at last to know me, Donald. I thought you understood that I am at a stage in my life where my standing in the art world must assume a paramount place in my consideration."

Donald began to open his mouth in protest but was silenced by Pearle's raised hand. "Since you have managed to so completely misconstrue my nature, allow me to put it in terms you cannot misinterpret. Far from caring whether or not I benefit monetarily from your miserable biography, Donald, I would give all of my fortune to some modern-art dunghill and go penniless and happy into my dotage if it meant preserving my reputation."

Donald opened his mouth and then closed it again. When he did that, Pearle rose from behind his desk.

"I can see that our little talk has come to an end—unhappily for you, I perceive, yet satisfactorily for me." He walked around his desk and started for the door. "I don't expect we'll be chatting again. I believe you know the way out."

Donald became aware of a person lingering just outside the partially open door to the study. He suspected it was Louise, the ever-present houseguest. She often lurked. Whoever it was, was staying just out of sight.

"I've been sweating over your *authorized* biography for eight months now, sir, but it doesn't necessarily have to be an authorized biography."

This piece of information, delivered to Wallace Pearle's departing back, brought him to a halt at the door, where he turned. "What do you mean?"

"What I mean is that it would be great if you chose to co-operate and be candid with me about this issue, but if you don't, it's not the end of the story. I can write your bio with or without your permission."

"If you print that lie, I'll have my attorney drag you through the courts. I'll ruin you."

"That 'lie' is contained in an official police report, currently on file and still open, in fact, since the murder was never solved. And you, I'm afraid, are what we journalists refer to as a 'public figure,' which means that you are fair game." Donald watched Pearle's expression harden into stone.

"Well, then, our attorneys shall do battle."

Donald teetered on the tipping point and then decided to go ahead. "I have one other thing to say. If you refuse to co-operate and force me to go ahead with an unauthorized biography, I'll be forced to spice things up using the only other information I have—information regarding your involvement with a man named Edward Fitzner."

The painter stared wide-eyed at Donald for several seconds before whispering, "How do you know about that?"

Donald understood that an essential tactic in successful negotiating is providing your adversary with an honorable way out. This was especially true with a proud man like Wallace Pearle. "I would never put any of it into the book if I had any other option, if I could assume that you're at least going to consider my proposal."

"Answer me!" Pearle shouted. "How can you possibly know about that?"

Donald ignored the question. "I'm going to do you the favor of taking your reaction as a yes." He rose to his feet. "It'll be to both of our benefits to let things settle down for now. I'll be in touch to arrange another interview at your convenience. We'll discuss how to incorporate Ellie Myers' murder into the book."

Suddenly Donald heard a voice near the door and looked over to see Roberta Pearle talking quietly to whoever had been listening just out of sight. Then Louise walked past the open door, departing quickly, and Roberta glanced inside.

"I'm sorry. I'll see that you aren't disturbed further."

Roberta left, pulling the study door closed behind her. Without saying another word, Wallace Pearle opened the door and left.

He's right about one thing, Donald thought. *I do know my own way out.*

Chapter Seven

Wallace Pearle stood beside his desk in the early evening silence of his office and listened to the soft, puttering ring in his ear and the click when the connection was made.

"Hallo." The voice that answered sounded sleepy and a bit tinny.

"Edward?"

There was a pause at the other end. "Yes, who's this?"

"It's Wallace, Edward."

"Wallace, my God." Another pause. "Do you know what time it is?"

Wallace glanced at the antique brass ship's clock on his desk. "Yes, it's seven o'clock."

"In America, perhaps. It's one in the A.M. here."

When the other man said nothing further, Wallace continued. "I'm sorry, but I'm afraid we may have a problem."

"A problem? What sort of problem?"

"A young man, a local writer with more ambition than brains, has been poking around and has somehow learned about you."

"A writer knows about me? Do you mean a reporter? Are you sure?"

"Yes. He mentioned you by name, in fact, though I'm not sure how much else he knows."

"It doesn't matter. Anything is too much. Can you deal with it?"

"Deal with it, how?"

Wallace could hear the exasperated intake and exhale on the other end. "Wallace, I don't have to remind you that it is in both of our interests to keep things undisturbed. You have as much to lose as I."

"I have much more to lose, Edward."

"Surely there's some way you can secure his silence."

"We spoke. The price he demands is intolerable."

"What price is that?"

"It's difficult to explain. It would cost me my reputation."

"You're an ass, Wallace."

"Nonetheless."

There was another pause, this time longer. "I'm coming over."

"Here, to America?"

"Somebody has to take things in hand. I'll book a flight as soon as possible. I'll gain six hours flying west, so I expect I can be there by Sunday evening."

"Will you want to stay here, on the estate?"

"Are you ringing me on your own line?"

The question caught Wallace by surprise. "Yes," he finally admitted.

"Then I might as well. I shouldn't think it would matter now. Try not to botch things too badly until I have a chance to reason with this young man."

There was a final click, and Wallace collapsed into his chair, staring at the dead phone in his hand.

Chapter Eight

June 1983

Ellie Myers stood beside the Steinway baby grand and stared at the Brahms "Clarinet Sonata in F Minor," which stared back at her from her music stand. She was waiting for Wallace to complete his preparations to begin their duet. She licked her lips, wetting the reed of her clarinet, and discovered that if she leaned over toward the Steinway far enough, she could see her reflection quite clearly in the high gloss of the piano's ebony finish.

A month had passed since Ellie had been hired as Wallace Pearle's personal secretary, and the entire time had been a maddeningly inevitable march toward the event in which she was now hopelessly entangled: their first duet together. It had all begun harmlessly enough during her interview, with the innocent observation that she had played the clarinet in college, but then had spiraled quickly out of control. Over the past weeks she'd been relentlessly focused on trying to work her way into her new position as Dragon Lady of the atelier, but Wallace had been just as relentless in his insistence that they play together. And the thing was that, as far as the job was concerned, Ellie was actually getting it. She was assuming an ever-increasing role in overseeing the day-to-day operation of the school as well as maintaining Wallace's financial relationships with the select galleries around the country that handled his art. The work was challenging, she was meeting interesting people, and the pay was sufficient to allow her to dream of the day when she would actually be debt free. Then, with everything going so swimmingly, Wallace had caught her in a moment of weakness and finally pressed her into playing this duet. As a result, for the past two weeks it had been home every night after work to practice her clarinet, which she hadn't touched in four years.

The thing that made it bad, really bad, was that she'd heard Wallace play the piano several times over the past month, and he was impressive. The same artistic sensibilities that had made him a talented painter apparently also served him musically. And the way he attacked the pieces made his passion for the music all too evident to Ellie. So now, after being put off for a month, this world-famous artist, this accomplished pianist, this cultured, handsome gentleman was about to hear her play for the first time. She fingered the clarinet keys nervously while she scanned the sheet of music and wondered, if she threw up on the Steinway, would she still have a job in the morning?

Ellie noticed a small box, long and thin, lying on the table next to the piano. Still waiting for Wallace, she picked it up and opened it. Inside was a necklace, an amazingly beautiful necklace with a large blue stone set in what appeared to be platinum.

"My father was made ambassador to England in 1961." Wallace had noticed Ellie gazing into the box. "He gave that necklace to my mother to wear on the occasion of their first visit to the White House to have dinner with President Kennedy and the First Lady."

"It's exquisite."

"It's a sapphire."

"Do you usually leave jewelry like this lying around the house?"

"I'm sending it to the jeweler. I happened to notice that one of the prongs was loose, and it could use a good cleaning." Wallace rubbed his hands together lightly and placed them on the keyboard. "Are you ready?"

Ellie reverently placed the necklace back in the box and picked up her clarinet. All the nervous tension she had been trying to put out of her mind washed over her, and then, before she had a chance to think about it, she was playing. And she wasn't lost, and she wasn't missing any notes; playing the Brahms sonata about four hundred times at home had apparently paid off. Her tone could have been a little more refined, but at least she hadn't hit any squeakers—yet. Ellie was even able to summon the presence of mind to soften her volume when *pianissimo* was indicated in the music. She listened to the piano and tried to blend her clarinet with it but found that, although the reading came easily, the musical expression was more elusive.

During a pause in her part, Ellie dared a glance at Wallace and found him looking directly at her. She thought his expression was positive, maybe even a little too positive. Did his gaze convey something beyond the music? Receiving special attention from a man as charming and accomplished as Wallace Pearle was a heady experience for Ellie. She wasn't displeased by it, nor was she exactly surprised at the attention. A week earlier at the end of the day, when she was getting ready to leave for home, her Chevy Nova had become temperamental and refused to start. Wallace had insisted on giving her a lift in spite of the fact that Marie, the housekeeper, was going downtown for groceries and had offered her a ride.

During the drive her boss had turned on the charm, and

whenever he did that, the high beams could be dazzling. He was full of questions about her college days, not just her education but also her personal experiences in Madison. Did she go to the cinema? (Yes, he actually called it the cinema.) Was she inordinately passionate about any of her classes? Where did she do her laundry? His manner had been surprisingly candid and familiar, or at least Ellie got that impression. When he shared an impromptu confession with her about shoplifting a pint of Bell's Whiskey from a liquor store when he was a lowerclassman at Oxford, he seemed uncharacteristically awkward. Then, when they'd arrived at her apartment and she was about to get out of his car, he had reached out and touched her arm. A tiny gesture, quite harmless, and natural in the context of the small talk, but one that had left an impression on Ellie.

That was the day their business relationship began to evolve. Wallace started sharing his personal opinions on artistic matters with her, something he rarely did with anyone other than his students and never with someone as unschooled in art as Ellie. He began slipping in small personal questions in the course of their daily routine. After Dieter Stolze, a well-known German painter, had visited the atelier Pearle, Wallace asked her if she thought he wore a toupee and if she liked his mustache. Yes and no, she had answered, and was surprised to find them both laughing together. Wallace had an undeniably powerful intellect, and their interactions often reminded her of an adult trying to amuse a child. But more and more often the crinkles around his smile seemed genuine, and she found herself attracted to the boy who peeked out from behind his eyes.

Ellie dragged herself back from her musings and refocused on the sheet music, cautioning herself against allowing her concentration to lapse again. Naturally the thought immediately caused her to lose her place on the page. However, they still managed to bring the piece to a unified, if somewhat shaky, finish. She lowered her clarinet and, with the sustain from Wallace's final note still sounding, rushed to declare her inadequacies in the hope that it would release him from feeling an obligation to do so.

"I'm afraid I missed a couple of notes at the end."

"Did you?" Wallace said. "I hadn't noticed."

Like heck, you didn't, thought Ellie, but she appreciated his saying that, anyway.

"You played your part wonderfully," she said. "This piece is much more difficult for the piano." *Oh, brother! Can you maybe think of* one *thing to say that isn't obvious to him already?*

Wallace shuffled his sheets of music into order and placed them back in their folder.

"Not that difficult—one section, perhaps. You did quite well actually, Ellie. It's only our first time playing together, but it was a good start."

Ellie smiled and managed to relax enough to accept the compliment gracefully. "Thank you."

"And good beginnings are important."

He said this looking into her eyes, lending the words weight beyond their musical significance.

"I think so too," she said. And then she added, "I'm really rusty. I wish I could have—I mean, I wish my playing could have been a little more in sync with yours."

"We'll work on it, but we were together. You know, Ellie, in the same sense that seventy musicians can unite to create a symphony, two people can also unite to create something special. We were together because we created a whole that was greater than our individual selves, and, like a work of art, it will endure in our memory."

Ellie felt a surge of . . . what? "I love the way you put that."

Wallace rose from the piano bench and gently took her right hand in his left. "A musical duet is not unlike a dance,

Ellie." He drew her toward him and placed his right arm loosely around her waist.

Almost without realizing it, Ellie placed her left hand on his shoulder. She looked up into his eyes and allowed Wallace to lead her through a brief dance turn, which brought a smile to her face.

He released her. "And with enough practice, eventually two dancers must grow closer."

This observation certainly merited some response from Ellie, but her mind chose that moment to go on vacation, taking with it her ability to speak intelligently. She finally managed to say, "Do you dance as well as you play the piano?"

"That is not for me to determine." Wallace placed a hand under Ellie's chin and gently tilted her head up toward him. "When it comes to judging one's dancing prowess, the only opinion that matters is the partner's." He wasn't holding her or preventing her from drawing away, and yet she didn't. Then he leaned forward slowly and lightly kissed her lips.

Chapter Nine

Sunday

T he nose wasn't quite right—a bit too large, and the subtle bump midway up wasn't so subtle. Dexter Loomis considered trying to fix it, but while he thought about it, the painting continued to dry. Watercolor is not a medium for procrastinators; he had to decide. Recognizing that spontaneity is part of watercolor's charm, his first impulse was to leave it. Besides, a lucky accident might balance it out later.

In the course of trying to break away from landscape painting and teach himself portraiture, Dexter had learned that you're supposed to spend ninety percent of your time looking at the subject, not the painting, so he was dutifully staring at Ann Summer's photograph. Since she'd gone back to Madison, all she'd left behind were a few photographs and Asta. The pictures prevented Dexter from forgetting the tiny bump on her nose or how green her eyes were, and Asta was a relentlessly cheerful reminder that you should never try to buy a pet for someone else.

Not having Ann to pose for the painting in person wasn't a problem; the photos were fine. In fact, having a live model might actually have been a distraction, and having Ann there definitely would have been a distraction, though a welcome one. As Dexter stood in the middle of his converted bedroom/painting studio, trying to decipher the patches of light and shadow that played across her face, dozens of Ann's expressions stared back at him. He saw her grimacing at her partner, Zack's, factoid of the day, laughing at Dexter's lame magic tricks, and haunted by the report of her father's suicide. Dexter stepped back from the painting and gave his thick hair a vigorous rub.

"I don't know. What do you think, Asta? Have I done her justice?"

Asta's ears perked up at the sound of her name, and she tilted her head sideways, making her appear skeptical.

"Maybe you're right. The nose is probably a little too much."

Dexter considered the profile of the nose again and decided that Ann didn't deserve to look like the Wicked Witch of the West. He picked up a Kolinsky No. 1, his smallest sable brush, and dipped it into the water. Then he wiped it on a paper towel, drawing off most of the moisture and leaving it slightly damp. Ann's face was profiled against a medium blue background, so Dexter picked up a tiny amount of that color from his palette. He was working with "dry brush," so the underlying layer of paint would not bleed through the newly applied, thicker, dryer paint. With one careful stroke of fresh blue background paint, he redefined the outline of Ann's nose, relieving the severity of the bump just a bit. He stepped back again and examined the result.

"And that, Asta, is how the Wicked Witch of the West became Annie, the Beautiful Witch of the North. I think I'll title it *The Imperfect Proboscis.*"

Asta got up off the floor, a short trip for such a small dog, and barked.

"What's that, Asta? No, I don't suppose she is a witch,

even a good one. Say, what do you think the chances are that Annie would want to come back to Higgins Point?" Dexter looked down at his dog, but she chose to remain silent on the subject. "You're probably right. Beyond everything else, she's a homicide investigator—no chance she's coming here without a dead body waiting for her. And that's a bigger sacrifice than even I'm willing to make."

Asta settled back down, apparently content for the moment to coast on the anticipation of the walk she knew was in her near future.

"It's okay, though. I'm doing all right. And I've got you, don't I?"

Dexter suddenly noticed the *Felix the Cat* clock on the wall. The tail was swinging, and the eyes were rolling, and it was almost 11:00 A.M. He had to get over to the Daily Grind. Grady would already be sitting at an outside table, waiting to lose yet another chess game. He tested the surface of the watercolor paper with the back of his fingers. It seemed dry, so he removed the masking tape that held it to the board.

"You know, Asta, men don't need women nearly as badly as women think they should. I'm sure there are laboratory results somewhere that support that. I think I can honestly say that I'm content being single." Dexter carried the painting across the room, where he opened a folder and carefully placed the watercolor with the three other paintings of Ann Summer.

Chapter Ten

Dexter parked his Jeep under the shade of an oak tree on Cedar Street and walked up to Main, turning left toward the Daily Grind Espresso Cafe. A half block away he could see Grady seated in front of a chessboard at an outside table, reading the paper. The Sunday morning weather was perfect for June, low humidity and reasonably warm, with a light breeze off the St. Croix River. Dexter paused in the shade of a maple and took a moment to inhale the smells of Higgins Point, letting the aroma wafting from the bakery across the street wash away the sense of loneliness that always seemed to follow a painting session with Ann Summer's photograph.

Piled on top of his mild, female-induced depression was Dexter's ever-present sense of guilt. He'd settled it on himself, and it was always there, like the permanent click in his jaw that was the result of a punch he'd received in high school for mouthing off to the wrong guy. He understood that even though he wore the badge of police chief, ten months of law enforcement classes do not a peace officer make. Determination and good intentions can only take you so far; eventually some measure of actual competence must enter the mix. Even a town as tiny as Higgins Point deserved a real cop. Dexter had accepted the job on a temporary basis last year, as a favor to his friend Mayor Dick Evenson, who had promised to hire a full-time professional as soon as he could. But when Dexter took a hand in solving the murder of Dick's daughter, the mayor decided that he liked his police chief right where he was, inexperience and all. So, lacking the resolve to quit the job on his own, Dexter stayed right where he was and tried to enjoy the morning, while he thought about Ann Summer and worried about being busted for impersonating a police officer.

Just as Dexter began walking again, Grady Penz stood up, stretched, and stepped inside the Grind. By the time he returned, Dexter was sitting at the table in front of the white pieces and had moved his king's pawn forward. One thing neither one of them ever forgot was whose turn it was to play white. Grady set his new cup of coffee next to the chessboard, settled his long frame into his chair, and glanced at Dexter, who was leaning forward over the board, his chin resting on one cupped hand. He pushed a black pawn forward two squares, to oppose Dexter's pawn. Without a word passing between them, the two men settled in and made several moves over the next ten minutes, enjoying the relaxed sort of silence that only good friends share.

Eventually Cindy Holt, one of the Grind's older waitresses, came out and set an unsolicited cup of coffee next to Dexter. Grady, who hadn't made a move for several minutes, chose that moment to pick up his knight.

"Thanks, Cindy," Dexter said, and then addressed Grady, "It's about time."

Grady paused with the knight poised above the chessboard, his eyebrows raised. "This is a game that favors a man with patience."

"You're going to have to put it down sometime."

"I figure if I hold it long enough, you'll forget where I picked it up from."

Dexter said, "Ticktock, ticktock," which brought a scowl from Grady, who finally placed the knight back on the board, threatening one of Dexter's exposed pawns. Dexter immediately pushed another pawn forward to protect the one that Grady had threatened.

Grady went back to studying the board for a minute and then leaned back suddenly. "What the hell is this?"

Dexter also sat back. "What?"

Grady pointed at the board. "You got two white bishops."

Dexter looked, and, sure enough, where he should have had one bishop on a white square and one on a black square, both were currently resting on white squares. He smiled. "Well, what do you know? Looks like one of my bishops crossed the color line."

Grady folded his thick arms across his chest and scowled at Dexter. "As a black man in America, I want to register an official protest. I got enough to worry about without having to play against two white bishops."

"I thought you guys were African Americans now."

"I'm black."

"Actually, you're more like a chocolate brown."

"I don't need you to tell me what color I am—I'm burnt-sienna, but that's beside the point." Grady gestured at the board with one large hand, and it was as if he were waving a frying pan at Dexter. "What are you going to do about this?"

"Do about it? What do you want *me* to do about it? I suppose now you want reparations."

"Yeah."

"All right. I'll put one of my bishops back on a black square."

"And I get to choose which square."

"No way," Dexter said. "Before that happens, I'll leave 'em both on white."

"That suits me. I guess it's my move." Grady quickly reached out and moved one of his own bishops so it was threatening Dexter's queen.

"Fine. They'll stay on white," Dexter said, and he moved his queen out of danger, onto a long diagonal, where it applied pressure on one of Grady's rooks.

Following this emotional flurry of moves, the game stalled while both men took their time studying the new holes their rash behavior had left them in. Ten minutes later neither man had moved a piece, and a shadow suddenly appeared across the board, cast by a man standing on the sidewalk next to them. Grady glanced up and then immediately returned his attention to the board, but Dexter had to look twice. The man standing ramrod straight presented a striking figure. He had a head of close-cropped, steel gray hair, a prominent mole high on his left cheek, a strong jawline, and a very commanding presence. He grinned at Dexter, and his mouthful of pearly whites pushed everything else out of Dexter's mind except the thought that he hadn't seen his uncle, Delmar Loomis, since his Aunt Myra's funeral, three years earlier.

"So how's my favorite nephew?" Delmar's rich, gravelly New York accent seemed way out of place in rustic little Higgins Point.

"Uncle Delmar, what a surprise." Dexter rose out of his chair and shook hands with his uncle. "How'd you find me here?"

"I stopped by your house, but you were gone—just some dog yappin' at me through the window. So I stopped in someplace called Janet's and mentioned your name. They handed me some cock-and-bull story about your being Higgins Point's police chief. Could've knocked me over with a feather. I can't believe I got family who's a cop, and a police chief at that."

"I'm afraid the rumors are true, Uncle."

"You're Dex's uncle?" Grady asked.

"That I am. The name's Del." He extended his hand to Grady, who shook it without getting up.

"Oh, sorry," Dexter said. "This is my buddy, Grady Penz. Grady, meet my uncle, Delmar Loomis."

"So when did you quit the engineering gig, Dex?"

"I haven't worked for Curran County for almost a year. But what brings you to Higgins Point? Oh, sorry, have a seat. Want some coffee?"

"Nah," Delmar said, patting his stomach, "I'm all tanked up." He dragged a chair over from a vacant table, sat down, and glanced at the chessboard. "Hey, white's playing with two white bishops. You guys know that?"

"Yeah, we worked it out," Dexter said.

"Well, don't quit playing on account of me."

Dexter picked up one of his white bishops and captured an offending rook, which earned him a look from Grady. He noticed that his uncle hadn't answered his question and decided to try it again. "So what brings you to Higgins Point?"

"Hey." Delmar reached over and rubbed Dexter's hair. "Do I need a special reason to visit my favorite nephew? Any chance you could put me up for a few days, Dex?"

"Well, yeah, of course, anytime. Glad to have you."

"That's really great, cause this sad old bag of bones is tuckered out and could really use some downtime."

Dexter looked at his uncle's barrel chest, and the phrase "sad old bag of bones" didn't really seem to apply. When Dexter was growing up, Delmar had always been extremely friendly and supportive, but somehow intimidating at the same time. Maybe it was because he was always Dexter's best cheerleader, he felt it was okay to make Dexter the butt of his jokes too. Or maybe it was Delmar's close bond to his brother, Dexter's father, that he felt gave him privileges with his nephew. Whatever the reason, the pattern was established early in their relationship: when Dexter's uncle snapped his fingers, Dexter fell into line.

"Make yourself at home. There's beer in the fridge. Oh, and that dog you mentioned is named Asta. Don't worry, she's a peach."

"I get along great with dogs. Did you say your house isn't locked?"

"Nope. Don't lock my Jeep either, unless the gun's inside."

Delmar was studying Dexter as if he were some kind of Neanderthal in a diorama at the Museum of Natural History. "This fascinates me. Why not?"

"Simple. Kids used to smash out my Jeep window, maybe once a year. I never left anything inside worth stealing, but they didn't know that until after they broke the window. Now they don't have to break in. They can take a look, see that there's nothing to steal, and leave me in peace. I haven't replaced a window since I stopped locking the Jeep."

"Dexter's got his own way of looking at the world," Grady explained, moving his queen in line with Dexter's king. "Check."

"Long as you don't forget and leave your keys in it, I guess." They all looked down at the board, and Delmar said, "It's looking like he's got you on the ropes, nephew."

"I'm lulling him into a false sense of security," Dexter explained.

"Hey, that's interesting," Delmar said.

"What?"

He pointed at the board. "You got one bishop on each color again."

Grady looked at the board and brought his hand down sharply on the table. "This time there's definitely gonna be reparations."

Chapter Eleven

T en minutes after leaving Dexter and Grady at the Daily
Grind, Delmar Loomis pulled up in front of Dexter's house.
He entered carrying his single suitcase. After quickly making
friends with Asta, he took a few minutes to survey the rooms
in the small cottage before finding what he was looking for.
In Dexter's front room there was a framed watercolor painting hanging above the sofa. It was a large landscape, thirty-
six inches by twenty-four inches with a coastline and some
kind of white birds in it, and it had Dexter's signature in the
lower right corner. Delmar took it off the wall, laid it on the
dining room table, and then opened his suitcase and removed
the Wallace Pearle canvas. He unrolled it and spread it out on
the table next to the watercolor, taking a minute to admire it.
Girl on a Window Seat, he thought, you need a temporary
home. He removed the spring tensioners from the back of the
watercolor frame and disassembled it. Then he placed the
Pearle canvas between the watercolor paper and the backing
board and reassembled it. When he was done, he hung the
painting back up on the front room wall and stepped back. He
and Asta stood side by side, staring at the painting.
  "That is one terrific-looking watercolor, huh, Asta?"

71

Chapter Twelve

Louise Dahlman was seated on the couch in the Pearles' spacious front room, located just off the foyer. At this time of day the couch was her favorite spot because the sheer drapes across the large windows let in just the right amount of afternoon sun. Reclining against silk cushions, Louise was reviewing the preparations for an upcoming luncheon fundraiser for Books for Africa, one of her favorite charities, when the doorbell rang. When she opened the door, the man standing on the porch took off his hat and smiled. His smile seemed oddly cold.

"Good afternoon. I'm here to see Mr. Wallace Pearle. I believe he's expecting me."

The gentleman's thick English accent surprised Louise. The man was of medium height, and his stocky build filled his proper-looking dark suit almost to bursting. Though he was nearly bald with a thin fringe of gray-brown hair above his ears, the tie done up tightly against his thick, muscular neck gave the impression of substantial strength.

"Certainly," she said. "Please come in."

The man stepped forward into the spot vacated by Louise.

"May I say who's calling?"

"You just tell him his old chum Eddie's here."

"Eddie?"

"Eddie Fitzner. I'm an old acquaintance of his."

When Louise's eyes widened in surprise, Fitzner took a moment to look her over. "Are you all right, then?"

"Oh, yes."

"Do I have the honor of addressing Mrs. Wallace Pearle?"

"No. I'm—my name is Louise. Please follow me, Mr. Fitzner."

Louise led him with quick, nervous steps across the foyer toward Wallace's study in the rear of the house, but Fitzner lagged behind, folding his hands behind his back and taking time to study the rich décor that surrounded him. He let out an appreciative whistle. "Old Wallace hasn't done badly for himself, I see. Not badly at all."

As they reached the great room, Roberta emerged from the hall that led to the kitchen. "Louise, I thought I heard someone at the—" She stopped when she saw Fitzner. "Oh, hello. I'm Roberta Pearle. May I help you?"

Before he had a chance to respond, Louise said, "This is Mr. Edward Fitzner. He's here to see Wallace."

Either Fitzner failed to notice Roberta's stunned expression, or he chose to disregard it, bowing slightly. "Pleased to make your acquaintance." He grinned. "More the merrier is what I say—maybe we'll pick up a few more stragglers on the way."

Fitzner took a small metal box out of his suit pocket and opened it. He extracted a white lozenge from it and popped it into his mouth and then held the open tin out to Roberta. "Mint?"

Roberta seemed to have recovered from her shock, but her quizzical expression prompted a word of explanation by Fitzner. "Altoids—good strong English mints."

She shook her head, and Louise declined as well.

He smiled and snapped the box shut, placing it back in his pocket. "Can you lead me to your famous husband, then?"

"Certainly. This way."

With the lady of the house available to assume the duties of hostess, Louise dropped back, content to follow at a distance. When they reached Wallace's study, Roberta peeked in through the open door and said, "Wallace—"

Before she could explain, Fitzner stepped around her into the doorway. "Wallace, old man, such a long time. So good to see you again."

Wallace Pearle stood up, stepped around from behind his desk, and walked across his study. He shook hands with Fitzner and mumbled something under his breath to him that Roberta couldn't make out.

"I want you to arrange a meeting for tomorrow if possible," Fitzner said. "The quicker we nip this thing in the bud, the better for all concerned, eh?"

Wallace reached around Fitzner and, without saying a word, closed the door, leaving Roberta and Louise out in the hall.

Chapter Thirteen

July 1983

By the time Ellie Myers had been Wallace Pearle's secretary for three months, two things had happened. The first was that Ellie had begun to be accepted into Wallace's circle of atelier students. Wallace held court nightly at group dinners, during which anecdotes, opinions, and debate flowed as liberally around the table as the house Chianti, providing Ellie with a fascinatingly candid view of the artistic process. They played duets twice a week as a rule, usually following dinner, accompanied by glasses of sherry and attended by any of the students who cared to listen. Over the course of many such evenings, Ellie had come to understand that, while Wallace held himself to high standards of formality in his speech and etiquette, his demonstrated tolerance for the behavior of others was indeed genuine.

The second thing that happened was that Ellie was proving herself indispensable, not only to the atelier Pearle and Wallace's business concerns, but also to Wallace himself. She was writing letters to his associates on his behalf, she was making decisions regarding his public appearances, and she had even become friends with Wallace's business manager, Eloise Whitney. Eloise, who had her main office on Fifth Avenue in New York City, was coming to trust Ellie's judgment and rely on her as her local eyes and ears and so was able to perform more of her duties long-distance from the Big Apple.

The increase in Ellie's responsibilities was naturally accompanied by an increase in the demands on her time. So when Wallace eventually offered her the use of a guest bedroom in the main house, she accepted. It just made sense that a room of her own on the estate would be practical. She still kept her apartment, of course, but gradually more and more of her wardrobe and belongings were finding their way to her new second home.

Ellie had come to understand how generous Wallace could be. One day in July he'd come to her explaining that he wished to establish an ongoing charitable donation for an organization called the Greater London Arts Association.

"They were very supportive during my undergraduate years at Oxford," he explained. "It was a time when I was casting about trying to find myself. Without their help and encouragement, I'd likely have wound up a lawyer and been relegated to a dry and barren life spent toiling before the bar. What I owe them is incalculable."

What Wallace owed them only he knew, but what he elected to pay them turned out to be a hefty monthly stipend. Wallace pointed out that in her position as personal secretary and Dragon Lady, Ellie already controlled the various accounts that ran both the household budget and the atelier.

"To your growing list of responsibilities, Ellie, I would like to add the task of seeing to it that each month a specific sum is entered into my personal account so I may be able to write a check to the Association."

This seemed strange to Ellie. Her systematic nature rebelled at the inefficiency of having to write a check every month, as opposed to, for example, making a single yearly donation. And why would Wallace want to be bothered with the task himself? But when she offered alternatives, her boss waved them off, saying simply, "It is my desire to do so." Still, Ellie recognized that the slightly eccentric nature of Wallace's request in no way diminished the generosity of the gesture.

It was a Saturday night in late July when Ellie stood in front of the full-length mirror in her room and shifted her evening gown in grave assessment. The gown, a gift from Wallace, had specifically been meant for a Minneapolis gallery opening that they were attending that night. It was stunningly chic, black, and obviously very expensive. Wallace knocked on her bedroom door and then opened it, and Ellie turned to face him. When he saw her, he stopped in the doorway, staring. The length of the silence flustered Ellie into nervous speech.

"The gown is so beautiful, Wallace."

He walked over to her, gently placed a hand on each of her shoulders, and kissed her. "You make the gown beautiful, Ellie, and I'm pleased that you like it."

"I do. Now I've got to decide what jewelry would look good with it." She reached across her dressing table and opened her mahogany jewelry box. She realized that she was embarrassed by the sparse selection, and that made her feel uncomfortable.

"Perhaps I can help." He walked around behind her and turned her so they were both facing the mirror. A necklace appeared in his hands. He placed it around her neck, his fingers lightly brushing her skin as he closed the clasp. When he lowered his arms, he remained behind her, both of them staring at the necklace. It was the one Wallace's father had given to his mother to wear to the White House. A sapphire set in platinum.

Ellie's startled expression found Wallace's face in the mirror. "I can't borrow this. What if something happened to it?"

"It's yours, a gift."

Ellie turned around, looking up into his face. "I don't know what to say," she said.

"The sapphire matches the color of your eyes," he said. "I want you to wear it when I paint you."

"You're going to paint me?"

"I am helpless before great beauty, Ellie," he said. He brushed the back of his fingers across her cheek, a habit he'd acquired. "Yes, I would like to paint you." He walked back to the doorway. "This is some affair you've arranged for us," he said. "They've actually sent a car. It's downstairs now."

Ellie turned back to the mirror for one last look and smiled. "I thought it would be a nice touch."

"We must be important."

"Do you think the mayor of Minneapolis would be there if you weren't attending?"

"I would like to believe that he's an art lover. Shall we go?"

"I just have to put on some cologne." Ellie picked up her bottle, and Wallace walked back over to her. He took the cologne, sniffed it, and read the label. "Opium, Yves St. Laurent. This is a strong scent for someone so young. I like the Amarige on you, myself. It's much lighter, more delicate."

"Really?" She'd discovered Opium in college. It had always suited her needs, so she'd never bothered looking any further. *Oh, well,* she thought, *who am I wearing this for anyway, him or me?* She set the Opium down and picked up the atomizer of Amarige, misted it into the air, and walked though it.

Chapter Fourteen

Monday

Ray Danvers wasn't what Donald Berglund had been expecting when he contacted the Two Bears Casino in northern Curran County to set up an interview with the general manager. Danvers' secretary, Deborah, had been businesslike and courteous to a fault when arranging things on the phone, and Danvers himself, undoubtedly a very busy man, had proven generous with his time. Still, with all the businesslike efficiency, Donald had arrived at the casino expecting to see some sort of acknowledgment that these people actually were Native Americans.

The Two Bears Casino itself did this to an extent; though the actual structure was modern steel-and-block construction, a rustic-looking timber-lodgelike facade had been tacked on. And two bears, representing the constellations Ursa Major and Ursa Minor, towered above the entrance. But once Donald had gotten inside and walked past the Council Feast Buffet and the Wigwam Room, featuring Chubby Checker appearing tonight, that was pretty much it for the Native American décor.

The offices that he glimpsed as he was led through the halls to Ray Danvers' office were full of laptop computers and wall charts and did little to identify the casino as a Native American business concern. And when he was finally ushered into the general manager's office, he glanced around, half expecting to see a tepee pencil sharpener or something equally corny, but was disappointed. Instead of moose antlers adorning the walls of the spacious room, a bank of twenty-four television screens filled one long wall, providing video surveillance of various areas of the casino.

Ray Danvers rose from behind his large, well-ordered desk and buttoned his suit jacket as he stepped around to shake hands. Danvers looked like the CEO of a Fortune 500 company. His suit looked European, his tie was definitely silk, and his black hair, going to a distinguished gray on the sides, was meticulously groomed, as though a barber attended to it every morning. His handshake was firm, and his eyes met Donald's squarely and held on, reminding Donald of successful politicians he'd had occasion to meet in the past. Donald was surprised. Though he hadn't seriously expected to be greeted by someone with a long ponytail, a buckskin jacket, and a bolo tie, he also hadn't expected someone quite this poised.

"Mr. Danvers, thanks for taking the time to talk to me," Donald said. "I know you're a very busy man, and I appreciate your being willing to fit me in."

"Not a problem, Mr. Berglund." Danvers' voice was soothing and pleasant, and he spoke without hurrying. "After reading your newspaper article last week, I believe it may be in both of our best interests to meet."

The welcoming timbre of his voice seemed to invite Donald to appreciate the reasoning behind his words and agree with him. Donald understood that the Two Bears tribe wasn't foolish enough to trust the operation of a business concern worth in the neighborhood of two hundred million dollars a year to some rustic hick. Of course this guy was smooth. Donald had done a bit of homework and knew that Ray Danvers had a couple of master's degrees under his belt. He sensed an icebreaker.

"Was there anything specific in the article that caught your attention?"

"Have a seat, Mr. Berglund." Danvers indicated the over-stuffed leather chair that faced his desk and then walked around and resumed his own seat. "Would you like some coffee?"

"No thanks." Donald sat down, placing the manila envelope he was carrying onto the desk.

Danvers leaned back, took a slow breath, and tented his hands as if to say, *here is the church, here is the steeple.* "It wasn't so much what you said in the article, Mr. Berglund; it was more what you left unsaid or, rather, implied."

"I simply pointed out that your operation has attracted the attention of an as yet unnamed out-of-state interest," Donald said, paraphrasing his own words.

"But what you implied was that this out-of-state interest wants to be taken in as a full partner."

Donald shrugged, unable to keep a tinge of pride out of his voice. "I have a source with connections in Atlantic City who owed me a favor. He says the word is that certain people are sniffing around for a chance to buy in, and these particular people are always full partners."

The general manager smiled. "Buy in? To this operation? The Two Bears band of the Chippewa is a sovereign nation, Mr. Berglund. We have agreements in place with both the state of Wisconsin and the National Indian Gaming Commission in Washington—agreements that we take very seriously."

"Of course you do," Donald said. "But the real question is, how seriously does the Manzara family take those agreements?"

"Manzara? Are you referring to organized crime?"

"Are you telling me that you didn't know who the unnamed interest was?"

Donald watched as Danvers took a pack of cigarettes from his desk drawer and lit one. Did he notice a tinge of nervousness in the gesture?

"I can assure you, we are not handing our casino over to a New Jersey mob."

"They might be a handy source of capital—I mean, if you needed some. For instance, if your profits were off substantially, like, for three straight quarters. It's a funny thing about business; you can be profitable, but in today's business climate, if you're not as profitable as expected, you're toast."

Danvers took a drag off his cigarette, blew the smoke at the ceiling, and smiled at Donald. "Someone's been crunching numbers. I'm beginning to suspect, Mr. Berglund, that you've come here to ambush me."

Donald ignored the comment. "The only drawback is that accepting capital from a new investor might mean giving up some control over the operation. And in the case of this particular investor, past history guarantees that that'll be the case."

"But your premise assumes interest on our part, interest that simply does not exist."

Donald crossed his legs and sat back in his chair. "Tell me something, Mr. Danvers. Who would you—I mean, your tribe—contact if you thought you were being squeezed?"

"Squeezed? By the mob?" Danvers looked as though he were about to dismiss the question, then seemed to change his mind. "Our first call would be to the state gaming commission, of course."

"And then?"

"The National Indian Gaming Commission and certainly the governor."

"Have you contacted them yet?"

"Of course not. There's no reason to."

Donald slid the manila envelope that he'd brought with him off the desk and opened it. He withdrew an eight-by-ten photograph and tossed it onto the desk between them. "This picture was taken last Tuesday at the Sportsman's Bar in Hudson."

Danvers leaned forward in his chair and studied the photo but said nothing.

"Just four men having a friendly drink. Two are members of your tribal commission, but of course you know that. The third is a New Jersey resident with the unlikely name of Pete 'The Pick' Gumbusky, and the fourth is none other than the celebrated Alfonse 'The Python' Manzara. I believe you also know that."

The Two Bears general manager stared at the photo but still said nothing. Donald continued. "The silent treatment isn't going to make these people disappear."

"You're assuming too much, Mr. Berglund; they're just having an innocent drink in a public place."

"Is that your official response? An innocent drink?"

Danvers sighed and set his cigarette down in a glass ashtray fashioned to look like the two bears constellations. He got up slowly from his seat, picked up the photo, and walked around his desk to face Donald. "Is this all you were concerned about, this photograph? Everything's fine, Mr. Berglund. If members of our commission are approached in public, they can hardly be condemned for it. Guilt by association was a bad idea during your Communist witch hunts in the fifties, and it remains a bad idea today."

Donald rose from his seat, having received the message loud and clear that the interview was over. Danvers placed one hand on Donald's shoulder as they walked together to the door. With his other hand he produced a pair of tickets, which he handed to Donald along with the photograph.

"Please be our guest in the Wigwam Room. I think Chubby Checker is appearing tonight."

Donald accepted the tickets but handed the photo back. "Keep the picture—it's a copy. But do me one favor: give me a call when you come to your senses. Or, better still, do yourself a favor and call the Feds."

Chapter Fifteen

"**Y**ou told Bob Tilsen you voted for Wyatt Earp?"

Frank Kahler, a reporter with the *St. Paul Pioneer Press,* wasn't exactly going out of his way to kill the sarcasm in his voice. He was sitting on Phyllis Biederman's desk and talking to Dexter from across the room.

Dexter shrugged. "He mentioned that he didn't get a campaign contribution from me, so I told him I didn't vote for him."

"And you told him you voted for Wyatt Earp instead?"

"He said he ran unopposed."

"*And then* you told him you voted for Wyatt Earp?"

"I guess. Yeah. How'd you hear about it, anyway? There wasn't anybody there but the two of us."

"Are you kidding? He's telling that story all over the office up at the County Center," Kahler said, laughing. "Brilliant."

Dexter searched for a snappy comeback but came up dry, and the moment passed. He wrote it off, content that a line would undoubtedly occur to him at three in the morning, so at least he had that to look forward to. He shuffled the deck of cards he was holding and turned his attention back to Grady, who was sitting beside him at his desk reading Chief

Coffer's report on the 1984 Ellie Myers murder. Seeing her in the photograph of the painting and then having the conversation with Donald Berglund had gotten Dexter thinking about Ellie Myers to the point where her case was starting to suck him in. For a while this morning, after soundly thrashing Grady at chess, Dexter had tried to concentrate on locating pawnshops in the cities where the thief might have tried to unload Roberta Pearle's jewelry. But the murder of his babysitter had proven too strong a draw. And now Grady was apparently hooked too.

"She was poisoned," Dexter pointed out.

"Shh." Without looking up from the report, Grady waved a hand at Dexter as though he were a fly.

"The autopsy found traces of extract from a poisonous plant in her blood."

"Hush, boy."

Dexter gave it about five seconds. "It was belladonna."

This time Grady did look up from the report. "I'm not to that part yet, okay?"

"Sorry." Dexter leaned over, seriously invading Grady's personal space, and looked at the report. "Belladonna's an ornamental plant that's also called deadly nightshade, I Googled it. Supposed to be fairly common in gardens."

"Yeah, I know about belladonna."

Dexter shuffled the cards again. "The report says Coffers had his eye on Wallace Pearle as a suspect. They found some belladonna growing in his greenhouse at the time of the murder, but they couldn't connect him to actually using it, so they never charged him. How do you know about belladonna?"

Grady flipped a page of the report. "I'm a medical tech, remember? I studied poisons a couple of years ago. They went through all the common plants: belladonna, Jimsonweed, curare, hemlock, and rhododendron. And you're right, belladonna's common in lots of gardens."

"They never found out how the poison got into her system."

"Dex, when you asked me if I wanted to take a look at the report, you never said anything about an audio book." Grady flipped another page, read for a minute, and said, "They never charged Pearle."

"Lack of evidence. And if you were paying attention, you would have just heard me say that." He held the deck of cards out toward Grady. "Pick a card."

"You said that writer—what's his name again?—wanted to include this report in his biography?"

"I'm not sure. I think he's just looking for anything that has to do with Pearle's relationship with Ellie Myers. And his name's Donald Berglund."

"You gave a copy of that report to a writer?" asked Frank Kahler.

"Yeah," Dexter said.

"An unsolved homicide? Did you at least charge a copy fee?"

Dexter decided he was sufficiently mature to ignore the comment, but Kahler persisted.

"Uh-oh. Never mind releasing confidential police info, there was no copy fee. Looks like a financial scandal brewing at city hall."

Dexter got out of his chair, walked over to Frank Kahler, and held the cards out to him. "Pick a card, any card."

"Say what?"

"Just pick a card."

"He's practicing for tonight," Grady explained without looking up from the report.

"What's tonight?"

Phyllis provided the explanation. "Every year Dexter puts on his amateur magic show for the folks at Clintondale. It's really popular."

"Clintondale—that's your retirement home here in Higgins Point, right?"

"It's over on Mason Street. It also has an assisted-living

section and an intensive-care section." Dexter was still holding the deck of cards out to Kahler. "You gonna pick a card or what?"

Kahler looked down at the deck in Dexter's hand and shook his head. "Some other time, Chief. We gotta go." Kahler stood up, and Phyllis joined him, walking to the door.

Dexter spread his hands. "Where's the fire?"

"We're taking my mother to the IMAX theatre at the Minnesota Zoo," Phyllis explained. "There's a feature on Mt. Everest."

Grady looked up from the report and grinned at Kahler. "Meetin' the mom, huh? Guess things must be gettin' serious."

"Is this the first time you're subjecting your mother to Frank, here, Phyllis?" Dexter asked.

Phyllis smiled. "Uh-huh."

Kahler grimaced and said, "Need-to-know basis, Phyl. Don't tell these guys our business."

Dexter walked over and tossed the deck of cards onto his desk. "What's with this secretive attitude, coming from a member of the Fourth Estate? I tell you I'm shocked, Grady. Shocked and appalled."

Phyllis paused at the front door, while Frank Kahler waved a hand in the air. "Yeah, yeah. Let me know when you actually dig up something on the burglary."

"See you tonight, Kahler," Dexter said.

Kahler lowered his arm. "What are you talking about?"

"Aren't you going out with Phyllis?"

"Yeah."

"Well, she never misses my show. Do you, Phyl?"

"Nope," she said, smiling at Kahler as she led him out the door.

"Time for you to go," Dexter called after them. "The mother's waiting."

A second later, as if it was a revolving door, Delmar entered. Dexter grinned. "Hey, Uncle Delmar."

"Dex, and uh . . ."

"Grady Penz," Dexter reminded him.

"Yeah, Grady, right."

"Do you need anything, Uncle Delmar?"

Delmar shook back his gray sharkskin suit jacket and straightened his shirt collar, which was opened to the second button, exposing a tanned chest full of hair. He looked around Dexter's office as if he was considering purchasing it. "Hey, you know what? Since we ain't on some kinda kiddie TV show, why don't you knock off that 'Uncle Delmar' stuff, and just call me, Del, okay?"

"Sure, no problem . . . Del," Dexter said, having just a little trouble getting it out. "Are you enjoying Higgins Point?"

"Oh, yeah, sure. Everything's great. Only I got a little bored hangin' around your place. Thought I'd wander into town, but I'm havin' a little trouble findin' it. Higgins Point's a great place if you want to get lost and never be heard from again."

Grady set the report down, apparently finished with it. "We like it," he said.

"Anything ever happen around here?"

"In fact, we just had a little excitement," Dexter said. "There was a burglary Friday night."

Delmar flipped up the hinged countertop and stepped into Dexter's office. "You know, I heard something about that. They were talking about it over at the cafe, at Janet's. They got great coffee by the way. So, you guys get a lot of crime out this way?"

"Not really," Dexter said. "This is my first burglary."

"Your first one. No kiddin'? If I knew that, I would've got you somethin'."

Dexter got up and walked to the coffeepot. "Like some coffee, Uncle—uh, Del?"

Delmar walked over to Dexter's desk and sat down in the vacated chair. "Thanks anyway. Just had a cup at Janet's, like

I said." He put his hands, hands that Dexter thought looked as if they could crush walnuts, on Dexter's desk, palms down, and looked sideways at Grady.

"So this is what it feels like to be a cop. Pardon me, to be the top cop in town."

Grady took a sip of coffee and said, "You'd have to put on the badge to get the full effect."

Delmar grinned at Grady. "Yeah, I guess you would. You're a medical technician, right, Grady?"

"Yup."

Without a desk to sit behind, Dexter sauntered to the counter and leaned against that. "You know, Del, I hardly ever get to see you," Dexter said. "I don't think you ever mentioned what you do—I mean, for a living."

"Oh, you know, Dex, a little of this, a little of that. Nothing too exciting."

Noting the way his uncle tended to dress, Dexter decided to take a guess. "You're in sales, right?"

"Yeah, sure. You could say there's some sales, and some acquisitions too."

"What do you acquire?" Grady asked.

"Oh, whatever happens to be—hey, what have we here?" Delmar picked up a set of handcuffs that were sitting on a corner of Dexter's desk. They were shiny steel and made a serious-sounding *ching* when he shook them.

Responding to some subliminal resentment at having his uncle handling his police gear, Dexter stepped over to the desk with the intention of applying a bit of misdirection. He picked up the deck of cards, shuffled them, and held them out to his uncle. "Pick a card, any card."

Delmar looked at the cards and then grinned at Dexter. "You serious?"

"Yeah. I'm doing a magic act tonight, and I can use the practice, and Grady's a terrible subject, for reasons too numerous to go into right now."

Grady shook his head, and Delmar said, "You're doing a magic act? I got a better trick you can do tonight. Hold out your hands."

"Oh, I don't know, Del." Dexter stepped back and, without realizing it, put his hands into his pockets.

Delmar picked up the cuffs and pushed the chair back as he stood up. "C'mon Dex. You got a key around here someplace, right?"

"Sure. Of course I have a key."

"Well, then, let's have it."

Dexter took the key out of the top drawer and handed it to his uncle, who put it into his pocket.

"Okay, now gimme your hands."

There was something about Delmar, something that, if asked, Dexter couldn't have put a word to, but something that made him see his uncle's request as perfectly reasonable. Without really believing he was actually doing it, Dexter extended his hands.

"Atta boy." The cuffs locked on with a thick, clicking ratchet. Dexter noticed that Delmar was careful not to tighten them too much. Apparently he had learned how to handle handcuffs in his sales position. Delmar grabbed both of Dexter's wrists and gave them a firm shake. "They on good?"

"Uh, yeah, I believe so."

Dexter looked at Grady, who was both shaking his head and grinning. "Don't look at me, brother. You're the one who's wearing handcuffs in his own jail."

"Okay, Del, so now what? What's the trick?"

At that point the door opened, and Sheriff Bob Tilsen walked in. Dexter actually saw Tilsen's right hand, in the tiniest gesture, start for his sidearm before he read the situation and relaxed. He paused in the doorway for just a second while he surveyed the three men, and then he slowly closed the door behind himself. He was carrying a manila folder, which he tossed onto the counter.

"Insurance photos of the Pearles' jewelry, Dex. Figured they'd come in handy if you're checking pawnshops." He looked at Delmar. "Who's the arresting officer?"

"This is my uncle, Delmar Loomis," Dexter said. "Del, this is Sheriff Bob Tilsen."

Delmar stepped back from Dexter and nodded at the sheriff. "Pleased to meet you. Hey, those must be the photos from that burglary I heard about this morning."

"They are," Tilsen assured him. "And your nephew is going to solve the case for us—that is, if he can get out of the cuffs. Right, Dex?"

Dexter, who was busy staring at his uncle's pants pocket where the key was, wasn't going to dignify that comment with a response. Instead, he held up his hands and whispered to his uncle, "Hey, Del, why don't you—"

But Delmar ignored Dexter and stepped over to the counter across from Tilsen. He opened the folder that lay on the countertop between them and whistled while he paged through the photos. "There's some fancy-lookin' baubles here. Looks like this Pearle lady's got good taste."

Tilsen was studying Delmar. "I hate to sound like a cliché, but haven't I seen you someplace before?"

Delmar looked at him and raised his eyebrows. "I got that kinda face."

"No, really. You look familiar."

"I was back here a few years ago for my sister's funeral. Maybe you saw me then."

"Who's your sister?"

"Myra Taylor, Dex's aunt, the one who left him the house." He closed the folder. "You guys got any leads yet?"

Tilsen shrugged. "Nothing much. We think we know how he got inside. She was your sister, and she left her house to Dexter?"

"Dex's dad was out of the picture," Delmar explained,

"and Myra knew I moved around too much to own a house. So how did he get in?"

"The usual way, through the garage. We're not sure how he got past the dog, though. So what do you do that keeps you moving around, Delmar?"

"Uh, excuse me, Del." Dexter held up his hands and rattled the cuffs to get his uncle's attention.

"They take anything besides the jewelry? They break open a safe?" Delmar asked.

"Not the safe, but they took a painting."

"An expensive one," Dexter added, "worth a quarter of a million dollars."

Delmar whistled again. "Is that a fact—a quarter of a million? Hey, you guys ever think maybe it was a gang did this?"

The sheriff shook his head. "I doubt it. A gang would have left more behind. We don't have any prints, fibers, footprints, nothing."

"It sounds like you guys are up against a real pro. He took jewelry and art from an occupied home and got away without leaving a clue. That's pretty impressive. You think you're gonna find this guy? I mean, he's probably long gone by now, right?"

Tilsen was staring at Delmar. "Yeah. I doubt he'd be stupid enough to hang around. But we've got some irons in the fire. We have a better than even chance of catching him. Funny, I don't recall mentioning that the home was occupied."

"Yeah, sure, you did."

Dexter cleared his throat and held up his manacled hands again. "Uh, Del."

The sheriff looked at Dexter and grinned. "Guess you'd better release your prisoner. Sounds like he's had enough. I have to go. Dex, Grady. Nice meeting you, Delmar. Just wish I could remember where I've seen you before."

After Tilsen was gone, Delmar picked up the folder of

photos and tossed them onto Dexter's desk, then stepped over in front of Dexter and held his wrists. "Okay, you want out, you gotta say 'uncle.' "

Dexter tried to smile.

"Hey, just kiddin', Dex." He produced the key and unlocked the handcuffs, massaging Dexter's wrists as he did it. Then he tossed the cuffs onto the desk. "You're free to go." He winked. "Just don't leave town." Delmar walked around to the other side of the counter. "I gotta go too. You guys, take it easy."

"Wait a minute, Uncle. You were supposed to show me a trick with the cuffs. So what's the trick?"

"A trick? Did I say that?"

"Yeah."

"Look, I really gotta go. What time you got, anyway, Dex?"

Dexter glanced down at his left wrist and suddenly realized his watch was missing. When he looked up, Delmar was dangling it from a finger and smiling. He placed it on the counter. "I'll just leave this here in case you need it. Afternoon, gentlemen."

Delmar stepped out and closed the door, and Dexter walked over and put his watch back on. "Not a bad trick, I guess."

Grady nodded. "Pretty good. You gonna use it tonight?"

"Ha-ha, very funny." Dexter was looking at Grady a little strangely.

"What's the problem, Dex?"

Dexter shook his head. "Just wondering where the sheriff knows my uncle from."

Chapter Sixteen

At 8:30 P.M., the main assembly hall of the Clintondale Commons Senior Living Facility on Mason Street was rocking to the rafters. Stainless steel wheelchairs were lined up wheel to wheel along the sides and in the back, and the walking wounded, as some of them liked to refer to themselves, filled perhaps fifty chairs in the center. Two dozen white uniformed attendants stood around the periphery, and IV trees and oxygen canister dollies stuck up like pussy willows in a swamp. The center of the attention was Dexter Loomis, aka The Great Dexterini, draped in a purple cape and brandishing a magic wand. The occasion was the annual Clintondale Magic Show, an extravaganza that had grown over the years from Dexter's practice of visiting the home periodically to perform magic for the residents.

Dexter, with the assistance of Grady Penz, currently had three of the ambulatory residents up onstage, each clutching a playing card to their chest as if they were never going to give them back. Spreading his arms wide, Dexter walked quickly across the makeshift stage and then spun around, causing his purple cape to flare out for dramatic effect. He wasn't fooling himself; he realized that, to the normal viewer, the collection of lame tricks that constituted his "magic act," were mind-numbingly inane, but he also understood that these Clintondale shows were all about getting the residents out and active. Just because they were advanced in years didn't mean that they still didn't get a kick out of seeing and being seen.

Dexter used a cordless microphone to address the crowd. "Okay, each one of you has—" A loud squawk from the PA brought pained grimaces from the audience. One of the attendants in the back reached over to the amplifier and adjusted the volume down slightly. "Each of you has looked at your card and knows what it is."

Alfred Cherny, who was a little odd, in that he had a habit of spontaneously disrobing at inappropriate times, took another quick peek at his card.

Dexter pointed at Mrs. Addison, the first person in line. "Your card," he announced, "is the seven of spades." Mrs. Addison just stared at him. "Go on, you can show everyone your card now." She continued to stare. "It's okay to show it now. Go on." She glanced at her card again and finally held it up.

"The seven of spades," Dexter announced, drawing comments from the audience.

"What'd he say?"

"Didn't he do this trick last year?"

Dexter pointed at Mr. Cherny in the middle. "Your card is . . ." Pausing to elevate the suspense, Dexter held a hand to his forehead, indicating intense concentration. ". . . the jack of diamonds." Once again the audience got into the spirit of things.

"I think he's going to do it."

"Go for it, Al."

Mr. Cherny was indeed reaching for his belt buckle when an alert Grady Penz, who had assisted Dexter with this show in past years, hurried over and gently assisted him offstage.

Dexter walked back across the stage again, waving his

arms, and aimed his wand at Benny Dobson, the third subject. "And last but not least, your card is . . . the king of clubs."

Benny held his card up, revealing the king of clubs, and farted.

The other residents started clapping.

"You tell 'em, Benny."

Grady retrieved the cards from Mr. Dobson and Mrs. Addison and helped them return to their seats.

Dexter raised his arms dramatically. "And now, for something special."

Sensing something special, the crowd grew so quiet that the only sound to be heard in the hall was a chorus of wheezing from the asthma contingent.

"As I'm sure you all know, Ole Nordstrom turns one hundred years old today!"

Dexter nodded to Grady. Amid general applause, Grady and one of the attendants went to the front row, where Ole was seated, and helped him to his feet. Grady guided him forward toward Dexter, while the attendant wheeled the dolly that held the canister attached to the clear plastic tube that fed oxygen into Ole's nostrils. He made his way slowly up to Dexter, managing to cover the last few feet under his own steam.

"Mr. Nordstrom owned and operated a family dairy farm in Jackson County for more than fifty years," Dexter announced. "Joining him for this occasion are his two remaining sons, five of his grandchildren, seven great-grandchildren, and, yes, one great-great-grandchild! I'm sure I speak for everyone here, sir, when I say that it's an honor to help you celebrate your one hundredth birthday."

Ole, who had long since forgotten that he was ever a farmer, adjusted the volume on his hearing aid, leaned over toward Dexter, and said, "What?"

Ole's relatives had filed onto the stage during Dexter's

speech. They patted their patriarch on the shoulder, then shuffled off to the side, where they stood respectfully.

"Mr. Nordstrom, I wonder if we could get you to help us out with a magic trick."

Dexter signaled Grady, who brought over a chair and placed it next to Ole, facing the audience.

"Just take a seat, Mr. Nordstrom, and relax." Ole sat in the chair, and Dexter produced a black silk bandana. He waved it around and then placed it over Ole's eyes, stimulating further crowd reaction.

"Oh, my God, they're going to shoot him!"

As soon as the blindfold had been tied into place, Dexter nodded to a pair of attendants at the back of the room, who went out of the hall and returned pushing a wheeled cart. On the cart was a giant birthday cake that held one hundred blazing candles. The management had arranged to disarm the smoke detectors in the hall just long enough to bring in the cake and blow out the candles. Someone turned the lights down, and everybody watched in silent awe as the huge cake was wheeled through the crowd toward the stage. When the cake had been positioned ten feet in front of Ole, Dexter removed the blindfold and then signaled the crowd to begin singing "Happy Birthday to You."

For such an outpouring of affection from his fellow residents, Ole demonstrated remarkable restraint.

Dexter placed his hand on Ole's shoulder. "Ole?"

There was no response.

"Mr. Nordstrom?"

Ole remained completely motionless. Someone brought the lights back up, and Dexter noticed that Ole's chin was resting on his chest. He hoped Ole was taking a nap, but when he bent down to check him, Ole's staring eyes made him doubt it.

"Uh . . ." Dexter looked helplessly at Grady.

Grady stepped over and checked for a pulse in Ole's

neck. After a few seconds he removed his hand and shook his head.

Dexter whispered to Grady. "Is there anything we can do?" Two attendants were already putting the body into a wheelchair and hurrying him away to try to resuscitate him.

"They'll try," Grady said, "but at that age—it's just his time."

Dexter's shoulders sagged; he felt incredibly useless. The attendants began assisting the residents back to their rooms, and as they slowly filed out, Dexter was painfully aware of the way they looked at him. Grady was blowing the candles out, so the smoke detectors could be reactivated, when Dexter's cell phone went off. It was a state police dispatcher cordially inviting him to a traffic accident.

Chapter Seventeen

It was 9:15 P.M. when Dexter and Grady walked over to the shoulder of County Road J and looked down the embankment at the activity ten feet below. Bathed like a circus ringmaster in the light of a nearly full moon and the hit-or-miss beams of half a dozen flashlights, Sheriff Bob Tilsen was cautioning his deputies to be sure to take enough photographs. He'd obviously paid attention to how his old boss, ex-Sheriff Moses Hicks, used to handle things. The object of everybody's attention was a light blue Volvo that was hubcap deep in weeds and had apparently attempted to embed itself in an elm tree. The car looked vaguely familiar to Dexter. When he and Grady climbed down the bank, Tilsen saw them coming.

"Howdy, Grady. We've got things pretty much covered here, Dex."

"Well, that's just great. Grady gets a 'howdy,' and all I get is a 'piss off.' "

Tilsen grinned. "Sorry about that. Howdy, Dex."

"Howdy."

"Now piss off."

Dexter nudged Grady. "Do you detect just a hint of Moses

Hicks' Southern drawl there? Because I swear for just a second I was experiencing déjà vu."

At his towering height, Grady was one of the few men who could look down on Dexter, and he looked down on him now. "What you're experiencing, Dex, is a case of selective memory. See, you remember that I'm black, but you forget that I'm from Chicago and therefore don't have any personal experience with any Southern drawl."

Dexter gave up on Grady and turned to Tilsen. "As police chief, I think I ought to take a look around, don't you?"

Tilsen made the same face that Dexter used to get from kids on the playground when they didn't want to play with him.

"Bob, technically, the Higgins Point city limits run right along the Curran County easement on County J." Two deputies accompanied by the medical examiner were just going past carrying the stretcher bearing a covered body. Dexter asked them to stop for a minute. "What was the cause of death?"

The ME looked at Dexter for a second and then, with a straight face, said, "He was in an auto accident." Then he added, "Severe head trauma."

Dexter pulled the sheet back and couldn't prevent a tiny intake of breath when he found himself staring down at the ruined face of Donald Berglund, the writer. He'd spent a grand total of maybe fifteen minutes with this guy, but for some reason the shock hit him in the gut, as if he'd lost a friend.

"Was it the impact with the windshield?"

"No, actually it was the impact with that." The ME pointed at an eighteen-inch wide oak tree that stood perhaps thirty feet beyond the elm that had brought Donald Berglund's Volvo to the fatally sudden stop, catapulting him through the windshield.

"No seat belt?"

"No seat belt."

"So, technically," Dexter pointed out, "he was still alive when he left his vehicle, here on county land, and he died when he hit that tree over there—beyond the easement, in Higgins Point."

The ME made a funny face. "I don't know if that tree's in Higgins Point or not, but I'm pretty sure he died when he hit it."

Dexter looked at the sheriff, and neither man spoke. Tilsen finally blinked. "The vehicle's sitting on county land, Dex."

"But the ME says he died in my town."

The sheriff turned to the ME. "Why do you encourage him?"

"You gentlemen can settle this between yourselves, but you'll have to excuse me—I have to get this body on ice. I've been told to get over to Clintondale to collect Ole Nordstrom." The ME looked pointedly at Dexter. "He turned one hundred today."

His expression told Dexter that he'd already heard about the unfortunate circumstances surrounding Ole's passing. Dexter kept his mouth shut until the ME and the deputies had carried Donald Berglund's body away; then he turned to the sheriff.

"Don't worry, Bob, I'm still inviting you into the investigation."

"Investigation?" Tilsen snorted. "What's there to investigate, why he fell asleep?"

"What makes you think he fell asleep?"

"Didn't find any alcohol in the car," Tilsen pointed out, "but we'll have to wait for the toxicology report to be sure. I suppose he could have hit a deer."

Dexter stepped over to the crumpled Volvo. "Hey, Grady, let me see your flashlight a minute." Grady handed the flashlight to Dexter, who used it to examine the front grill of Donald Berglund's car. After a minute he announced, "No deer parts or blood in the grill, and no dead deer in sight."

"Maybe he swerved to miss a deer," Grady suggested, "and went off the road."

"It's possible, I suppose," Dexter said as he started examining the driver's side of the car.

Tilsen shook his head. "You looking for signs of a side impact? So, what, now you think somebody ran him off the road?"

Dexter ignored the question, and the sheriff called out to two deputies standing at the edge of the road. "You guys find any skid marks up there?"

Both officers shook their heads.

Tilsen asked Dexter, "Any signs of scraped paint on the Volvo?"

Dexter straightened up. "I don't see any evidence of paint scrapes or a side impact."

"There's no skid marks because he never saw a deer, and there's no dents because he wasn't run off the road. He just fell asleep. If it's not dramatic enough for you, that's tough."

Dexter leaned in the passenger side window and guided the beam of Grady's flashlight around the interior. There was a box of fried chicken from the Main Street KFC lying on the floor, a spilled-out soft-drink cup, and a thin spattering of blood left behind from Donald's impact with the windshield. During the past ten months that he'd been a law officer, Dexter had been to several accident scenes, and it never failed to amaze him what thousands of pounds of steel traveling at high speeds could do to the human body.

"Seems like a stupid place to take a nap to me."

"Well, aren't we Mr. Sensitive?"

Dexter pulled his head out of the Volvo just in time to hear someone say, "You know, that's just the kind of priceless quote I've come to expect from the chief of Higgins Point's one-man police force."

Looking up, he saw Frank Kahler making a halting descent down the weed-covered embankment. He clutched a small white notepad in one hand and was waving it around to maintain his balance. *Great,* Dexter thought, *now I get to read* that *in the paper tomorrow.*

"What's up, folks? I passed the meat wagon on the way here. Anybody live?"

Grady shook his head.

"Victims?"

Sheriff Tilsen stepped closer. "One. Local fella, I guess."

"Got an ID yet?"

"Ronald Berglund."

"Donald," Dexter almost shouted at Tilsen. "His name's *Donald* Berglund."

"Okay, Dex, *Donald* Berglund."

"He was a writer," Dexter added softly.

Kahler was scribbling on his pad. "Oh, yeah? What'd he write?"

Nobody said anything, and Kahler looked around the group for an answer, but Dexter was suddenly too fatigued to talk. Nobody else there except Grady had ever met Berglund, and he didn't seem to have anything to say either.

Kahler was writing and talking at the same time. "By the way, you guys know that the chief, here"—he gestured at Dexter—"is leaving bodies in his wake at Clintondale?"

"Just one body," Grady pointed out, causing Dexter to grimace.

"Only because he didn't get to finish his act," Kahler pointed out. "Given the chance, I'll bet he could clear out the whole intensive-care wing."

Dexter summoned the strength to try to change the subject. "How'd you find out about this accident so quickly?"

"Are you kidding? You didn't see me? Same way I found out about your Kervorkian magic act—I was with Phyllis at Clintondale."

A fresh wave of fatigue washed over Dexter. "Let's go," he said to Grady.

They clambered up to the top of the embankment and stepped onto the road just as Phil Launer was starting to unwind the winch cable from his tow truck.

"Taking it to your place?" Dexter asked.

Phil nodded. "It'll be there for a few days, till the state police are through with it."

Dexter and Grady walked back to Dexter's Jeep. After they got in, Dexter put the key into the ignition but didn't turn it. He just sat there, staring ahead. Grady must have known he was thinking about Donald Berglund.

"He seemed like such a lively little guy."

Dexter took a deep breath. "I only met him once." He thought he was going to say something else, but it didn't come, and he didn't feel like forcing it.

"Why don't you think it's possible he fell asleep?" Grady asked.

Dexter turned the key. *Because I don't want to,* he thought. But that only raised another question. Why didn't he want to believe that Donald Berglund just fell asleep?

Chapter Eighteen

September 1984

Greater London Arts Association
71 Knightsbridge
London WI
England

Dear Sir/Madam:

I am writing to you regarding the monthly donation that your worthy and deserving organization currently re-ceives from the Wallace Pearle atelier. In my position as personal secretary to Mr. Pearle, please let me assure you at the outset that Mr. Pearle's support and enthusi-asm for your Association remains steadfast, and no re-duction in the stipend is being considered. Rather, my reason for contacting you at this time . . .

Approaching voices caused Ellie's fingers to pause above the keys of her IBM Selectric II typewriter. Through the open door of her office, which was located on the first floor of the main house, a short distance down the hall from the foyer, came the temperate tones of Wallace's cultivated speech. It was time for the next semester of instruction to begin, and Wallace was taking the new crop of aspiring artists on a tour. Ellie could hear him as he explained the layout of the house while answering questions being asked by younger, nervous voices. As the group drew nearer, Wallace's voice grew louder.

". . . and the marble used in the foyer was imported from a quarry in Italy, near the birthplace of Michelangelo." Suddenly he appeared in her doorway. "And ensconced in her citadel of power, resplendent beneath the many-colored raiment of her authority, behold the Dragon Lady of the atelier, Miss Ellie Myers."

Ellie nodded. Her smile was halfhearted; being referred to as the Dragon Lady by Wallace had begun to lose some of its charm, now that they were so close. He guided the five students to the doorway in front of him, and Ellie was mildly surprised to see among them a female student. She appeared to be in her early twenties, and Ellie was dismayed to note that she was both tall and attractive. She had a fine complexion, longish, gently curled auburn hair, and large expressive eyes. Ellie was further dismayed, though not exactly surprised, to see Wallace's hand casually resting on her left shoulder. In the sixteen months since Ellie had entered the sphere of Wallace's considerable influence, she'd come to understand certain things about his needs—chiefly, that they wouldn't be denied.

"At the conclusion of our little tour I will take my leave and place you in the competent hands of Miss Myers, who will show you to the cottages, which will be your homes for the next few months. At that time Miss Myers will also answer any and all remaining annoying questions."

Ellie took a deep breath and rose from her chair to face her five charges, their smiles fading by a barely discernable amount. This was the third group she'd handled since assuming the duties of Dragon Lady, and the routine was just beginning to feel tolerably comfortable.

"Welcome to the atelier, and please call me Ellie. I'm here to assist you in any way I can and help make your time here both enjoyable and rewarding. You should feel free to call on me with any questions or needs regarding your living quarters, meals, or our general routine here on the estate." Did she just see Wallace's hand actually massage that girl's shoulder? "I also manage the supplies for the atelier, so if you find you have any special requests in that area, I can take care of them for you. I believe your tour will last—what, another twenty minutes?"—she looked at Wallace, who nodded—"ending in the studio, where I will meet you and show you to your rooms, which are actually individual cabins and quite comfortable."

At the conclusion of Ellie's brief speech, Wallace removed his hand from the girl's shoulder and began herding the group down the hall toward the library. Ellie sat back down, returning her attention to the unfinished letter waiting in her typewriter. She was surprised when she glanced up and saw that the female student had returned to her doorway.

"Hello, I wanted to introduce myself. I'm Roberta Kaplan."

Ellie noted that she had a beautiful smile. She was obviously several years younger than Ellie's thirty-one but seemed to be playing the "two girls among the guys" buddy card, anyway.

"I'm pleased to meet you, Roberta," Ellie said in a cordial yet cool voice, designed to warn her off and send her down the hall.

"I'm sorry for interrupting you, but I just had to tell you how grateful I am for being given the opportunity to study here."

"Thank you, Roberta, but you weren't 'given' anything. These spots aren't doled out to just anyone, and I'm sure you wouldn't be here if you hadn't earned it." Though Ellie had to wonder exactly what sort of entrance exam Wallace had cooked up for young Miss Kaplan.

Roberta took a small step into Ellie's office. "It must be amazing being his personal secretary," she said.

She's trying to get into some sort of conversation with me, Ellie thought.

"I mean, working under someone as brilliant as Wallace Pearle—I can't even imagine . . ."

"Trust me, you will soon." Ellie wasn't exactly crazy about Roberta's reference to her working 'under,' Wallace.

"Watching the two of you just now, I—well, I probably shouldn't say anything."

"It's okay," Ellie said, resigned to the fact that they were now in a conversation.

"It's just that when I saw the way you looked at each other, I sensed a vibe between the two of you. You know, like maybe you're more than just his secretary."

Ellie was beyond surprised. She opened her mouth to speak, but the inappropriateness of Roberta's comment robbed her of her ability to respond. She had to remind herself to close her mouth.

Roberta's sculpted eyebrows rose in concern. "I'm sorry. I shouldn't have said anything, but I can understand it. I mean, a man like Wallace Pearle—he's practically an icon."

Still struggling to form a reply, Ellie realized that her hesitation had crushed any possibility she might have had of denying it. And she sincerely wished that this person would stop saying Wallace's name. "Well, personal secretary is my title—Roberta, was it?"

"Yes. Roberta Kaplan."

Ellie smiled. "You'd better hurry along, Roberta. You don't want to get left behind."

Roberta backed out the door. "I apologize if I put my foot in my mouth. I didn't mean to offend you. And don't worry, I can be very discreet." Then she was gone.

Ellie stared at the empty doorway for a full minute, wondering if she'd imagined the whole exchange. Finally she shook her head and turned her attention to completing the waiting letter.

Rather, my reason for contacting you at this time is regarding the manner of the monthly payments. I would like to propose switching to a single annual donation, which would be the equivalent of the twelve monthly checks you currently receive. I expect that such an arrangement would benefit your organization as well as ours, since it would allow you to count on the funds, and plan their use accordingly. Please indicate by post at your convenience if such an arrangement would be satisfactory to you.

Sincerely,
Ellie Myers, Personal Secretary
Pearle Atelier

21 Pearle Lane
Higgins Point, WI 54016
USA

Ellie wasn't in the habit of disregarding Wallace's wishes, but she saw no reason that his generosity toward the Greater London Arts Association should place a needless burden on his time. She was convinced that by stepping in to prevent his having to attend to this detail every month, she was not meddling but merely inserting a bit of efficiency into the process.

Chapter Nineteen

Tuesday

"What are you writing?" Grady was looking over the top of the newspaper at Dexter, who was sitting at his desk, head bent over a tablet of paper.

Dexter answered without looking up. "My to-do list."

"To-do list, huh? What do you have on it so far?"

Dexter tossed his pencil onto the desk and sat back, rubbing his neck and rolling his head. "Let's see, number one, solve Ellie Myers' murder."

"The twenty-year-old murder? Right. What else?"

"Number two, solve Pearle burglary. That's still on the list from Saturday."

"Anything else?"

"Number three, send flowers and an apology to Ole Nordstrom's family."

"On the list since last night?"

"Right."

"Is that it?"

"Number four, look into Donald Berglund's accident." He

111

looked up at Grady. "They're not necessarily in chronological order."

Grady studied Dexter for a moment before he spoke. "Tell me something, Dex. How would you go about getting six elephants into a Volkswagen?"

Dexter thought about it and then shrugged. "Well, I suppose, three in the front and three in the back. Why?"

"That's what I thought you were gonna say."

Grady disappeared behind the newsprint again just as the door to Dexter's office opened. A pale-skinned man, who looked to Dexter to be about thirty years old, walked in holding a manila envelope. He was close to six feet tall, and the weight he carried suggested that his only form of exercise was probably lifting food to his mouth. He ran a hand through the thin brown hair that hung over his ears and looked first at Dexter, and then at Grady, and then back at Dexter again. Then he suddenly turned around and left. Through the window Dexter could see him out on the porch, reading the brass plaque next to the door. When he walked back in, Dexter leaned back in his chair and waited.

"I'm looking for the police chief."

"If you find one, let me know," Grady said, and he went back to his paper.

"That'd be me." Dexter shot a look at Grady.

The man looked at Grady, in his brown EMT uniform, and then back at Dexter. "You're the Higgins Point Chief of Police?"

Dexter pointed at the area of his khaki shirt that normally would have held his badge. "That's what it says"—and realized that he'd left it at home—"would have said here." He looked around for some papers to straighten, but the only thing on his desktop besides his computer and a chess set was his to-do list.

He tapped importantly on his keyboard for a few seconds and then settled back in his chair. "What can I do for you?"

Grady's newspaper rattled, and Dexter swore he could hear him rolling his eyes.

"My name's Eugene Otto. I'm here about Don Berglund."

Dexter's posture lost its slouch. "Sure, last night's accident."

"He's my roommate—was my roommate."

Grady lowered his paper, and Dexter rose from his chair. He walked over to the end of the counter and raised the hinged top. "Step into my office, and have a seat."

Eugene Otto nodded and walked to Dexter's desk. He laid the envelope he was carrying on the desk and sat down in the wooden chair. As Dexter walked back to his chair, he studied Eugene's face. His complexion was ashen gray, and his eyes, which had the puffy look of not having been closed for a while, seemed way beyond fatigue. He had obviously taken his roommate's death hard, but there seemed to be something else, something beyond simple grief. Dexter flipped his pad of paper over to a clean page and spoke while he wrote down the name.

"Okay, Mr. Eugene—"

"Otto, O-T-T-O."

"Right," Dexter said. "Okay if I call you Eugene?"

"Sure."

"What can I do for you, Eugene?"

"I have some information."

"About last night's accident?"

"Maybe—not exactly. I'm not sure. What I mean is, Don's accident might not have been an accident."

Dexter and Grady looked at each other. "If it wasn't an accident, then what was it?" Dexter asked.

"He might have been murdered."

Dexter leaned forward. "Murdered?" He gave Grady a significant glance. "By who?"

Eugene shifted in his seat and cleared his throat. "By *whom*. Ah, sorry, the mob," he said quietly.

"Excuse me?"

"He said, 'the mob,' Dex," Grady said, smiling. Then he went back to reading his paper.

Dexter couldn't think of a tactful way to put this, so he just said it. "We only have about five hundred people here in Higgins Point, Eugene. If there was a mob here, I probably would have noticed."

Eugene shook his head. "I'm talking about a New Jersey mob, the Manzara crime family."

Dexter wrote this down. "You think mobsters came all the way out here from New Jersey to murder Donald Berglund?"

"I think it's possible."

"Why would they do that?"

"Because of the story he was working on."

"He stopped by here on Saturday and mentioned that he was writing a biography of Wallace Pearle. He wanted a copy of an old police report. What's that got to do with New Jersey mobsters?"

Eugene had started shaking his head as soon as Dexter mentioned Wallace Pearle and had kept shaking it until Dexter finished. "No, not the biography. I'm talking about his other project."

"What other project?" Dexter asked, as Grady's paper came back down.

"Don wrote a piece last month for the *St. Paul Pioneer Press* about outside interests trying to muscle in on the Two Bears Casino."

"I remember the column," Grady said, "but I don't recall anything about any New Jersey mob; that's something I'd remember."

"His first article didn't mention Manzara by name because he hadn't come up with hard evidence—until recently."

"What evidence?"

"A photograph of a couple of Two Bears' tribal council members having a drink with Alfonse 'The Python' Manzara and one of his enforcers."

"The Python? Sounds like some kind of professional wrestler."

If Eugene found Dexter's remark funny, he didn't let on. "He's also called 'Nine Fingers' Manzara, but I bet not to his face."

"I've heard of him," Grady said.

"I expect most folks have," Eugene said.

"There wasn't any evidence of a gunshot wound," Dexter pointed out, "and I didn't find any signs of a side impact or skid marks that would indicate he'd been run off the road."

Eugene shrugged. "They call it *organized* crime for a reason—they have all sorts of ways of doing things."

"The sheriff thinks he fell asleep."

Eugene shook his head.

"No?"

"Not likely. Don always kept himself wired on coffee and cola. He's never come close to falling asleep behind the wheel."

"We were also thinking he might have swerved to avoid, a deer," Dexter offered.

"I doubt it. Don's reflexes aren't—weren't—that good."

Dexter smiled thinly at Eugene's black humor. "Alcohol?" he suggested.

"Don was allergic to alcohol, couldn't touch it."

"So you're serious. You're here because you think the mob was involved?"

Eugene's gaze was steady. "Manzara's famous for never having been photographed. I think they found out about the photo and whacked Don before he could use it in his second article. And I think they're going to want the photo back. I'm just an average guy—I'm not some kind of hero. Frankly, the idea of these guys coming around to the house to get it is enough to give me writer's block."

"Writer's block?"

"What?"

"You said writer's block."

"Yeah."

"Are you a writer too?"

"Yeah, are you?"

"No, I mean too, like your roommate."

"Yeah, we were both writers."

"What do you write?"

"Fiction."

"Fiction?"

"Crime fiction."

Dexter tossed his pencil onto the desk again and leaned back, while Grady leaned in a little closer and asked Eugene the same question that had occurred to Dexter. "You mean you spend your time makin' up stories about fake crimes?"

Eugene held up a hand. "Now, hold it. I know what you guys are thinking."

"What I'm thinking," Grady said, "is that you have some kind of overdeveloped imagination. Real life ain't no mystery novel."

"Look, Don uncovered a possible connection between an Atlantic City mob and a local tribe's casino operation. Yesterday he went to the Two Bears Casino to interview the general manager and show him the photo. A day later Don's dead; that doesn't sound like much of a mystery to me."

"Okay," Dexter admitted, "you might have a possible motive. Got anything else to support it besides the photo?"

Eugene shook his head. "How much more do you need?"

Dexter took a slow breath. The truth was, he didn't need a great deal of convincing. "What was this casino boss's name?"

"Ray Danvers."

Dexter wrote the name down.

"And while you're looking into things, you might ask 'The Python' what he's doing right over in Hudson. When he tells you he's here for the fly-fishing, see if you believe him."

"This 'Python' character is in Hudson?"

"Donald mentioned that he's staying at the Hudson House."

"Mobsters at the Hudson House," Dexter recited as he wrote it down. "Got it. By the way, if Donald was investigating this connection like you say, I suppose I should take a look at any papers or notes he might have left behind."

Eugene nodded. "No problem. I talked to Don's folks this morning, after they identified his body at the funeral home. They didn't sound too eager to collect his things."

Eugene Otto gave Dexter his address and phone number and thanked him.

After he left the office, Grady picked up his newspaper again. "You really gonna investigate this thing, Dex?"

"You heard me tell him I would," Dexter said. "I'm going to start with another look at the car, and don't gloat, you're coming with." He flipped his pad open to his to-do list, and circled item number four—look into Donald Berglund's accident. Then he crossed out *accident* and wrote *murder?* above it.

Chapter Twenty

Phil Launer's Garage was located on Kelsey Street about a half block off Main. He didn't pump gas, just repaired cars. He didn't think there was enough profit in retail gas for an independent operator. Besides, Higgins Point already had two big chain gas stations, and they didn't do repair work. The building Phil worked out of was an old, abandoned Arco station. The gas pumps had been removed years earlier, but the concrete islands were still there, and Phil had several cars waiting for repair parked around them. The ancient, and most likely leaky, underground tanks were also still there. Tired of running into his ex-wife at the Econo Foods, Phil wanted to sell the property and move his business to St. Paul, but he knew that if he found a buyer, they'd test the soil, and he'd have to pay to fix whatever was down there. So Phil stayed in Higgins Point in his repair shop, which was where he was when Dexter and Grady drove up.

They got out of Dexter's Jeep and walked over to examine Donald Berglund's Volvo. The elm tree's imprint was an almost precise semicircle, eighteen inches across, sculpted into the front passenger side. The thought occurred to Dexter that when an unstoppable force meets an immovable object, occasionally it stops anyway. Phil had towed the wreck to his station and left it on the side lot, where it was currently keeping company with a smashed-up silver Taurus. Phil emerged from his shop and was watching now as Grady and Dexter slowly went over the exterior of the car, trying to account for every dent and scrape they found. When they were done, they were both convinced that the car had not been encouraged to leave the road by another vehicle.

Next, Dexter decided to take advantage of the daylight to take a closer look at the car's interior. He found the same box of KFC chicken and soft-drink cup that he'd seen the previous night. He sniffed the cup—it had contained some kind of cola, now dried onto the rubber floor mat.

Phil walked over to Grady and poked him in the ribs. "Musta been somethin' he ate, huh?"

Grady looked at Phil but didn't answer. Dexter picked the box of chicken off the floor of the car and emptied the contents onto the ground. There were two uneaten pieces of chicken, cups of coleslaw and mashed potatoes, both unopened, napkins, and a cellophane bag with plastic utensils in it, still sealed. To this, Dexter added a gnawed drumstick that he picked up from the driver's side floor.

Grady cleared his throat. "Ah, Dex, if you're hungry, we can stop on the way back to your office."

Dexter fished the sales receipt out of the pile and examined it. It placed the drive-thru sale at 8:45 on Monday night, about half an hour before the wreck was discovered. He tossed the receipt back onto the ground, and then something occurred to him. He picked it up again and studied it. "This receipt is for a four-piece dinner," he announced.

Grady was standing with his arms folded, waiting. "What?"

"I said, this was supposed to be a four-piece dinner."

"So what?"

"So there's two uneaten pieces here and a drumstick bone. Where's the fourth piece of chicken?"

Phil chuckled, shaking his head, and turned to walk back into the garage. "Guess he's got a refund coming," he said over his shoulder.

"Seriously," Dexter said, "where's the fourth piece of chicken?"

"Dex, I don't think you're allowed to say 'seriously' before you ask a question like, 'where's the fourth piece of chicken.' "

"The way I see it," Dexter said, "is, we have an accident that hasn't been explained, and the only thing we've found so far that's out of the ordinary is this receipt."

"That ain't necessarily out of the ordinary. He might have got overcharged at the drive-thru. Or maybe he tossed a bone out the window when he was finished with it."

"Then why didn't he toss this one out?" Dexter asked, indicating the drumstick.

"Could be he was in the middle of doin' just that, and that's how he ran off the road."

"All I know at this point is what I don't know. I don't know why Donald Berglund ran off the road, and I don't know what happened to the last piece of chicken. What if they have something to do with each other?"

Dexter tossed the contents of the dinner back into the box along with the drink cup and took it with him back to his Jeep. "I'm going to drop this off at the county lab for testing," he said in response to Grady's questioning look. And then he added, "Just a hunch." Though as hunches went, he was ready to concede that this one wasn't one to bet the farm on.

Chapter Twenty-one

It was four-thirty in the afternoon when Delmar Loomis showed up at Dexter's office. He found a small sign hanging on a hook, which read OFFICE CLOSED, WILL BE BACK AT:, and below that was a little plastic clock face with two hands. The grommet at the center of the clock face had apparently worked its way loose, so both hands hung straight down. Delmar wasn't too surprised when he tried the doorknob and found the place unlocked. *I love this town,* he thought as he let himself in. He walked over to the coffee table in the back corner, poured a cup of weak coffee, and then sat down behind his nephew's desk.

All things considered, Higgins Point was turning out to be a great little vacation spot. With the possible exception of Sheriff Tilsen, who seemed convinced that he'd seen Delmar somewhere before, everybody had been great to him. Hell, he might come back here every year for a little R & R, and if his visits just happened to coincide with a local crime wave, what's the harm? Delmar lit a cigarette and then stretched out, putting his feet up on the desk and folding his hands behind his head. He was just getting settled in to wait for Dexter's return when the door opened and a tall brunet in a short skirt and a tortured red cashmere sweater walked in. Delmar judged her to be in her early forties but very well preserved, with legs that looked like they went all the way up to heaven. She closed the door and approached the counter, carrying her head high, like she had some spirit in her.

"The sign outside says you're closed," she announced in a flat, matter-of-fact voice. "When I saw you sitting in here, I assumed you'd forgotten to take it in."

Delmar's only response was to leave his feet right where they were on the desk, take a slow draw off his cigarette, and blow a stream of smoke up toward the ceiling.

The woman's composure seemed slightly shaken by this reception, and faint lines of concern appeared on her forehead. "You allow smoking in here?"

Delmar thought about that. "Sure. Why not?"

She hesitated for a moment and then tossed her thick brown hair with reddish highlights back and said, "Oh, well, then." She produce a pack of cigarettes, tapped one out, and placed it between her lips—lips that Delmar noticed, with approval, were covered with bright red lipstick. He dropped his feet to the floor, got up, and walked over to the counter, extending his lit Zippo. She leaned into his flame, and when she straightened up, she was looking into his eyes.

He snapped the top shut. "Is there something I can do for you, doll?"

She worked a tiny bit of tobacco out between her lips and reached up and plucked it off her tongue, a socially acceptable gesture between fellow smokers. While she did this, she took her time looking Delmar over. She seemed to take in everything from his silver hair down to his Italian shoes.

"You don't dress like a police chief," she said.

Delmar smiled. "Just because a guy sleeps here, don't mean he has to buy his clothes here."

She thought about this for a second and then smiled back. "I suppose that's true." She took a drag off her cigarette.

"My name is Valerie McBride. I'm an investigator with Templer Mutual. We insured the items stolen from the Pearle residence."

"Oh, yeah, sure, the burglary. You're an investigator?"

"I am, and I just got to town. I was hoping you could bring me up to speed on the case—on anything you might have found out so far."

"Oh, the case. Sure, okay, let's see . . ." Delmar walked to the end of the counter and raised the hinged top. "Why don't you step over to this side and park it in the chair right over there, while I hustle you up a cuppa coffee."

She walked past Delmar slowly and took the offered seat across from Dexter's desk. "Thanks but no thanks on the coffee," she said.

"That's probably for the best. It's terrible." This got a smile out of her, and they both took another drag on their cigarettes, Delmar admiring her sweater as she inhaled. "You talk to the sheriff yet?"

Valerie McBride shook her head and pulled a pad and pen out of her purse. "I've been over to the Pearle estate, and the sheriff is next on my list. But I usually like to start locally. I assume you've been contacting the pawnshops?"

"Of course," Delmar lied, "both sides of the river. We'll work our way west and check every one of 'em in Minneapolis and St. Paul before we're through." Delmar was momentarily thankful that he'd already shipped the jewelry to his fence in L.A.

"Tell me, in your opinion, was this an inside job?" she asked. "My experience is that a large percentage of insured thefts are."

Delmar gazed into Valerie's large brown eyes. The eye shadow, umber with just a hint of orange, was just about right. "Inside? Naw, I doubt it."

"Do you think someone from the cities came over?"

"I'll tell you what I think. This job's got all the earmarks of a pro from somewhere like . . . Miami, for instance. Or maybe a gang. And by now they're probably long gone, back to F-L-A, sippin' cold drinks under a hot sun."

Valerie hesitated a minute and then wrote something on her pad. "What about the art? Have you developed any leads on that yet?"

"Forget about the painting. That'll get smuggled out of the country, go for about thirty cents on the dollar, and probably end up in a private collection on top of some mountain in Switzerland."

"You seem a little pessimistic about tracking down the stolen objects. Maybe we should concentrate on the crime scene. The Pearles told me that the consensus was that the thief got in through the garage door."

Delmar shrugged. "That makes the most sense—drug the dog, and use the garage door."

"The dog was drugged?"

"Wasn't she?" *Ouch,* Delmar thought, *watch yourself.*

"The Pearles hadn't mentioned that, but maybe the sheriff knows about it. It would certainly help explain how the thief got past him."

"Her."

"What?"

Delmar almost bit his tongue. "I think somebody told me the dog was a bitch." Unlike a house, which Delmar never broke into without first knowing exactly how he was going to get back out of, he'd foolishly entered this conversation without an exit plan, and he was feeling a little exposed.

"I assume the Pearles provided you with an inventory of the pieces that were stolen?"

"Oh, yeah, I think it's around here somewhere."

"And copies of the photos I was shown?"

Delmar recalled the photos of the jewelry he'd seen the day before and saw an opportunity for his exit. "Pictures? Probably."

"Probably? What does that mean?"

"That means I don't know. You'll have to ask Dex."

"Dex, what's a Dex?"

"Dex is Dexter Loomis, my nephew, the Higgins Point chief of police."

Valerie shook her head. "You mean to tell me you're not the police chief?"

Delmar allowed a slow smile to spread across his face. "Honey"—he spread his hands—"do I look like the police chief of some crummy little town?"

Valerie's smile betrayed her confusion. "I . . . didn't think so. But didn't you tell me—"

"I never told you who I was because you didn't ask. I guess you assumed I was a cop, and while I'm certainly flattered, honey, I am definitely not a cop."

"Then who are you?"

Delmar leaned across the desk a little and winked. "Whoever you want me to be, doll." That did it; that brought the blush right out through her makeup. "Tell me, where are you staying while you're here in town?"

"I'm, uh—" Valerie reached up and unconsciously touched her hair. "I'm at the Best Western in River Falls."

"I didn't think you looked like the Motel 6 type. So, Miss Valerie McBride, how about you and me gettin' together sometime for a little dinner? Say, tomorrow night?" Delmar could see that half of Valerie was thrown by the suddenness of his suggestion, and the other half was intrigued.

"I, uh—that is, I'm—tomorrow night? Wednesday?"

"Yeah. A little steak, a little wine, and you can tell me all about what it's like to be an insurance shamus."

"Well, I—well, okay. I'm in Room 206."

"Eight o'clock okay with you?"

Valerie rose from the chair. "Eight o'clock would be fine—Delmar, did you say?"

"Call me Del. I'll swing by and pick you up around eight."

"All right, Del."

"Yeah, like that. I like the way you say that."

He lifted the countertop for her and walked her to the door. "Tomorrow night, eight," he said, and he stood in the doorway, taking a moment to admire the view as she walked to her car. After she drove away, he went back into Dexter's office, tossed the rest of his coffee down the sink, and washed out his cup, placing it in the cupboard where he'd found it. He took another look around the room, wondering if his nephew had actually come up with anything on the Pearle job yet. Probably not, he decided. He's bright, but it's only been a few days.

He was on his way out the door when the fax machine came to life. He stood there and waited while it spit out two pages. The first was a cover sheet identifying the sender as a technician named Marilyn Dobner from some toxicology lab. The second page was some kind of chemical analysis. It said that the fried chicken they'd tested contained some kind of poison that came from a plant that Delmar couldn't pronounce but that was spelled *Tanghinia venenifera.* He placed the pages back in the fax machine and let himself out, leaving the door unlocked just as he'd found it. The entire time he'd been in Dexter's office, sitting at his desk, handling the countertop, the fax pages, and the coffee machine, he hadn't left a single fingerprint. It wasn't done consciously; it was just habit developed over the span of four decades in the business. *I always knew chicken was no good for you,* he thought as he walked away from the office.

Ten minutes after Delmar left, Dexter and Grady arrived back at the office, and Dexter spotted the fax immediately. He read the report, then smiled and handed it to Grady. After taking a moment to savor Grady's reaction, he sat down at his desk and made three calls. The first call was to the county medical examiner to arrange for an autopsy to be performed on Donald Berglund's body. The second one was to the

Franklin Funeral Home, to stop the service that had been scheduled for Wednesday. The third was to Sheriff Tilsen's office to make sure they'd also received the toxicology report. Tilsen assured him that they had, and they were already arranging to question the KFC employees who were on duty Monday night. When he was done, Dexter leaned back in his chair with his hands folded behind his head.

"Looks like you got a homicide after all," Grady said. "Feel like goin' to Dick's Bar for a beer?"

Dexter declined the offer, and after Grady left, he sat in his office tossing his tiny Nerf basketball into a plastic hoop and thinking about Donald Berglund. Why would somebody want him dead? After he'd thought about it long enough, he reached for the phone to make a fourth call.

Chapter Twenty-two

Wisconsin DCI Agent Ann Summer, her arms folded, leaned against the doorway that led out to the solarium and tried to keep a straight face. She was listening to her partner, Agent Zack Rose, address the four people whom they'd gathered in the spacious, mahogany-paneled library. Zack stood in the center of the room, a professional investigator with an eyebrow ring, spiky hair, and a plaid sports coat over a Megadeath T-shirt. There was also the ever-present earpiece hanging from his left ear, connected to the cell phone at his belt.

"You all know one another, so I'm going to get right to the point. Three of you are innocent citizens, inconvenienced by our request that you meet with us here today on Dr. Vincent Gardener's estate." This generated indistinct murmurs indicating general agreement. "And one of you"—at this point Zack held up a garden trowel sealed in a clear plastic bag—"is guilty of burying this trowel in Dr. Gardener's chest. Pardon the pun."

One of the men leaned over and said something to the woman seated to his right.

"What was that, Mr. Caine?"

Roger Caine rounded his eyes in innocence. "Nothing," he said. He looked, for a second, the way he must have looked in the sixth grade when he was called to task for talking out of turn in class.

Laura Bentley, the woman to whom Caine had directed his remark, smiled and said, "He simply said it wasn't actually a pun," which earned her a look from Caine.

Zack walked across the library toward them, tapping the plastic-encased trowel on his fingers. "Roger Caine," he said thoughtfully. "Bachelor, sportsman, heavy drinker, the victim's financial advisor—and secretly gay."

The lone snort of laughter amid the chorus of surprised gasps came from Ann Summer, who was already beginning to regret caving in to her partner's plea to try to "wrap up" the murder of the good doctor in this manner. The thing was that after two weeks of probing, Ann and Zack had come up with four suspects, all houseguests of the victim on the weekend he died, and all with motives for wanting Dr. Gardener dead. But after trying to sort out the logistics of who was where and when on the night of the murder, and after examining the meager forensic evidence left behind, they still had next to nothing. Zack's plan was to flush out the killer by fooling him—or her—into thinking that the investigators knew more than they really did. Zack called this technique an "Agatha Christie," but Ann preferred to refer to it by its traditional name, a "Hail Mary." All four suspects were gathered in the library, waiting for Zack's brilliant train of logic to pull into the station and unravel the mystery for them. Dr. Gardener's widow, Frieda, was not a suspect and was elsewhere in the house. She alone had no monetary reason for wanting her husband dead, since the bulk of the couple's fortune had come from her.

Roger Caine had turned both crimson and silent at Zack's unexpected disclosure of his sexual orientation. Zack consulted his notes.

"Dr. Gardener suffered a series of financial setbacks over the past several months," he pointed out. "He couldn't have been too happy with your management of his money, Mr. Caine. We found an envelope in his safe that contained photographs of you walking into the Brass Rail, a well-known gay establishment in Minneapolis. It's possible that he intended to get even with you by passing them around to your other clients."

Laura Bentley was leaning back and beaming at Roger Caine. "Why, Roger, you duplicitously macho little stinker, you! I never suspected. I think it must have been your unfortunate wardrobe that convinced me you were straight."

Caine glared at her, and Zack turned his attention to her. "Ms. Laura Bentley, horsewoman, gourmet cook, the victim's attorney, and well-known lesbian."

"But not necessarily in that order," she offered.

"We had a very interesting talk with Phyllis Conners recently."

Laura Bentley's smile faded at the mention of the name.

"She's been your partner for—what?—about two years?"

Laura Bentley placed a cigarette between her lips, tilted her head sideways, and lit it. She put the lighter into her pocket, took a long drag, blowing the smoke up toward the ceiling, and returned her gaze to Zack without answering.

"Ms. Conners described a nasty little scene where you accused her of having an affair with . . . Dr. Gardener, of all people. It seems reasonable to assume, doesn't it, that you may not have had your client's best interests at heart?"

Laura Bentley casually tapped the ash from her cigarette onto the silk Persian carpet. "The man was a breeder and a pig, but I was still his attorney, and business is business. I didn't kill him."

"You disgust me," announced Dr. Darryl Pinkman. "And you know Frieda doesn't allow smoking in the house."

Zack glanced over at Ann as if to ask, *How am I doing?*

Ann shrugged with her eyebrows. Zack stepped over to Dr. Pinkman and consulted his notepad. "Dr. Darryl Pinkman, avid fly-fisherman, orthopedic surgeon—to several Green Bay Packers—and colleague of the deceased."

"And *friend* of the deceased—and staunch heterosexual," Pinkman added, fingering the crease in his pin-striped suit pants.

"Would it shock you, Doctor, to learn that in examining Dr. Gardener's files, we came across a letter by him, apparently never sent, that detailed a shocking lapse by you in surgery? A lapse that prematurely ended the career of Scott Lacina, at the time one of the top receivers in the NFL."

"Things are rarely so cut-and-dried on the operating table," Dr. Pinkman assured him.

"And yet the letter does exist," Zack insisted.

"But was never sent, as you pointed out. Vincent well understood the medical uncertainties in treating the human body."

"Maybe he did, and maybe he didn't. And maybe his murder was your way of making sure his letter never got a stamp."

Dr. Pinkman smiled condescendingly. "If you're considering medical malpractice as a motive, Detective, I think you should talk to Bobby. He actually had the dubious experience of going under Vincent's knife."

All eyes followed Dr. Pinkman's gesture to a corner of the room, where Bobby LeDeux sat quietly, sipping a gin and tonic and slowly turning the three-foot, floor-mounted globe next to him. When Zack approached him, Bobby removed his hand from the globe.

"Bobby LeDeux, former Detroit Red Wing, one of the top centers in the NHL, patient of the victim, and currently on tranquilizers for a chronic nervous condition brought on by—this is just a guess—a destroyed right knee."

Bobby narrowed his eyes at Zack. "Vincent didn't ruin my knee," he said. "A cheap shot by a Toronto defenseman did that. Vincent tried to repair it."

"Are you that sure?"

Bobby LeDeux took a sip of his drink. "I'm not mad at him," he said. "I'm just thirsty."

"Look here," Caine said, "if you have something to tell us about Vincent's death, then tell us."

"I agree," added Bentley. "I've got to be back in Milwaukee by four o'clock to take a deposition."

Zack held up his hands. "Take it easy. You'll all get where you're going—except one of you." Zack consulted his notepad. "Dr. Pinkman, you were the one who claims to have discovered the body in the greenhouse."

"I don't 'claim' to have discovered him. I did."

"And the reason you were in the greenhouse at nine o'clock was to smoke a cigar?"

"Bobby suggested a drink and a smoke. Frieda doesn't like smoke in the house." He threw a dismissive look at Laura Bentley, who responded by exhaling a stream of smoke in his direction.

"So on a two-hundred-acre estate, you just happened to pick the one spot currently occupied by a corpse to have a smoke."

Dr. Pinkman's sigh communicated his fading patience. "It was starting to rain. We wanted to be indoors but out of the main house."

"And Bobby LeDeux—"

At this point the French doors that led to the main hallway burst open. Frieda Gardener stood swaying in the doorway, a martini glass in one hand and a chrome tumbler in the other. The time-honored tradition of wearing black during an appropriate period of mourning apparently held little sway with her. She was dressed in a hot little red number with a neckline cut low enough to make Laura Bentley sit up and smile.

When she spoke, her voice contained an aristocratic slur. "Are you people still here?" She took two unsteady steps into the room and addressed Zack. "When you asked if you could use the library, I didn't think you meant all night."

Ann watched Zack struggle for a way to handle this unscheduled monkey wrench.

"Mrs. Gardener, I, uh, that is, we, we're just getting started. We're trying to get to the bottom—"

"For two weeks you've been poking and prodding into our affairs." She took a sip of her martini. "I think it's time you wrapped it up and moved on, don't you?"

"Mrs. Gardener, I'm about to reveal—"

"Fiddlesticks. You're not about to reveal anything, and stop calling me Mrs. Gardener. It's annoying." She smiled suddenly. "Call me Frieda." She indicated the houseguests. "They all do."

"Okay, *Frieda,* if you'll just let me have—"

"Let you have a little more time? For what?" She took another sip, draining her martini glass, and paused to freshen it from the tumbler. "To pin the thing on one of them?" She took a sip and waved the tumbler in an arc that took in the whole library. "Who the hell are *they?*" I'll tell you who *they* are. Lawyers and bankers—clerks who worked for Vince. Another quack doctor and a broken-down goalie—or something." She spotted the cigarette in Laura Bentley's hand. "You bitch."

Frieda took another sip, which turned into a gulp, draining the glass. When she tried to freshen it again, the tumbler was empty. Without a thought she threw it across the room, where it smashed into the brick fireplace. The violent impact seemed to sober her up momentarily.

She looked at Zack and raised her chin. "I killed him."

"Excuse me?" Zack took a small step toward her, and Ann uncrossed her arms and stood up straight.

"I said, I killed him. I stabbed the bastard in the back first and then buried the trowel in his wheezy old chest"—she looked down at her empty martini glass, momentarily distracted—"and left it there."

The fact that Dr. Gardener had been stabbed in the back was information that had been intentionally withheld. It was something only the real killer would know, and it convinced Ann that Frieda was telling the truth. The one person they hadn't suspected had done it.

"May I ask why?" Zack said.

"Because"—she hesitated, swaying slightly—"he was such a Twinkie."

Frieda walked over to the bar in a corner of the library and started mixing another batch of martinis, when suddenly the theme song from *Mission: Impossible* drifted up from Ann's purse. All eyes in the room turned toward her while she dug her cell phone out and flipped it open.

"Agent Summer."

"Annie, it's Dexter."

Ann opened her mouth to answer but just stood there. Dexter was the only person other than her late father who ever called her Annie. The immediate rush of elation she felt at hearing his voice after all this time quickly changed into questions.

"Annie?"

"Sorry, Dexter, hello."

"Did I catch you at a bad time?"

"No. We're finishing up a case, but it's okay." There was a brief pause. "It's been a while." *It's been a while?* You haven't so much as talked to the guy for six months, and you can't think of anything better to say than, "It's been a while?"

"Yeah, it has."

Dexter hesitated, and there was dead air for a moment. *Say it!* thought Ann. *Say it, you tongue-tied moron. Tell me you miss me.*

"I have a problem I was hoping you could help me with."

"Problem?" Ann felt a letdown coming. "What kind of problem?"

"Well, believe it or not, it looks like we have another homicide in Higgins Point."

Ann took a deep breath to keep the disappointment out of her voice. "You want the DCI there?"

"I was hoping maybe you and Zack could come—that is, if you're not tied up."

Getting asked back to Higgins Point and Dexter after all these months just to run a homicide investigation felt to Ann a little like being taken to the prom by her cousin. She glanced over at the bar, which was now occupied by the murderess and the four previous suspects, all making drinks together. Zack stood off to one side, waiting for Ann to finish her call before he broke up the party.

"I'll call my director. I'm pretty sure he'll make us available."

"That's great, Annie. I appreciate it."

"It's Tuesday now. I have a hunch we'll spend tomorrow taking statements and doing paperwork. We can probably be there by Thursday afternoon. Is that okay?"

"Sure. Thursday."

"Just make sure you don't bury the body in the meantime."

"Did Zack tell you to say that? It'll be nice to see you again—you and Zack."

Did Ann detect something in the hesitation in his voice? "It'll be nice to see you too, Dexter—you and Grady."

"So, you're finishing a case, huh? When you get here, maybe you can tell me about it."

Ann was a little surprised at how comfortable she already felt talking to Dexter after . . . everything. "Not that much to tell, really. I guess you could say that Frieda did it with the garden trowel in the greenhouse."

Chapter Twenty-three

October 1984

Ellie Myers was not in a good mood. Sitting at her desk, she gazed out her office window over the expanse of the west lawn and watched Wallace and Roberta Kaplan, the new student, as they strolled together down by the studio. They were walking and talking—wasn't that strolling? Granted, Roberta was his student, but her demands on his time and attention went beyond needy, and Wallace's willingness to comply was providing more and more of a trial for Ellie. Since moving into her cottage at the beginning of the term, Roberta hadn't hesitated to make herself right at home. She had been on the estate only five days before talking Wallace into hiring a friend of hers to replace the maid. Marie, their old housekeeper, had announced two weeks earlier that she was planning to move back to San Antonio to be near her son and to make life miserable for her new daughter-in-law. Roberta's friend, Louise Dahlman, had moved onto the estate and taken to the job like a pro. In fact, she was sharing a cottage with Roberta.

These thoughts ran through Ellie's head as she ran

through the day's mail, creating three piles; personal correspondence for Wallace's attention, bills, and professional matters dealing with the business side of art. Then one letter caught her eye; it was addressed to Ellie, and it was from the Greater London Arts Association. It had been at least four weeks since she'd written them suggesting they change their monthly stipend to a yearly one, and she'd all but forgotten about the matter.

She forced Wallace from her mind for the moment and opened the letter, expecting to hear how delighted they were with her suggestion, but what she found puzzled her. They had no idea what monthly contribution Ellie had referred to in her letter; however, they, of course, knew of the famous Wallace Pearle and were delighted to hear that he would be donating money to their organization. Monthly or yearly, it made little difference to them.

Ellie sat back in her chair and pondered the letter. If Wallace wasn't writing checks to this organization, then why had he asked her to make sure the funds were available in his account each month for that purpose? And where was the money actually going? In her capacity as Dragon Lady of the atelier, Ellie had been given full access to all the accounts. Her curiosity piqued, she decided to look in Wallace's checkbook register to see if she could trace the funds. She rose from her chair and glanced out the window just in time to see Wallace following Roberta into her cottage. She waited until she saw the door close behind them and then, with lips pressed firmly together, walked over to Wallace's study.

As the Association's correspondence had indicated, Wallace's check register showed no checks written to them. After a brief examination, however, Ellie did find checks in the correct amount, written on the first of every month, beginning in July of 1983. But the checks were to someone named Edward Fitzner. Who was Edward Fitzner? Ellie would have assumed that he worked for the Great London Arts Association, except that they claimed not to have been receiving any money. She flipped open Wallace's Rolodex and found a card for Edward Fitzner in it, containing his phone number and a London address. She took down this information and returned to her office.

Ellie dialed the number from the card and then rose from her seat and paced behind her desk while the connection was made. She heard a series of soft, puttering rings on the other end, and eventually a man's voice answered.

"Hallo."

"Mr. Fitzner?"

"Yes."

"Mr. Edward Fitzner?"

There was a brief hesitation. "Yes."

"Mr. Fitzner, my name is Ellie Myers, and I work with Wallace Pearle, in the United States." There was no response to this from the other end, and Ellie wasn't sure how to proceed. "May I ask, please, if you're associated with the Greater London Arts Association?"

This was met with total silence.

"Mr. Fitzner?"

A hollow click indicated that the line was dead, and Ellie was left staring at the receiver in her hand. After a few seconds she set the phone down and sat back down at her desk. She thought about the call and about the possibility of a substantial amount of misdirected funds. Finally she dug out her personal phone book and opened it to Kathleen Withington. Mrs. Withington, a very nice lady, was a resident of London as well as her mother's pen pal of many years. Ellie had met her once several years ago, when she'd accompanied her parents on a trip to England. The ring tone in the receiver had the same funny, soft, puttering sound, and then Mrs. Withington's voice came on the line.

"Hello."

"Mrs. Withington?"

"Yes."

"It's Ellie Myers, Margaret's daughter—from America."

"Ellie, is that you, dear?"

"Yes. We haven't spoken in quite a while, Mrs. Withington. I hope everything's well with you."

"Oh, yes, and you must certainly call me Kathleen." Ellie could hear her telling someone, probably her husband, that Margaret's daughter was on the line. "Oh, my goodness, are you here in London, Ellie?"

"No, I'm calling you from Wisconsin, in the United States."

"I see. Is it snowing there?"

"Not quite yet. It's still early October." Why did everybody always think it should be snowing in Wisconsin? It suddenly dawned on Ellie that she hadn't paid any attention to what time it was in England before placing the call. "Have I called at a bad time? What time is it there?"

"It's a quarter past nine, dear. It's fine." There was a slight pause, and then Kathleen said, "Is Margaret all right?"

"Oh, yes, we're all doing fine. I'm sorry if I scared you."

"No, of course, dear. Not at all."

"The reason I'm calling you, Kathleen, is that I'm trying to find out about a man who lives in London, a man named Edward Fitzner. And I wondered if maybe you could help me—I mean, since you live there."

"I don't understand, dear. What sort of things do you want to know about this Mr. Fitzner?"

"Well, uh—wait one moment, okay?" Ellie had just spotted Louise Dahlman, in her new maid's outfit, standing outside the open door to her office. She rose from her chair, walked across the room, and smiled at Louise before gently closing the door. "I'm sorry about that—just a minor interruption. What were you saying?"

"Do you mean information like an employment query?"

"Yes," Ellie said, seizing on the offered description.

"Anything you could find out about him would help me greatly."

"Would you want me to check the police records?"

This caught Ellie by surprise. "You can do that?"

My nephew is a detective sergeant. I imagine he has access to all sorts of information. I could ask him to make an inquiry for me. Edward Fitzner, did you say?"

Ellie spelled the name for Kathleen and supplied the address from the Rolodex.

"I can't thank you enough, Kathleen."

"I'm glad to help, dear. Might I ask why you want to know about this man?"

"Oh, it's for my employer," Ellie explained, keeping it vague. "I work for Wallace Pearle. I'm his personal secretary."

"Wallace Pearle, the American painter?"

"The one and only."

"My goodness, dear, that's wonderful. I'm delighted to hear that you're doing so well."

"And I'm glad to hear that you are all well," said Ellie. "Shall I give your regards to my mom?"

"Of course, and I'll be in touch when my nephew has something to report."

"That'll be great, Kathleen. Thanks again."

"Not at all, dear. Ta-ta."

"Good-bye."

Ellie placed the handset back on the phone and leaned back in her chair. She decided that there was no real reason to bother Wallace with this; he clearly had enough on his mind. She made a phone record of her call to Kathleen Withington and placed it in her drawer, along with her original letter to the Great London Arts Association and their reply. Then she returned her gaze to the still-closed cottage door and settled in to wait for them to emerge.

Chapter Twenty-four

Wednesday

Dexter's visit with Donald Berglund's parents was awkward, sad, and mercifully short. When they invited him into their small home on Division Street in River Falls, the front room had the somber air of a place of mourning, and Mr. and Mrs. Berglund had the deflated pallor inevitable in parents who'd had to identify their son's body under morgue lights. The first words out of Dexter's mouth were his sincere condolences, followed quickly by an apology for postponing their son's funeral in order to accommodate the autopsy. The twelve hours that had passed since Dexter spoke to them on the phone had obviously done little to lessen their pain. It had only allowed the initial shock of the homicide to subside enough for the real bone-crushing pain to flood in, accompanied by anger that increased by the hour.

Dexter asked them about their son's newspaper article regarding the Two Bears Casino. They'd read it, of course, as they read everything their son wrote, but had no idea if its contents might have posed any personal danger for him. He never mentioned anything about it, they said, nor did they think he would have been likely to. Donald had been out of their house for many years. Though he maintained a good relationship with them, he had long since fallen out of the habit of disclosing his day-to-day concerns to them. Dexter pointed out that angering an organized crime family probably went a little beyond "day-to-day concerns." Still, there was nothing to report.

Dexter asked if Donald had been in the habit of keeping any of his research materials at their house—papers, perhaps notes of some kind? The answer was no, but it prompted a brief tour of Donald's former upstairs bedroom. He saw the usual personal effects of children gone on to live their own lives. Old toys, posters, records, juvenile books, and plastic car models.

Knowing that he intended to visit Donald's house next, Dexter asked permission to examine their son's papers. He didn't have to spell out why; they readily agreed, telling him he could take anything he liked. Dexter promised to return everything to them when he was through.

After leaving the Berglunds' home, Dexter stopped by the grocery store in downtown Higgins Point. When he asked a cashier if he could have a few empty boxes, she sent him to the back of the store, where he drew a crowd. Several employees, including the manager, peppered him with questions about Monday's auto accident. Somehow they'd heard rumors that it hadn't been an accident. He managed to escape with the boxes while dodging the questions.

It was 10:00 A.M. when he stepped up onto the wooden porch and rang the bell of the house that Donald and his roommate rented on Raymond Street. He saw the closed curtains in the front window stir slightly and then heard the lock being released. Eugene Otto, looking considerably worse than when he'd stopped by Dexter's office, peered out, blinking in the morning sunlight. He obviously hadn't shaved since his roommate was murdered.

"Good morning, Eugene. Mind if I come in?"

Eugene stuck his head out the door like a turtle and looked down at the boxes Dexter was carrying. Then he glanced up and down the street, apparently concerned that a mobster might slip into the house along with Dexter. When he was satisfied it was safe, he pulled his head back inside and said, "Come in."

Dexter carried the boxes inside, and Eugene closed the door behind him, threw the dead bolt, and then peeked out through the curtains again.

"If they want to find you, Eugene, they will. Draperies aren't going to stop the mob."

That ill-advised attempt at humor drew a sour look. "Have you started investigating them, like I asked you to?"

Dexter ignored the question, looking around him. The front room was strewn with plates, glasses, and miscellaneous articles of clothing. Eugene halfheartedly picked up an undershirt and a sock and then looked sheepishly at Dexter. "I never realized how much of the housework Don did."

Dexter thought he looked lost in his own front room. "I'm going to question those New Jersey boys later today. You said they were at the Hudson House, right?"

"I was hoping you were here because you'd already talked to them." Eugene tossed the clothes onto a chair.

"One thing at a time. I just finished talking to Donald's parents."

Eugene nodded. "I know what you mean. I was with them when they went to the morgue to identify Don's body." He ran a hand through his thinning hair. "Don and I've been buddies since junior high." Eugene walked into the kitchen. "Can I get you some coffee? I just made a fresh pot."

"I'm going to pass on the coffee, but thanks anyway." Dexter followed him into the kitchen, and Eugene's voice floated up from behind the open refrigerator door.

"How about some pop? We have—there's Coke, Diet Coke, and Mountain Dew."

"Maybe a Coke," Dexter said, only because accepting it seemed friendlier than rejecting it. "Thanks."

The kitchen looked like the front room but with an empty pizza box on the table, more dishes, and fewer clothes. Eugene handed a can of Coke to Dexter and then opened one for himself, apparently having changed his mind about the coffee.

"Been eating in?" Dexter indicated the pizza box.

Eugene nodded. "I usually make my own pizza, but I haven't been in the mood lately. No fun cooking for one." That drew a silent nod from Dexter, who was accustomed to cooking for one. "I guess you're here to take a look at Don's stuff."

Dexter nodded again. "Yeah, whatever he was working on, to see if there might be a connection to his murder."

Eugene shook his head. "I told you what I think. Just because the mob used poison instead of a bullet doesn't mean it's not a homicide. Don's just as dead."

"How'd you know Donald was poisoned? We just found that out ourselves yesterday afternoon."

"I'm a crime writer, remember? I have friends in the sheriff's department." Eugene took a drink of Coke and sat down at the kitchen table.

"I'd like to look around in Donald's office."

"Second room on the right," Eugene said, pointing down the hall. "Everything's in there. Don was too organized to leave loose material lying around the house. By the way, if you want to examine his computer, his password is Y-R-E-T-S-Y-M."

Dexter jotted this down on his pad and looked at it. "That's *mystery* spelled backward," he said.

Eugene just nodded and shrugged. Dexter thanked him and picked up his boxes and his Coke and walked down the hall, leaving Eugene sitting at the kitchen table staring at the pizza box.

Donald Berglund's office was a converted bedroom, and

at first glance Dexter felt overwhelmed by the task of examining its contents. Much of the material that filled the small room consisted of reference books, phone books, manuals, and archived newspapers and magazines. In addition, there were shelves containing the typical array of office supplies. When Dexter actually began sorting things out, however, he realized that Donald really was—or, rather, had been—a very organized person.

After eliminating the extraneous material, what was left was fairly clear-cut. There was a file cabinet in one corner. The top drawer contained a series of manila folders, each holding one of Donald's previously published investigative journalism pieces along with his original notes. One folder contained a six-month-old article exposing a bribe that was used to grease the wheels for a liquor license in Higgins Point. Another contained a year-old piece in which Donald had uncovered illegal campaign contributions to the Wisconsin Republican Party. Apparently the payoff was seven million dollars worth of state-issued no-bid contracts for highway bridge repair work. Among these files Dexter also found the *St. Paul Pioneer Press* article that Donald had written about the Two Bears Casino. Although it contained no mention of organized crime, it detailed financial hardship in the form of disappointing gaming profits that had made the casino vulnerable to possible takeover by unspecified "outside interests." Dexter put the entire collection of articles into one of his boxes.

Donald had dedicated the second drawer of his file cabinet to his Wallace Pearle project. The notes for the biography contained interviews with what looked to be dozens of people, and there was also a hard copy printout of the computer manuscript-in-progress. In the back of the drawer Dexter found something that made him pause in his search. There was a separate section entitled *Ellie Myers* with several pieces of paper inside. He took a moment to indulge his tattered memories of a cute, sixteen-year-old with a soft voice telling him that he could stay up an extra half hour if he behaved himself and didn't tell his parents. When he leafed through the pages, he noticed that one of them had the name *Sara Ulmer* at the top followed by a question mark. Now who was Sara Ulmer? It all went into the box.

Donald's writing desk held a desktop computer and had a single drawer. In the drawer Dexter found another manila folder with notes for what obviously would have been the second piece on the Two Bears Casino, along with an eight-by-ten photograph of four men sitting in a restaurant—clearly the photo Eugene had referred to. This also went into the box.

A search of the closet yielded only more office supplies and an old cardboard box lying on the floor. Dexter popped open the folded flaps of the box and looked inside. It contained a hodgepodge collection of personal effects and reminded Dexter of the box he'd carried away from the Curran County engineering office on his last day there. A dusty black instrument case lay on top. Dexter guessed it was a clarinet and opened it to find he was right. So Donald had played the clarinet. Great, another piece of information to make his death more personal. There was a desk clock and calendar, a cup full of pens and pencils, a lamp, and a dusty assortment of items typically used to personalize an office. Dexter couldn't see anything that looked as if it might pertain to Donald's research, so he closed the box and placed it back on the floor of the closet.

He invoked Donald's password and spent the next hour searching his computer files. He found the Wallace Pearle manuscript, the beginning of the second casino article, and not much else. Apparently Donald didn't believe in maintaining old computer files. Or perhaps he liked to store his material on disks and then delete it from the hard drive. At any rate the computer looked like a cold trail.

Satisfied that he had given Donald's office a reasonably

thorough initial look, Dexter gathered up the two boxes he had filled and brought them out to the front room, where Eugene was lying on the sofa reading the paper.

"All done," Dexter announced, setting the boxes down near the door.

Eugene folded the paper, set it aside, and stood up. He looked as if he didn't know what to do with his hands. "Find everything okay?"

"Sure. Hey, Eugene, do you remember my mentioning that Donald stopped by my office, looking for info on Ellie Myers' murder?"

Eugene nodded. "Sure."

"I wonder if he ever mentioned to you whether he came up with anything."

Eugene shrugged. "I just know Don was looking for some way to cash in on her—you know, for book sales. Last week he spent a whole day in Superior looking through county records."

"Superior? What was he looking for up there?"

"He never said. But I know when he read the police report you gave him and found out that Wallace Pearle had been a suspect in the Myers' murder, he figured he'd found something he could use."

"He was going to publish that?"

"He was on the phone to Pearle an hour after he got back from your office, setting up a meeting. He said he expected a tough sell. Said he was going to have to 'hardball it' with him. Don was serious; he didn't want to get stuck with a three-hundred-page doorstop."

"Are you telling me they had a disagreement two days before Donald was murdered?"

"I don't think it turned out to be much of a disagreement. When he came home, Don said it was all taken care of. You know, Don was stepping on more serious toes than some big-bucks painter's."

"I know, the mob." Dexter bent down and fished the eight-by-ten photograph out of the box. "By the way, is this the photo you were worried about?"

Eugene stepped closer. "Alfonse Manzara, yeah. The only existing photograph of him."

Dexter tossed it back into the box and picked them both up. "When I'm done with this stuff, I'll return it to Donald's parents."

Eugene held the door open for Dexter. "Great. And I'm glad you're getting that photo out of here. Good riddance."

He seemed to breathe a little easier as soon as Dexter and the photo were out the door. Dexter didn't have the heart to point out that the mob would have no way of knowing that the photo had been removed from Eugene's house. Eugene stood in the doorway for a minute staring at Dexter, and then suddenly he looked up and down the street and disappeared inside. Dexter thought his expression looked a little funny.

Chapter Twenty-five

"I didn't say the case was solved." The forced calm in Sheriff Bob Tilsen's voice utterly failed to conceal his regret that he had bothered to call Dexter Loomis to his office to share information on the Berglund homicide.

"You said, 'I think we have a winner,'" Dexter quoted. "I'm assuming a 'winner' is a murderer, as strange as that sounds." Dexter and Grady were both seated in the sheriff's office, Grady leaning back in his chair and Dexter sitting forward in his.

"It's possible. Hey, Dexter, look what we have, will you? We questioned the six employees who were on duty in the KFC on Monday night. None of 'em says they know anything, but one of 'em, this kid named Dennis Stowell, turns out to be the son of Leonard Stowell. I don't have to remind you who he is—he's a local celebrity. He's currently serving thirty months at Oakhill Correctional for cooking the books in the Celtic Insurance meltdown. So Dennis Stowell's old man's doing time, and his family's destitute because of the fine the court laid on him. And who exposed Mr. Stowell's financial shenanigans? Donald Berglund. It's a solid revenge motive."

"I finished going through Berglund's old articles earlier today," Dexter said. "I didn't think any of them provided a compelling motive."

"Revenge is a motive, and we have the fact that Berglund was a regular customer at that KFC, which means the Stowell kid could have depended on his coming by at least semi-regularly and planned it out, and that's opportunity."

"Berglund's Celtic Insurance article came out eighteen months ago," Dexter pointed out.

"But because of his appeals, Leonard Stowell didn't actually go to prison until four months ago."

"I don't know . . ." Dexter turned to Grady, who hadn't said a word. "What do you think?"

Grady looked at both men. "I think I'm gonna avoid eatin' at that particular KFC for the foreseeable future."

Giving up on Grady, Dexter tried once more to reason with Tilsen. "I'm just saying that you should keep an open mind. It's too early to close off inquiries in other directions."

"And I suppose one of those 'other directions' includes a certain New Jersey crime family?"

Dexter shrugged. "The victim's roommate seems convinced. I know it sounds far-fetched, but what if he's right?"

"Far-fetched would be generous," Tilsen pointed out.

"But according to Eugene, they're actually here in town."

"The mob?"

"A couple of 'em, staying over at the Hudson House."

"Mobsters are staying at the Hudson House?"

"Alfonse 'The Python' Manzara and one of his enforcers," Dexter explained.

"Hey," Grady said, "they have to sleep somewhere. And by the way, Sheriff, how come you guys didn't know they were here?"

Tilsen scowled at Grady. "What are you doing here, anyway? Don't you have a job?"

"I'm going to have a talk with them later," Dexter announced.

Tilsen redirected his scowl at Dexter. "I want you to stay as far away from Manzara as possible. We've got a suspect in the Stowell kid, and we're almost there. We've got motive and opportunity. We're getting a warrant to search the kid's home, the family car, and his locker at school. If we can come up with traces of the poison he used, that Tanghina venen—something, we'll have the means."

"His locker at school?"

"Yeah."

"How old is this guy?"

"He's seventeen."

"A school kid is your big suspect? Keep your options open, Bob—that's all I'm asking."

"And stay away from Manzara, Dex—that's all I'm saying."

Feeling that he'd done everything he could to deliver his message, Dexter got up to leave, followed by Grady. When he opened Tilsen's office door, a tall, shapely brunet was standing in the doorway.

"Oh, M-Miss McBride," Tilsen sputtered, coming to attention more quickly than Dexter thought possible. The sheriff rounded his desk to greet her, spewing introductions on the way. "Miss McBride, this is the Higgins Point police chief, Dexter Loomis, and Grady Penz, an EMT out of New Richmond. They were just leaving."

At the mention of "police chief," Valerie McBride's eyes lit up, and she zeroed in on Dexter. "So *you're* Chief Loomis," she said, which gave Dexter the uncomfortable feeling that he was expected to know this woman.

He glanced at Grady and the sheriff. "Uh, yeah, I'm Dexter Loomis. You're Valerie McBride?" The manner of Dexter's phrasing had the unintended effect of making it sound as though he'd heard of her before.

"I am." She thrust her hand toward him, gazing levelly into his face. "I stopped by your office yesterday afternoon."

"Oh, right." Dexter now understood that she was reminding him that they'd met yesterday, but he couldn't for the life of him recall the meeting, a distinct impossibility in a town as quiet as Higgins Point. He took in her rather low cut blouse, high heels, tight skirt, and tousled reddish brown hair that, for some reason, struck Dexter as vaguely Italian, and thought, *I would remember.* "Did we discuss the burglary?"

Concern knit her eyebrows together. "We didn't discuss anything, Chief Loomis. You weren't there."

"Oh, I wasn't there. I've never seen you before."

"No, of course not." There was a brief pause while everybody's confusion sloshed around a bit before reaching a common level, and then Valerie McBride went on. "I spoke with your Uncle Del. But I'm glad I ran into you. I wanted to see if you've made any progress on the burglary."

"The burglary? No. We've got our hands full with the murder. You know my Uncle Del?"

"Yes, I do. A very interesting man. In fact, we're having dinner tonight. What murder?"

"Donald Berglund," supplied the sheriff, trying to find a way into the conversation. "Died Monday night. Did you say you're having dinner with Delmar Loomis?"

"He was a local writer," added Dexter. "One of his projects was a biography of Wallace Pearle. I have the manuscript at home."

Tilsen looked at Dexter. "How did you get Berglund's manuscript?"

"He was writing about Wallace Pearle?" Valerie looked from Dexter to Tilsen. "And he was murdered right after Pearle was robbed?"

"When you put it that way, you make it sound like there's

a connection," Dexter said, the tone of his voice making it clear he didn't think one existed. To Tilsen he said, "I told you, I'm going through Berglund's papers, looking for anything that might have given someone a reason to kill him."

"You removed material from the victim's house without my permission?"

"Did this Donald Berglund spend much time at the Pearle estate while he was writing this biography?" Valerie asked.

Dexter's head swiveled back and forth. "Yes, and possibly," he said. And then to Valerie, he added, "Did you just say you were having dinner with my uncle tonight?"

"Yes," she said to Dexter. "He said something about steak. I'm just a little bit curious what he does for a living." To Tilsen she said, "So Wallace Pearle's home was robbed on Friday night, and a man who had frequent access to it was murdered on Monday?"

All three men stared at her.

"Yeah, so?" said Tilsen.

Valerie crossed her arms, almost squeezing her chest out of her blouse. "Was this Berglund fellow's access to the estate sufficient for him to have acted as an inside accomplice?"

"This '*Berglund fellow's*' name was Donald," Dexter pointed out, perhaps a bit too forcefully, "and he wasn't a thief. And I'm embarrassed to have to admit that I have absolutely no idea what my uncle does for a living."

Valerie released her chest and held up her hands in a gesture of peace. "I don't mean to denigrate a homicide victim, but whoever pulled this job got away with a serious haul. Honor among thieves doesn't go very far in my experience, and it wouldn't be the first time I've seen a job end in a double-cross."

"We think it was probably a local kid, works in the KFC," explained the sheriff.

"Or New Jersey mobsters," added Dexter.

"What!" Valerie's head went back and forth. "KFC and mobsters?"

"I can sure tell you're new in town," said Grady.

"Are you guys serious?" Valerie looked at Dexter. "And is your uncle single?"

Chapter Twenty-six

Wallace Pearle was an eminent man, famous, wealthy, and a pillar of society; his wife had gone out of her way to see to it that Dexter understood that fact. Whereas private citizen Dexter Loomis would be very reticent to intrude on the great man's privacy unannounced, Police Chief Loomis was perfectly happy to pop in and surprise him. He rang the front bell at six o'clock and was admitted by Mrs. Pearle, who directed him to Wallace's study. Upon entering, he found the painter seated behind his desk, looking at something under a magnifying glass.

Dexter reintroduced himself to Wallace, to remind him who he was, and apologized for arriving around dinnertime. Wallace assured Dexter that it wasn't an issue, as they were dining out tonight. He invited him to step around his desk and see what it was that he'd been examining so closely. He handed the glass to Dexter and held the object, apparently some sort of ring, steady for him. Dexter bent over and was a little surprised to realize he was looking at three tiny Oriental figures, carved in jade, engaged in a fairly inventive sexual act.

"Ancient Chinese pornography," Wallace explained.

"Rather a naughty passion of mine, I'm afraid. I've always been fascinated by the idea that an ancient civilization whose culture we hold in such high regard had its earthy aspects as well."

"I guess we're all human," Dexter said, handing the glass back to Wallace.

"Very true." He accepted the magnifying glass from Dexter and placed it, and the ring, in his desk drawer. "To what do I owe the honor, Officer Loomis. Or is it Chief Loomis?"

"I answer to either."

"Fine, then, Chief it is. May I assume that your presence here is an indication that you've made progress on the theft?"

"Not exactly, but we're working on it," Dexter lied. "Actually I'm here about Donald Berglund."

Wallace's face darkened. "Oh, yes. Roberta told me earlier today that she'd learned he'd been killed in an auto accident. Tragic."

"Yeah, it's a shame," Dexter said, remembering again the thin, quick-talking, enthusiastic fellow squirming in his office chair. "He seemed like a nice guy."

"Then you knew him?"

"I only met him once. He stopped by my office looking for information, which actually brings me to why I'm here. I understand he was working on your biography."

"Yes, that is correct."

"And the two of you had a meeting recently—a meeting that didn't go too smoothly?"

"What an odd question. May I ask what prompted it?"

"It's true that Mr. Berglund died in a car accident, but it looks as if his car went off the road because he was poisoned."

"Oh, my God." Wallace sat down in his chair very slowly, a stunned expression on his face.

Dexter studied his response, trying to gauge the honesty

of the man's emotion. "I'm sorry if I shocked you," Dexter said. "There's no reason you should have known that." *Unless it was you who poisoned him.*

"Donald was murdered," Wallace stated numbly, and then he marshaled his thoughts and refocused his eyes on Dexter. "Naturally you're interested in anyone who might have argued with him recently. May I ask, how did you find out about our . . . discussion?"

"His roommate, Eugene Otto. He told me that Donald had mentioned to him that you two were having some kind of disagreement over his book."

Wallace took a moment to consider his response. "I— we—" He paused and started again. "Donald came by on Saturday to discuss the biography. He'd somehow gotten the idea that it would be advantageous for book sales if it were to focus on the death of Ellie Myers, an old . . . friend of mine. To that end, Donald had obtained a copy of an old police report listing myself as a possible suspect. The crux of our disagreement was whether he would include that information in the book." Wallace paused for a moment, his face slowly clouding over. "I must apologize for being so slow, I only just realized that you must have been the one who provided Donald with that report. Would that be a correct assumption?"

Dexter nodded. "I provided the report—and I've read it."

"Did you mistakenly believe that you were serving the law by divulging such baseless slander as that?"

Dexter realized that Wallace had a point, and possibly a legal one, since the case was officially still open. "I'm sorry for any trouble that may have caused," Dexter said, trying to finesse the issue. "I certainly see your point."

Wallace spread his hands. "Isn't it natural for any innocent person to object to a public airing of unsubstantiated charges?"

"Of course, sir, but just to be clear, you are telling me that you had an argument with Donald two days before he was murdered."

"I'm a peaceful man. I would never dream of harming Donald, regardless of what he decided to include in the book; that's what I have an attorney for. In any case, we resolved the dispute peacefully—Donald got his wish to include the material in question."

"What made you give in, if I may ask?"

Wallace smiled. "Donald can—could—be very convincing."

"Okay, fair enough," Dexter said, and then he caved in to an irresistible urge. "Ellie Myers seems to be the lightning rod here. Mind if I ask you a few questions about her?"

"I have nothing to hide, Chief Loomis."

"How long did you know her before she died?"

Wallace Pearle leaned back in his chair and took a briar pipe and tobacco pouch out of his desk. "Do you mind?"

Dexter shook his head, and Wallace continued. "About a year and a half." He inserted the pipe into the pouch, filled it, and packed the tobacco.

Dexter did the math. "She died in December of eighty-four, so you met her—"

"In May of eighty-three, when she applied for a position as my personal secretary. When she arrived for the interview, I recall expecting someone older." Wallace put a match to the pipe and sucked on it for a few seconds until the smoke came freely, then exhaled and inhaled fresh air. "She was twenty-nine, as it turned out, though she appeared younger than her age. The painting that was stolen recently from the great room, *Girl on a Window Seat*—that was Ellie, painted about three months after she arrived here."

Dexter nodded, dredging up his hazy recollection of Ellie, revived by the photograph shown to him by Mrs. Pearle. "So she came to work for you as your secretary?"

"She very nearly didn't. On our first meeting I was struck

by her bluntness. She had a vigorous handshake and direct eye contact, all that. It raised my suspicions immediately."

"Suspicions of what?"

"That she didn't know the first thing about art. I quizzed her a bit, which confirmed my suspicions, and it was at that point, when I'm sure she thought she had blown the interview, that she became, well, flirty."

"She flirted with you?"

"She was a personable young woman, and dressed in an appropriately businesslike manner, but I'm afraid she allowed her desire for the position to color her judgment."

"How did she flirt with you? I mean, what did she do?"

"Nothing too outrageous—touched my arm when she addressed me, laughed at my comments, that sort of thing. Excuse me, I don't mean to be rude, but is this pertinent to your investigation?"

"It turns out that I actually knew Ellie Myers," Dexter explained. "When I was about six, she used to watch me for my mother."

Wallace lowered his pipe and looked at Dexter. "Extraordinary. Your babysitter. I had no idea."

Dexter smiled. "Just one of those coincidences. Actually, I barely remember her, apart from my six-year-old crush, but I am curious about her."

That elicited a gentle chuckle from Wallace. "Where was I?"

"I believe you were fighting off Ellie Myers' advances."

"Perhaps that's putting it a bit uncharitably. As I recall, she showed me her resume, which was—how shall I put this—thin."

"I see," Dexter said.

"I handed her resume back to her and was on the verge of putting an end to the interview, when she happened to mention that she played the clarinet." At this point Wallace placed his fingers over the dying pipe to choke it and puffed several times. "As it happens, I harbor a great passion for classical piano and have been an ardent student of it all my life. When she assured me that she did indeed play classical, I'm afraid that I became carried away with visions of duets, and I hired her on the spot."

"You hired her because she could play the clarinet?"

"Silly, I know, but she seemed to be a fairly organized individual, if a bit forward, who would likely grow into the position. I'm afraid I was seduced by the prospect of having a musical partner close at hand."

"Was it worth it? I mean, could she play?"

"It was a full month before she would agree to attempt even the most rudimentary student pieces. Each day I would ask if she wished to play, and each day she would delay the inaugural event with one pretext or another. Fortunately for her, she possessed considerable personal charm, even in her refusals."

"But eventually you played together?"

"It was in June, on a Saturday morning, as I recall. By this time I was quite curious to see how well she would play—not that it mattered, really, because she was working out fine in the job. A week earlier we'd selected a suitable duet by Brahms, so Ellie could prepare. I must confess that when we finally played together, it raised more questions than it answered."

"How so?"

"It wasn't the music; she found the notes, or, rather, most of them. Her performance on her instrument was mediocre at best, and her technique was uninspiring. It was what she did after we had finished. . . ."

"What did she do?"

Wallace laid his pipe, now gone out, in the ashtray. "She had just put her clarinet in its case, and I was still gathering my music together. I believe we were discussing what other pieces we might try. I remember that she was wearing a very nice skirt and blouse, a bit open at the neck, if you know what I mean. At any rate, she walked over to where I was seated at the piano, leaned over, and kissed me."

"Right out of the blue? Just like that?"

"I'm afraid so, as you say, right out of the blue. To this day I can conjure up the scent of the perfume she was wearing."

"And this was without any encouragement from you?" The look that Wallace bestowed on Dexter told him that such a question was unnecessary. "Anything happen as a result?"

"Not immediately." Wallace tapped the unburned tobacco from his pipe into the ashtray and chose not to elaborate.

"But eventually you became lovers," Dexter prompted.

"Yes, eventually." Wallace's voice faded just a bit, and then he seemed to gather strength. "After a few months she took a room in the main house. It seemed to make sense, since we were working so closely together. It was around that time that I painted her."

At this point Roberta Pearle opened the door to the study. "Wallace, our reservations are for seven o'clock. You should start getting ready. Officer—I'm sorry."

"Loomis, ma'am."

"Officer Loomis, I apologize for interrupting you."

Dexter rose from his seat. "That's quite all right, Mrs. Pearle. I still have another stop to make tonight myself."

Wallace also rose behind his desk. "If you wish to speak with me again, I will certainly make myself available."

He extended his hand to Dexter, who shook it and thanked him for his time, thinking that Wallace still looked a bit shaken from the news of Berglund's murder. Mrs. Pearle escorted Dexter down the hall, toward the front entry. Just as Dexter got to the foyer, he almost collided with a solidly built man coming around the corner from the direction of the kitchen.

"Excuse me," Dexter said.

"Not at all. Completely my fault, old chap," the man replied.

He was carrying a folded-up newspaper and a plate with what looked like herring on it. Dexter looked at Mrs. Pearle and waited to be introduced. It took her a few seconds to comply.

"I'm sorry. Officer Loomis, meet Mr. Edward Fitzner."

Fitzner tucked the paper under his arm and held out the hand that wasn't holding the plate. "Officer, 'eh? Pleased to make your acquaintance."

"Likewise," Dexter replied, shaking his hand. There was an awkward moment when nothing was said, so Dexter plunged ahead. "Friend of the family?"

Fitzner looked at Mrs. Pearle. "Yeah, you could say that. I'm a friend of the family. Just over from England."

"Are you staying here on the estate?"

"I am indeed, sir." He glanced at Mrs. Pearle. "Enjoying your famous American hospitality."

"Are you here on business or pleasure?"

He winked at Dexter and grinned. "That's right. You a constable, then?"

"Now and then," Dexter said, smiling back. "Well, anyway, nice meeting you."

"My pleasure entirely."

Edward Fitzner took his plate of food and disappeared in the direction of the great room, while Dexter and Mrs. Pearle entered the foyer. When they arrived at the front door, Dexter paused.

"I'm sorry for being such a nuisance, Mrs. Pearle, but since I'm here anyway, there's one other thing I should ask your husband."

Mrs. Pearle smiled. "Perhaps I can help you."

"Maybe you can. Do you know where your husband was on Monday night?"

Roberta had a perplexed look on her face. "What an odd question."

"Just something I wondered."

She crossed her arms. "He was home with me all evening."

Dexter thanked her for her patience and stepped onto the porch. As he walked to his Jeep, he considered how plausible it was that Wallace Pearle would have poisoned Donald Berglund just to keep the public from learning that he had been a suspect in a murder twenty years ago. He couldn't see it. And the fact that Ellie Myers had played the clarinet was something that he now realized he had already known. She had played in her high school band. He realized that the clarinet in the box in Donald's closet had probably belonged to her. Could, in fact, have even been the same horn she occasionally used to bring over to his house when she sat for him. He made a mental note to pick up the box. Now he was faced with leaving one highly unlikely suspect to talk to another equally unlikely suspect, Alfonse "Nine Fingers" Manzara.

Chapter Twenty-seven

"I got to be crazy, lettin' you talk me into questionin' somebody with a name like 'Nine Fingers' Manzara," Grady said.

"I need backup," Dexter explained as they walked down the long, carpeted hallway toward the rear of the Hudson House, a Best Western motel located on the I-94 frontage road in Hudson. "You're my go-to guy, so quit complaining. Heck, you should be honored."

Dexter had flashed his badge at the college student night clerk and learned that Alfonse Manzara and his bodyguard were staying in Room 130, the hotel's only Jacuzzi suite.

"Armed escort's what you need, not a med tech," Grady pointed out as they walked down the hallway with raised, red velvet wallpaper. "Bodyguard'll do some good before the violence commences. A med tech's only useful afterward."

Dexter noticed that Grady had grown increasingly agitated since he picked him up after leaving the Pearle estate. "Stop worrying. I just want to ask old 'Nine Fingers' a few questions."

"Right. See, that's the part I'm talkin' about, askin' the man questions. Ever think about maybe writin' him a letter? Why do they call him 'Nine Fingers,' anyway?"

Dexter shrugged. "Beats me. You want me to ask him?"

Grady moaned as they finally stopped at the end of the hall in front of Room 130.

"Everything's going to be fine," Dexter said, knocking on the door. Both men tensed when they heard what sounded like soft gunfire inside the room. Suddenly the door opened, and the doorway was filled with a very tall, very wide individual. Dexter, at six foot three, and Grady, at six foot five, weren't accustomed to having to look up at too many people. This particular gentleman had a head of thick black hair combed straight back and shoulders broad enough to block their vision into the room. He looked at Dexter and Grady for a second and said, "We didn't order no room service," and started to close the door.

Dexter moved his foot inside to prevent the door from closing, just as he noticed the holster and the cannon hanging off the man's shoulder. *Oops,* he thought. The man was starting to reach out for some unspecified part of Dexter's anatomy, when a scratchy voice came from behind him.

"Who is it, Pete?"

When the goon turned in the doorway to answer the question, Dexter caught a glimpse of a lone man sitting in a chair in front of the television across the room. The familiar *doink-doink* on the TV told Dexter that "The Python" was watching *Law and Order,* which apparently accounted for the gunfire they'd heard.

"It's room service, boss."

"Actually, I'm Chief Loomis," Dexter clarified.

The Neanderthal corrected himself. "It's some kinda Indian, boss." He turned back toward Dexter and narrowed his eyes. "I thought you said you was room service." The tone of his voice made it clear that he was very disappointed with Dexter.

"This is a motel," Dexter pointed out. "They don't have room service. And I'm not an Indian, I'm *Police* Chief

Loomis." Dexter was going to explain further, but a nudge from Grady prompted him to stay on point. "I'm investigating the murder of Donald Berglund."

The giant in the doorway glanced back at his boss, who was still watching television and hadn't bothered getting up, and then back at Dexter and Grady. "Who's Donald Berglund?"

"A local writer," Dexter explained. "He was doing some articles about the Two Bears Casino."

"Oh, yeah. That's probably the guy I saw take our picture. He tried to talk to the boss, but he didn't get too far."

"Why not?" Dexter asked.

"Because I prevented it. It's part of my job description," he added with an unmistakable touch of pride.

"I take it you're Mr. Manzara's bodyguard. What's your name?"

"Pete Gumbusky. Pete 'The Pick,' " he added, grinning.

"Do you have a permit for that weapon, Pete?" he asked, indicating the enormous gun in the giant's shoulder holster. Dexter's question brought another, harder nudge from Grady.

Pete took the gun out, allowing Dexter to identify it as a .45 automatic. "What, this thing? Yeah, got one around here somewhere." Then his mind seemed to reel off on a tangent. "Hey, you guys got any bears around here?"

"Bears?"

"This is Wisconsin, ain't it?" Pete waved the .45 around, and his eyes narrowed in a display of tense suspicion that no one should have to behold. "Don't you have bears here?"

"Most of the 'bears' we have around here," Dexter pointed out, "are cows."

"What if I was to pop one of 'em? You know, like in self-defense."

"Uh, no, Pete, you can't shoot the cows. If you were in a nasty mood, and you had to blow off a little steam, I suppose you might tip a couple of them over, but that wouldn't be very nice either."

"What the hell are you guys talking about over there?"

The bellow from in front of the television brought the nature discussion to a halt.

"It's some kinda Indian, boss."

"I'm—" Dexter cleared his throat and raised his voice above the television. "I'm Chief Loomis, Higgins Point Police."

Pete looked back at Dexter. "Oh, that's right." Then he looked at Grady. "So who's this other guy who don't say nothin'? He *your* bodyguard?"

"Yeah," Dexter said. "We call him 'The Hammer.'" Grady made a sound like a kitten being tortured.

"Well, what's he want?" Manzara's voice barked from inside the room. "Get him in here."

Pete reached out and grabbed Dexter's arm and pulled him forward. "The boss wants to talk to you." Grady followed, eager to avoid requiring Pete to lay hands on him too.

Alfonse "Nine Fingers" Manzara, a thin man with thinning hair, wearing a silk brocade smoking jacket, rose from his chair as Dexter approached. He rose to his full five feet four inches and looked up at the three men in front of him. "You guys look like you play for the Nets." He looked at Dexter. "You the cop?"

"That's right," Dexter said.

"Whaddaya want?"

"I want to ask you a question," Dexter said.

"We were gonna go to the casino," Manzara said to his bodyguard, "but this is better. Okay, shoot."

"I'm looking into the murder of a local writer, a guy named Donald Berglund," Dexter explained. "I'd like to know when you got into town."

"Been here in Hudson about a week. Did you say murder?

This is a business trip, not pleasure. I'm here smoothing out a few details."

"Well, Mr. Berglund was an investigative reporter, and he was writing articles exposing some of your activities, and I—"

"What activities? We're lookin' at pickin' up a few contracts at the Two Bears joint: garbage, maintenance, linen service. Just business. The trip's deductible, for Christ's sake."

"Still, it seems odd that you got into town, and a week later Donald, er, Mr. Berglund, gets murdered. So I wanted to ask you where you were on Monday night."

"Look, Sheriff—"

"Police Chief," Dexter corrected, and then added, "around nine o'clock."

"Yeah, whatever. I don't give a crap what looks 'odd' to you. Maybe you're some kinda nut, and everything looks 'odd' to you. You know what I'm sayin'?"

"Humor me. Where were you?"

Manzara spread his hands, like Christ above the altar. "I don't remember. Now, is there anything else I can help you with, or are we through here? You know, you miss five friggin' minutes of this show, and you lose track of the whole plot."

Dexter realized that if he wasn't willing to arrest the New Jersey mobster and drag him in for questioning—a prospect that was so daunting at the moment that his mind was incapable of grasping it—he wasn't likely to get anything of substance out of him. The man didn't have to talk if he didn't want to.

"Thank you for your cooperation," Dexter said.

"Good night."

Manzara turned around and walked back to his chair in front of the television, leaving Dexter like a bride at the altar. He and Grady walked to the door with Pete "The Pick" Gumbusky.

Dexter looked at Pete for a second and then motioned Grady ahead of him. "Go on. I'll be along in a minute."

Grady hesitated and gave Dexter a look and then left him alone at the open door with Pete.

Dexter endeavored to choose his words carefully. "Pete, I feel in the short time we've known each other that you and I, well, that we've bonded a little here tonight." Dexter moved his cupped hands back and forth as a visual aid to help Pete grasp the bonding process. "You know, maybe we're not that different, you and I." Dexter gazed into Pete's dark eyes, which looked like two deep pits and exuded the comprehension of a three-hundred-pound tuna. He forged ahead. "I'm curious about something."

"What?"

"What kind of retirement program does your organization offer?"

Dexter waited while Pete processed the question. "What organization?"

"You know, the gang. Do you have an IRA, stock options, maybe a flexible annuity?"

Pete looked as if he was getting a headache. He opened his mouth to speak, but Dexter cut him off. "Because I've heard that in your chosen profession sometimes it can get a little dicey around retirement time, and I know of a plan that beats the heck out of a bullet in the back of the head."

Pete looked at Dexter the way a New England oysterman would look at an oyster that had just spoken French to him.

Dexter lowered his voice discreetly. "What I'm talking about, Pete, is a time-honored career choice known as the witness protection program. It offers comfort, a stable environment, and security, and all you have to do to sign up is tell the truth. What could be simpler?"

When Pete finally finished processing Dexter's speech, he didn't say a word, just started closing the door.

Dexter stopped him. "I hope you'll make the correct choice and consider this valuable opportunity. Actually, I do have one last question, Pete—why do they call your boss 'Nine Fingers'?"

Pete "The Pick" Gumbusky, mob enforcer and personal bodyguard for crime family *patrone* Alfonse Manzara, glanced back at his boss, lost in television land, and then turned to Dexter. "Nobody I know calls him that," he said.

Chapter Twenty-eight

November 1984

Ellie Myers slid the slender silver blade in and jerked it sideways. The abruptness of the action betrayed the tension running just below the surface of her emotionless face. She laid the onyx-handled letter opener on the desk, blew into the envelope, and removed the contents. The letter was from the University of Wisconsin's Department of Fine Arts; they wanted *he whose name she would not speak* to address their graduating seniors next June. The suggested topic was to be "the reflection of a society's morals in its art." She almost gagged as she tossed the letter onto pile number one, for *he whose name she would not speak*'s attention. Let him decide. Then, on reconsideration, Ellie plucked the letter back off the pile and placed a yellow Post-it note on the front, on which she scribbled a note to remind herself to send a polite refusal to the school. Somebody with such an obvious lack of morals would not be lecturing the impressionable young minds of tomorrow on that particular subject—not if she had anything to say about it.

It had been two weeks since Ellie first spotted *he whose*

name she would not speak sneaking into Roberta Kaplan's cottage like a naughty schoolboy, and the revelation had not made for a pleasant fortnight. She hadn't bothered to actually confront him about it because she knew he would only deny it, and she had all the evidence she needed: Roberta no longer found it necessary to stop by her office to gush about her brilliant teacher, drop innuendoes, and gloat. That fact alone said it all. All in all, the estate was becoming hell on earth for Ellie.

She picked up the last envelope, and her gaze was immediately drawn to the distinctive stamps adorning its corner—English. The letter was from Kathleen Withington, her mother's pen pal in London. Given all the recent complications with *he whose name she would not speak,* Ellie had completely forgotten about their phone conversation two weeks earlier and her request for information on Edward Fitzner. With a guilty sense of adventure Ellie opened the envelope and read the two-page letter.

Kathleen said she hoped that all was well with Ellie and her family since last they'd spoken and then cut right to the chase. She expressed concern that Ellie was somehow involved with Mr. Fitzner, because he was clearly a very unseemly fellow. Kathleen's nephew in the police couldn't provide a copy of the actual police report, but he was able to furnish the following information. In July of 1981 Edward Fitzner was brought before the bar and charged with grand larceny and fraud, specifically art forgery. Apparently he had been peddling phony paintings around Europe—mostly in Switzerland, England, and Germany—for several years. The list of victims included some very well-to-do families. Fitzner was convicted and sentenced to twenty-three months in Brixton Prison in South London. He was released in June of 1983 after serving the full sentence, receiving no time off because he had refused to name his accomplice. The police realized that Fitzner had to have an accomplice, since he himself wasn't an artist.

Ellie paused, stunned. She recalled that June of 1983—the month of Fitzner's release—was one month before her boss's payments to him began. It seemed inconceivable that an artist as eminent as *he whose name*—oh, hell, as Wallace Pearle—would be party to any sort of art fraud. He might be an immoral sleaze, but a crook? But why else would he be sending money to the ex-felon? The conclusion seemed unavoidable: Wallace must have painted the forgeries that Fitzner had been selling around Europe. He must have been the accomplice the police never caught.

Ellie took a pad of paper from her desk drawer and put her suspicions down in writing. Then she gathered up the papers from the other drawer where she had placed them two weeks earlier. They included her original letter to the Greater London Arts Association, their reply, and Ellie's phone record of her conversation with Kathleen Withington requesting information on Edward Fitzner. She placed everything, along with Kathleen's latest letter, into a manila envelope and wrote *FITZNER* on the front with a felt-tipped pen. On second consideration she scratched out *FITZNER* and wrote *LONDON ARTS ASSOC.* below it. She placed the envelope in the bottom left-hand drawer of her desk and then leaned back and took a moment to stare out her office window at the cluster of cottages on the west lawn.

Gradually, over the past two weeks, Ellie had made up her mind to ditch Mr. Wonderful along with his job, but she had decided to keep her departure a secret until the last possible minute just to irk him. The question now became, what should she do with this information? Did her animosity toward Wallace extend to actually turning him in to the police? She'd have to give some thought to that. If she elected not to, was there any point in even letting Wallace know that she knew?

With Kathleen's letter, the mail was finished. Ellie rose from her desk and gathered up pile number one for Wallace's attention. His two-timing had been a body blow to Ellie's self-esteem, and performing her duties in a professional manner to the bitter end was one way to hold her head up. She left her office, nodding at Louise as she passed her in the hall.

Chapter Twenty-nine

Thursday

Dexter tugged at the front of his khaki shirt, fluffing it out, trying to get some air down his chest. He turned from the deputy sitting on his left to the deputy sitting on his right. "Does it feel warm in here to you?"

Deputy number one, a short, balding man with a shiny scalp, smiled. "Feels fine to me. You hot, Ed?"

Deputy number two's leather holster creaked as he adjusted his posture so his Glock didn't dig into his side. "Actually, I'm kinda chilly."

Dexter's gaze moved around the large, open office of the Curran County Sheriff's Department before coming to rest, once again, on the closed door at the far end of the room. Loitering outside Sheriff Tilsen's office were two Wisconsin state troopers. He glanced at his watch, certain that he'd been sitting there for at least thirty minutes, only to find it had been closer to ten.

"Is the air-conditioning working?"

Dexter had been summoned by a call from one of Tilsen's deputies, who had refused to give him a reason over the phone. The two deputies who were currently babysitting him had provided only a little information, none of it good. Several hours earlier, at approximately 5:00 A.M. Ray Danvers' body had been discovered in his car, parked behind Dibbo's Bar in Hudson. The word was that Danvers had been shot in the head.

Dexter was well aware of Eugene Otto's suspicions that gangsters had murdered his roommate because he was investigating some kind of mob/casino connection. The photo of the mobsters and the council members having a drink together was still in Dexter's desk drawer. If Eugene was right and they killed Donald for getting too close to the truth, it seemed fairly certain to Dexter that they'd also killed Danvers, probably because he wouldn't cooperate. And if they were willing to murder both of those men, wasn't it at least possible that they would go after Donald's roommate if they thought he knew too much?

"There's a guy named Eugene Otto," Dexter explained to deputy number one. "He lives at 213 Raymond. I'd like to have a squad car go by to check up on him."

"A welfare check? What's the concern?"

Dexter didn't want to go through the whole depressing thing right now, so he just said, "His roommate was Donald Berglund. He may be in danger too."

The deputy recognized Berglund's name as the first homicide they'd had in Curran County for quite a while. He looked at Dexter and then at deputy number two. "I guess he's not going to run." He hoisted himself to his feet. "Sure, we can do that. 213 Raymond. C'mon, Ed."

Just as they were walking away, Sheriff Tilsen opened his door, spotted Dexter, and called him over with a jerk of his head. He stood there holding the door open while Dexter walked across the room.

"Got some of your old friends here, Dex," he said as Dexter walked past him into the office.

Ann Summer and Zack Rose were seated in the chairs arrayed in front of Tilsen's desk. Ann looked trim and businesslike in a beige jacket, her brown hair just a touch longer than the last time he'd seen her. Zack hadn't changed at all. His hair was still uncombed, and his eyebrow ring was intact. He wore his standard plaid sports jacket over a T-shirt, and, of course, the cell phone earpiece still dangled from his ear. When Ann leveled her gaze at Dexter, her green eyes pushed everyone else out of the room, and he experienced a brief moment of profound self-consciousness. It was as though he couldn't judge his own facial expression. He tried a smile but wasn't at all sure it was convincing.

"Hi, Annie," he said finally, and then managed to remember to say, "Hey, Zack."

Zack snapped his chewing gum and grinned. "Long time no see, Chief."

"It's good to see you again, Dexter." Trust Ann to sound absolutely professional and in control.

"It's good to see you, Annie, but I wasn't expecting you until this afternoon."

"When they found the second body this morning, your DA decided he wanted us here ASAP."

"We sacrificed gas mileage for you, Chief," Zack pointed out.

"So, everybody's sure that the two murders are connected?" Dexter asked.

Sheriff Tilsen had closed the door and was returning to his seat behind the desk. Before anybody could answer Dexter's question, he said, "Dex, I want you to meet FBI Special Agent Robert Hatch. Agent Hatch, this is Higgins Point's police chief, Dexter Loomis. He's the one I was telling you about."

Dexter hadn't actually noticed the fifth person standing quietly in a corner. He was in the middle of nodding to Agent Hatch, when Tilsen's statement sank in, and he diverted his attention back to the sheriff. "You were telling him about me? What were you telling him?"

"Careful what you ask for," Zack said.

"Dex, do you recall our conversation yesterday afternoon?" Tilsen asked.

Dexter thought for a second. "You mean the part where you told me you were closing in on the KFC employee for Donald Berglund's murder? Because, frankly, Bob, I've been thinking about it, and I have to level with you, I don't think a high school kid would have done that. I mean, go to all the trouble of getting hold of the toxic plant that was identified in the report, and then reducing it down and extracting a useable poison. And then clock Berglund's trips to the KFC until he—"

"No," the sheriff said, speaking remarkably clearly through clenched teeth. "The part where I told you I didn't want you approaching Alfonse Manzara."

Agent Hatch cleared his throat and stepped forward. "Maybe I can help cut through the crap. Where were you at approximately nine-thirty last night, Loomis?"

Agent Hatch's question imposed quiet on the room and focused all eyes on Dexter.

"Where was I?"

"At nine-thirty last night."

"Well, let me see . . ."

"Because," Agent Hatch continued, "we very much like Alfonse Manzara for the murder of the casino manager. Our sources tell us that the Manzara crime family is looking to expand outside of Atlantic City, and he's been in Hudson for a week, leaning on the council members, trying to land some kind of service contracts. It's a classic first step onto a very slippery slope."

"I couldn't agree more," Dexter said. He looked to Ann for support and was surprised to see a concerned look on her face. *What does everyone in this room but me know,* he wondered. "I told Bob yesterday that the mob angle was—"

"So when Danvers' body was discovered early this morning," Agent Hatch continued, "your alert local law enforcement realized that he was important in the Chippewa gaming organization, and as such, his murder may have constituted a federal crime. They contacted the FBI, and we, in turn, immediately picked up Alfonse Manzara. Naturally, we asked him where he was last night when Danvers was shot."

Dexter looked around the room. Everybody was looking at him, except Zack, who had his head down and seemed to be shaking. Was he laughing? "So, where was he?" Dexter asked.

"Let me repeat my original question, Loomis. Where were *you* last night at nine-thirty?"

"You don't think I did it! Why would I—"

Agent Hatch stepped closer to Dexter and lowered his voice. "Would you please just answer the damn question?"

"Last night? Let's see, at nine-thirty I was—I was—uh." Dexter suddenly got it. "I guess I was with Manzara at the Hudson House—but only for ten, maybe fifteen minutes. I mean, how exact can the time of death be?"

"Exact enough, in this instance," Agent Hatch explained. We have two independent sources, both live in apartments above Dibbo's Bar where he was found, and both recall hearing what they thought at the time was a car backfire. They both put the time at precisely nine-thirty because an *Everybody Loves Raymond* rerun was just coming on."

"It's hard to find a time when an *Everybody Loves Raymond* rerun *isn't* coming on," Dexter pointed out. That observation earned only a stony silence from Agent Hatch. "So you're telling me that Manzara cited me as his alibi?"

"As strange as that may sound, that's exactly what I'm telling you. And you have just corroborated it, haven't you?"

Dexter suddenly understood what Manzara had meant the previous evening when he'd said, 'We were gonna go to the casino, but this is better,' He'd intended to make sure he was seen in public when his men were murdering Danvers.

"May I ask what you thought you were doing in Manzara's hotel room last night?"

"My being in Manzara's room did not get Danvers killed," Dexter pointed out. "He obviously had some of his men do that, and if I hadn't been there, he'd have had some other alibi in place." Dexter's rationale clearly had about as much impact on Agent Hatch as a tennis ball bouncing off a bank vault.

"We'll never really know, though, will we? Since you were kind enough to provide him with a very official alibi."

Ann gave Dexter a supporting smile, and he realized that this was probably an excellent time to keep his mouth shut. After a moment Agent Hatch returned to his original position in the corner of the room. "Let me be clear, Loomis. I don't want you anywhere near the Danvers investigation, *my* investigation."

"But Donald Berglund might have been murdered by—"

"And just for the hell of it, I don't want you anywhere near *that* investigation either. Now, go forth, Chief Loomis, and sin no more."

"Amen," Zack added, raising his gaze to the ceiling.

Ann punched Zack's shoulder and gave him a dirty look.

Dexter left the room and closed the door and was suddenly staring at Frank Kahler. His pen was poised above his notepad, and his eyebrows were raised, projecting innocent curiosity.

"So, Chief, would you like to tell our readers how it is that you came to provide the alibi for one of the most vicious thugs in America not currently behind bars?"

"How the hell did you find out about this so quickly?"

"It's my job, you know, like yours is to serve and protect. Boy, is this ever gonna be embarrassing for you."

Frank Kahler walked away, and Dexter started for the door, thinking that maybe he could still salvage the day—if he managed to get hit by a bus.

"That wasn't fair, Dexter." Ann's voice turned him

around. She'd apparently followed him out of Tilsen's office. "That was just Tilsen being himself."

"Sounded like it was Agent Hatch who had a problem with me."

"Tilsen went off about you for ten minutes before you arrived. He had Hatch primed."

"I am *so* glad I didn't vote for him." Dexter grinned, and when Ann returned his smile, suddenly Tilsen didn't matter anymore. "I asked you to town to help with the Berglund murder, Annie, but now it looks like I won't even be able to work the case myself. And with the FBI setting their sights on the mob, I suppose they're going to drag you away to help with the Danvers investigation."

"They did grab Zack, but I pointed out that it might be useful to leave one of us on the Berglund murder, in case they're connected."

"And the sheriff went for that?"

"Nope. He told me he wanted all of his 'assets' assisting the FBI. Then I pointed out that my boss assigned me to the Berglund case, and if he wanted to reassign me, he'd have to do the paperwork. We finally compromised. I'm going to split my time between the cases."

Dexter smiled. "I love a strong woman, Annie."

"You need a strong woman, Dexter."

"Whoa, this conversation suddenly took a left turn."

They looked at each other for a silent moment, and then Ann said, "How's Asta?"

"She misses you." It occurred to Dexter that his comment might be taken in more than one way.

"I miss her too," Ann said.

Two minutes with Ann and she had him feeling like a high school kid. "Where are you guys staying, anyway?"

"We've got rooms at a local bed-and-breakfast, but we haven't been there yet. Thought we should check in with the sheriff first."

"I've got an idea. Why don't you two come to my place for dinner tonight? My Uncle Delmar's in town—I'll introduce you."

Ann smiled. "I'd love to finally meet another member of the Loomis clan."

"And I can bring you up to speed on what I know so far."

"What you know about what?" Ann asked. "I just heard Hatch wave you off both cases. I'd listen to him, if I were you."

"By the process of elimination, that just leaves me with the twenty-year-old cold case."

"Cold case?"

"A woman named Ellie Myers, who was poisoned just like Donald Berglund."

"Are you serious?"

Dexter fixed Ann with his most steely look. "Annie, I'm a lawman. I'm always serious. Come by around seven tonight, okay?" Dexter noticed a funny look on Ann's face. "What's the matter, you forget where I live already?"

She shook her head. "It's just that after being away for six months, I'm starting to remember what it was like here in Higgins Point with you."

Chapter Thirty

Howard and Margaret Myers had moved from Higgins Point to Roberts, Wisconsin, in 1987, three years after their daughter, Ellie, was murdered. When Dexter got them on the phone, by way of introduction he pointed out that he was the same little Dex Loomis their daughter used to babysit for back around 1970. He then went on to explain that he'd recently reviewed the police report on their daughter's death and wondered if they would be willing to answer a few questions. The confused silence that followed his request brought a hasty apology from Dexter for dredging up painful memories, but in the end they agreed to talk with him.

The drive from Higgins Point took twenty minutes. When Dexter arrived, the Myerses welcomed him into their comfortable, neat-as-a-pin, two-bedroom rambler, seated him in the front room, and handed him a cup of coffee. Dexter could tell from their behavior that his call had precipitated a rush of speculation about finding their daughter's killer after all these years. Balancing the cup of too-strong coffee on his knee, Dexter cautioned them against expecting too much. After all, the crime had occurred more than twenty years ago.

"I know this is going to sound like a pretty basic question

after all this time, but do you recall your daughter ever mentioning anybody she might have had a problem with?"

Mrs. Myers hesitated and glanced at her husband, then said, "Just that Wallace Pearle." As it turned out, she tended to do the talking for both of them. "In fact, about a week before she died, Ellie told me the two of them were calling it quits."

"You mean their relationship?"

"Their relationship, the job, everything. Just before she died, she called us. She said she still had her apartment, but she wanted to stay with us for a little while. We arranged to come up and help her move back home. I guess they were arguing a lot, but she said she was just going to do one last recital with him."

"She told you they were arguing?"

"No, Lewis Coffers did. He was the police chief back then. He told us the cook and some of the students said they heard them fighting. We always suspected that Wallace Pearle murdered Ellie, and so did Lewis Coffers, but I guess he just couldn't prove it."

"So you never actually witnessed them arguing?"

Mrs. Myers glanced at her husband. "No. The few times we visited up there, everything seemed fine."

"I'm sorry again for bringing all this up," Dexter said.

"It's okay," Mrs. Myers assured him. "In fact, we were just talking about Ellie the other day with that young man who died in the car accident."

"You mean Donald Bergland? You met him?"

They both nodded, and she said, "He seemed like a nice man. We were sorry to hear about his accident."

Dexter knew that the weekly paper in Roberts came out on Friday, so they probably wouldn't learn that Donald Berglund's death hadn't been an accident until tomorrow morning. He decided to leave it that way. "Donald came to me looking for information about your daughter's murder," he explained. "Did he tell you he was investigating it?"

Mrs. Myers glanced at her husband. "Not exactly. He told us that he wanted to include Ellie in a book about Wallace Pearle. We got to talking—it felt good to talk about Ellie again—and when I mentioned that she used to play her clarinet with Mr. Pearle, he asked if he could see it. Well, we hadn't given it a thought in years. It took me a minute before I realized that it was still in the cardboard box we'd brought home from Wallace Pearle's house. We told Mr. Berglund that he was welcome to borrow it if he wanted."

"I believe I saw the box in Donald's office."

"We don't really care about the other things, but we would like to get the clarinet back; it's something personal of hers. Can you get it for us?"

"I sure can, Mrs. Myers. But would it be okay with you if I held on to it for a couple of days? I'm sure the police went through the contents of the box thoroughly in 1984, but I'd still like a chance to look them over. I'll be sure to return her things when I'm through."

"That would be fine, Chief, uh . . ." Mrs. Myers searched Dexter's shirt for a name tag but came up empty.

"Loomis, ma'am. But call me Dexter."

"Okay, Dexter, but I don't believe anybody ever saw the box until Mr. Berglund took it."

Dexter felt the tiny hairs on the back of his neck go up. "Are you saying it was missed in the original investigation? How can that be?"

"Well, when Ellie died, everybody thought she was sick from something. Took about a week before they figured out that she'd been poisoned. In the meantime we brought Ellie's things home and parked her car out back of the house. When they finally realized she'd been murdered, Lewis Coffers went all through Pearle's house, trying to find out how

Ellie got poisoned, but nobody gave a thought about her car, including us." She indicated herself and her husband, who was staring, unblinking, at Dexter. "It sat out there for—I guess about five years. We just couldn't bring ourselves to think about it. When we finally decided to get rid of it, we went through it, and that's when we found the box. It was in the trunk. Ellie must have put it there the night she died. She was planning on moving back home, like I said."

"And you never mentioned the box to Lewis Coffers?"

Mrs. Myers shrugged. "Five years had passed, and it was only some of her papers, her desk clock, her clarinet— things like that. We just put it in the basement."

Dexter's mind was racing. He—or, rather, Donald Berglund—had stumbled across possible new evidence in a homicide after twenty years. Who knew what might be in the box? If Donald had come into possession of the box only a few days before he was murdered, perhaps he hadn't gotten around to examining the contents. Dexter rose to leave, abandoning his still-full coffee cup. He thanked them both at the front door and then paused. "I'll let you know if anything develops."

Mr. Myers, who Dexter judged to be around seventy-five, leveled a penetrating look at him and chose that moment to finally speak. "Young man, I have no use for idle talk, but I'll be damn grateful for anything you can do in finding my daughter's killer."

Dexter smiled weakly and nodded, thinking to himself, *great, no pressure.*

Chapter Thirty-one

Dexter's uncle, Delmar, spun his spaghetti-laden fork against his spoon, set the spoon down, and paused. "I don't know, a little of this, a little of that," he said, and then shoveled it in. His face took on the expression of critical satisfaction reserved for cooks tasting and approving of their own food.

"A little of this, a little of that," Ann Summer echoed, smiling at his response to her question. "That covers a fairly broad spectrum." She lifted a forkful of spaghetti. "By the way, Delmar, this is delicious."

That sentiment was seconded by Zack Rose, who was seated across from Ann, on Dexter's right.

"The cook thanks you—and why don't you just call me Del."

Since the moment they'd sat down to dinner, Asta had planted herself like some tiny canine Buddha at Ann's feet, waiting for any offering of food from the table. As Dexter dug into his Caesar salad, he realized that he was annoyed by Asta's behavior. By the time he was halfway through his spaghetti, he'd figured out that he was annoyed because he was jealous. He fed this dog faithfully day and night, but

187

when the noncustodial parent breezed into town, any illusion of loyalty flew-right out the window. Dexter narrowed his eyes at his thankless pooch just as Delmar addressed him.

"So, nephew, you were about to lay out what the cops have got in this Berglund murder investigation so far."

"Which, as of this morning," Zack helpfully pointed out to Dexter, "you're no longer officially involved in."

"Or unofficially," Ann added, apparently in the interest of completeness.

Dexter smiled at Ann, seizing the excuse to gaze, if only briefly, into her green eyes. After all, Asta's demonstration of disloyalty wasn't *her* fault. When he'd invited Ann for dinner, he hadn't had any illusions about its being a romantic evening; he knew his uncle would be there, and he'd also asked Zack to join them. He had, however, envisioned himself in a central role, preparing a gourmet meal that he knew would please Ann—maybe salmon fillets with lemon-dill butter, roasted potatoes, and asparagus, things he knew she liked—and would leave him looking competent in her eyes. But once his uncle had heard the words "dinner guests" this afternoon, he hadn't let Dexter lift a finger. Within minutes he'd announced a suspiciously complete menu and was off to the store for groceries. Dexter finally decided that it was best to look at the bright side of this deviation from his plans; he was getting to know his uncle again after a long absence, the food was great, and he still got to see Ann. Aware that Ann and Zack had already received a full briefing from Tilsen on the Donald Berglund investigation, he laid his fork on his plate and addressed himself to his uncle.

"Okay, first up we have—"

"By the way," Delmar interrupted, "am I the only one here who's knocked out by that painting you did?" He waved his empty fork toward the living room. "The one above the couch with the seagulls."

"Uh, those are egrets," Dexter said. "And thanks."

"The white birds, whatever. It's an honor to have such a talented guy in the family. I bet your mother, God rest her soul, was proud as hell of you."

Dexter wasn't sure exactly how much information he wanted to include in his response. "It's a hobby I took up after she died," he finally offered.

Delmar's large features reorganized themselves into a tragic mask. "That's a shame, Dex. So she never saw your pictures?"

"No, I'm afraid not."

"You know something, Dex? I want to buy that painting. Who knows when I'll get a chance to stop by this burg again? This way I'll have something around to remember you by."

Dexter was caught completely off guard by his uncle's request, though he did have to admit to a certain rush of pleasure from the unexpected praise. "Geez, Uncl—uh, Del, if you like it that much, I'd like to give it to you."

"Aw, no. It's art. I ought to pay you something for it."

"No, I insist. It's yours," Dexter said, convincing himself that the painting should go to someone who admired it. "Be sure to remember to take it with you when you leave—end of story. Now, I was going to tell you about the Berglund case."

"Oh, right, wait a second." Delmar got up and walked into the kitchen to dish up another helping of spaghetti. "Anybody want some more?" This was met with a round of regretful smiles and the patting of stomachs. He returned to the table with a second full plate and sat down. "Okay, so you got any suspects yet?"

"Well, originally they liked Dennis Stowell, whose father is an accountant currently serving time in Oakhill Correctional for cooking his company's books. Since it was Donald Berglund who did the investigative reporting that exposed the scam, Tilsen figured the son might have decided to get even for his dad's unscheduled sabbatical. And he had opportunity—he works at the KFC where Donald received his fatal dose of poison."

"This Berglund was poisoned at a KFC?"

"The lab found poison on the chicken," Dexter explained, modestly omitting the part where he'd figured that out.

"They searched his locker at school," Ann added. "I guess they thought he might be stupid enough to leave a jar of poison lying around. They didn't find anything."

"His locker? You tellin' me he's a school kid?" Delmar's tone conveyed a healthy amount of skepticism. He spooned a little Parmesan cheese on top of his spaghetti. "Doesn't exactly sound like a sure thing to me."

"We kind of drifted off when the sheriff covered that part too," Ann agreed.

"And then," Dexter continued, "we have Alfonse 'Nine Fingers' Manzara."

Zack Rose's eyes lit up, and he started chuckling at something. When this behavior was met with three pairs of questioning eyes, he hurried to explain. "They did this thing on him on *Saturday Night Live* last year. Anybody see it?" Blank stares. "In the sketch they called him Alfonse 'Eleven Fingers' Mahony, and it was supposed to be in L.A., see. The cops were trying to fingerprint him, but they kept coming up with one print too many. They finally had to let him walk because they couldn't figure out how to deal with the paperwork. Funniest thing I ever saw." Zack glanced around at the table of staring faces and shrugged. "Well, maybe not the funniest thing, but it wasn't bad."

Delmar tore his gaze from Zack's eyebrow ring and returned his attention to Dexter. "Manzara, huh? No kiddin'? So why would some goomba garbage collector from New Jersey wanna come all the way out here just to whack a local?"

"How did you know that Manzara controls garbage contracts in New Jersey?" Ann asked. "What did you say you did for a living?"

"I got ears, is how I know about Manzara," Del explained, ignoring Ann's second question. "And what I hear is that he's exploring new revenue streams—you know, lookin' to expand. But that still don't explain why he'd punch some local guy's ticket."

"The victim's name is Donald Berglund," Dexter said, "and—"

"Allow me, Dexter," Ann said. "Mr. Berglund authored one article and apparently was about to publish a second one alleging that the Manzara crime family was trying to take over the Two Bears Casino. Given Manzara's well-known aversion to the limelight, the Feds think he probably decided to stop the bad publicity by going straight to the source."

"And it didn't help Manzara's case," Zack added, "when the casino manager turned up dead this morning."

Delmar arched his eyebrows and whistled softly. "Two guys in one week, huh? I guess Manzara's on a tight schedule. Sounds to me like you got your guy. So what are you messin' around with this high school kid for?"

"There's more," Dexter said.

"Really?" Delmar turned his toothy smile on Ann and poured more Chianti into her glass.

Dexter took some spaghetti onto his fork and started winding it up against his spoon. "Valerie McBride, the insurance investigator, thinks that whoever robbed Wallace Pearle's house might have murdered Donald. But you probably know all about that theory, Del, since you had dinner with her last night."

"Yeah, now that you mention it, I think she did say something about that."

"But since that would require Donald to have been working with the burglar," Dexter pointed out, "I don't think there's anything to it."

"So you figure this Berglund guy was on the square, a solid, upstanding victim?"

"Something like that," Dexter said.

"From the way Agent Hatch and the others were talking this afternoon," Ann said, "the investigation looks like it's heading toward New Jersey."

"And this Agent Hatch would be who?" Delmar asked.

"FBI," Dexter said.

Delmar nodded and chewed slowly. "Manzara shows up in town, and people start dropping dead. Sounds like an open-and-shut case to me."

Dexter decided not to muddy the waters by mentioning Wallace Pearle's argument with the victim, since it seemed unlikely that it would turn out to be anything important. And he certainly didn't want to bring up the subject of Ellie Myers' murder, especially before he had a chance to examine the box containing her belongings.

After dinner Delmar had key lime pie waiting in the kitchen for everyone. When they finished that, Dexter recruited Zack to help clear the dishes, while Ann went to the front room to reacquaint herself with Asta. Eventually they were all seated in Dexter's front room, where they drank coffee in an effort to coax some of the blood away from their stomachs and back into their brains. Dexter tried out some small talk in his head to see how it played before laying it out to the group. Had Ann been to any Brewers' games this summer? Was she dating anybody? Was she so busy dating somebody that she couldn't go to a lousy baseball game? Didn't whoever she was dating believe in baseball, for God's sake? Was this guy some kind of Communist? In the end he decided it might be wise if he left the small talk to the others and listened quietly while Ann asked Delmar about his cooking skills.

"Del, I'm impressed with the meal you put together tonight," she said. "Where did you learn to cook such good Italian food?" She glanced at Dexter. "Or is there some Italian blood in Dexter's family that I didn't know about?"

"No Italian blood," Del explained. "The Loomises are Norwegian and French."

"But now that I think about it," Ann said, "your accent even sounds a little Italian."

"My accent?" Delmar grinned, and his pearly whites contrasted with his tanned face. "I guess accents got more to do with where you been and who you hang out with than your nationality."

"I suppose that's true," Ann agreed. "So where have you been, and who do you hang out with, Del?"

Delmar laughed gently and took his time answering. "All over, and probably nobody you ever met, but that reminds me of something. Hey, Dex, Victor told me to say hi next time I saw you."

Dexter almost spilled his coffee. "Victor?"

"Yeah, he says hi."

Dexter felt utterly blindsided. "You've seen him?"

"We've . . . been in contact" was all Delmar would offer.

"Who's Victor?" Ann asked.

Dexter ignored her. "How is he doing? Is he okay?"

"Near as I could tell, he's doing fine."

"I don't understand. How can you be in touch with him?" Dexter asked.

"We got an arrangement."

"What kind of arrangement?"

"Dex, you're gonna have to excuse me if I'm a little stingy with the details. You understand."

Dexter nodded and took a deep breath. "Can you give him something for me? I mean, do you see him or just talk to him?"

"Sorry, we just talk. But I could pass a word along."

Dexter opened his mouth to speak and suddenly felt the way he had once in the second grade when he had been standing with his schoolmates, crowding around Santa in the school auditorium. Without warning Santa had turned and singled Dexter out from the group and asked him what he wanted for Christmas. Dexter's mind had shut down on that occasion too. "Tell him—tell him I said hi, I guess," he said weakly.

No more was said on the subject of Victor, and soon after Ann and Zack thanked Delmar and Dexter for dinner and rose to leave. Dexter walked them out to Ann's car, and as Zack slid into the passenger seat, Ann pulled Dexter aside.

"Dexter, this person your uncle was talking about . . ."

"Victor?"

"Yeah, what was that all about?"

"He's in the federal witness protection program. Been in it for several years. That's why I was surprised to hear that Del had talked to him."

"But who is he?"

"Victor's my father."

Chapter Thirty-two

November 1984

Ellie Myers was seated in the great room when she heard the chime of the front doorbell. There was a silent interval, and then another chime. When it was clear that she wasn't going to hear the sound of Louise's footsteps hurrying to answer the door, Ellie set down the art supply inventory list she was working on and went herself. She opened the door to a slender woman, perhaps in her fifties, wearing a gray cloth coat and rubber galoshes. The look of apprehension on her face caused Ellie to skip the pleasantries and invite her in out of the cold.

"May I help you?"

"My name is Francine Ulmer. I'm-I'm looking for my daughter, Sara."

It took Ellie a moment to process this. "Sara Ulmer? I'm sorry, but I don't think there's anybody here by that name."

"I was told she was here."

"Who told you that?"

She hesitated. "She could be using another name, but she's my daughter."

195

"You mean like an alias?" This didn't seem likely to Ellie. "Someone's here, on the estate, using a false name?"

"I don't know. I was told Sara was here."

Her concerned expression and the edge of desperation in the woman's voice convinced Ellie to humor her and try to sort it out. "How old is she?"

"Twenty-four."

Of the other three women who stayed at the estate, Barbara, the cook, was at least forty-five, which left only Roberta, the art student, and Louise, the housekeeper, both about the right age. "Is she a student here?"

"I don't know. I haven't seen her since—well, for about six years."

Ellie realized that both Roberta and Louise had similar coloring and, in fact, bore a slight resemblance to each other; they weren't going to get anywhere that way. "Would you please come with me?" Ellie led her through the house to the door that opened onto the west lawn. They stood on the back stoop, and Ellie pointed at the cottages. "Do you see that group of buildings?"

"Yes."

"Well, the one nearest to the right is shared by Roberta Kaplan and Louise Dahlman. Neither one is named Sara, but they're both about the right age. It's close to lunchtime, so they should be there now. You're welcome to go see for yourself if either one is your daughter."

Francine Ulmer looked at the cottage and then back at Ellie but didn't move.

"I guess six years is a long time, isn't it?"

Francine nodded.

"Do you want me to come with, or would you prefer privacy?"

"If she's there, I guess I'd like to see her alone—if it's okay."

"That's fine. Just follow the path."

Ellie gestured at the wide path connecting the outbuild-ings to the main house. It was kept plowed and clear of snow. Francine finally stepped off the stoop and began walking slowly toward the cottage. She turned suddenly and said, "Thank you, Miss . . ."

"Myers. I hope you find your daughter."

Chapter Thirty-three

Friday

Dexter opened the black instrument case and announced, "Clarinet." He pulled out the main section of the horn, fitted on the mouthpiece and the tailpiece, and was mildly surprised to note that a reed had been left in the mouthpiece when the horn was last stored away, presumably over twenty years ago. He held up Ellie Myers' assembled instrument, pointing the business end at Grady, and fingered the keys. "You know, I should have taken up the clarinet. Maybe it's not too late."

"I wouldn't go suckin' on that if I were you, Dex. Been layin' around forever."

Dexter lowered the horn. "True," he agreed, laying it back in its case on the desk.

"Clock radio," Grady said. He blew the dust off it and set it next to the clarinet.

Dexter reached into the box. "Pencil cup." He studied the multicolored beaded face staring at him from its side. "Looks like it's from Jamaica." He set it on the desk beside the radio.

When Dexter stopped by Eugene Otto's place to pick up Ellie Myers' box, he'd been glad to see that Eugene seemed calmer than he had on Wednesday. He told Dexter that he was sorry it hadn't occurred to him to mention that Donald didn't play the clarinet, but Dexter admitted he should have asked.

Grady reached into the box. "Rolodex." He handed it to Dexter. "If she knew her killer, his name could be in there."

Dexter flipped through it. "Along with about a hundred other people from twenty years ago."

"Hey, man, you want to solve a cold case, there's gonna be some legwork."

"Oh, and you know all about cold cases, huh? What are you, some kind of Sherlock Homeboy?"

The beginning of a smile passed across Grady's face before he caught it. "Yeah, and that makes you Wonder Bread, my faithful Caucasian companion."

"Hi Yo, Silver." Dexter handed the Rolodex back to Grady. "Check these people out, will you, and get back to me." Then he added, "By the way, I had dinner with Annie last night."

Grady set the Rolodex on the desk. "Man, you must love pain."

"What's that supposed to mean?"

"It means what it means. You must love beatin' your head against that brick wall."

"If you're referring to Annie, characterizing her as a brick wall is a little severe." He pulled a letter opener from the box. "Wisconsin Dells," he said, reading the handle. He held it up to the light to examine the blade. On CSI there was always some blood left on the blade.

"Maybe so, but you ain't been the same since she turned you out. And what do you think you're doin' with that letter opener? She was poisoned, not stabbed."

Dexter tossed the opener aside.

Grady pulled out a bottle of cologne, sniffed at it, and squinted at the label. "Says Amarige."

Dexter pulled Ellie's appointment book out of the box, thumbing through the pages. Under November he found the name Sara Ulmer and recalled also finding the name in Donald's notes. "Maybe we can run through her appointments, see if anything looks fishy. And she didn't turn me out."

"There you go with that 'we' again," Grady said, and he looked at Dexter. "If she didn't turn you out, then how come you're not together?"

"It was my call, not hers." Dexter felt a flush of embarrassment when he finally said this out loud.

It took a couple of seconds for the comment to work its way into Grady's head. When it finally did, he paused. "Did you just say what I think you said?"

Dexter cleared his throat. "uh—she didn't call it off. I did." He tried to focus on the contents of the box but was aware of an intense stare coming from Grady's direction.

"You mean to tell me that you been walkin' around for the past six months makin' sounds like a sick cow, and all the time you did it to yourself?"

Dexter remained silent, choosing to ignore Grady's obviously slanted characterization, but Grady wouldn't be deflected.

"Just when I thought white folks were startin' to make sense, you do somethin' like that."

"C'mon, you never thought white folks made sense."

"So why'd you do it, Dex?"

"Why'd I break up?" Good question. "I'm not too clear on that myself, actually. At the time it seemed like everything was happening so fast. I'd just been shot, remember. And then when Annie told me she was willing to leave the DCI and relocate, it shook the heck out of me. I guess I just got scared."

"Scared."

"Just an old-fashioned case of cold feet."

"She was willin' to leave the DCI for you, and you turned her out?"

"I gave her a puppy."

"So a puppy's about as far as you're willin' to go?"

"I guess I could have been more committed," Dexter admitted.

Grady pulled a Magic Eight Ball out of the box. "Trust me, Dex, you should definitely be committed. You ready to commit *this* time?"

Dexter took the Magic Eight Ball from Grady, shook it, and held it up. They both watched as the word ABSOLUTELY floated to the surface.

"And if she's willin' to give your sorry self another tumble, are you gonna tank again?"

Dexter shook the Magic Eight Ball and held it up again. The words NOT AT THIS TIME floated to the surface. He studied the Magic Eight Ball for a minute and then said, "How do you think she was poisoned, anyway?"

"The police report said belladonna."

"No, I mean, how did it get into her? The report also said they went through the entire estate, examined every cup and dish in the place."

"I don't know, what else do you put in your mouth—a toothbrush?"

"Toothpick," Dexter suggested.

"Mouthwash?"

"But not, unfortunately, in your case," Dexter pointed out. "Maybe chewing gum?"

"How 'bout a stamp? Maybe someone poisoned her stamps?"

"Possibly," Dexter said, and then he focused on the clarinet lying in its open case. Ellie Myers' clarinet . . . that she had played the night she died . . . that she had put into her mouth the night she died. He picked it up slowly, staring at the mouthpiece.

"I wonder how long poison stays toxic?"

Grady followed his gaze. "I'd guess forever, unless I

knew better," he said. "Maybe we ought to send that thing to the lab."

Dexter set the horn down and nodded. "Let's do that." He looked into the box, which was almost empty, and pulled out the last item, a manila envelope. A black felt-tipped marker had been used to obliterate something that had been written on it, and below that were the words *LONDON ARTS ASSOC.*

Chapter Thirty-four

Roberta Pearle's companion and perennial houseguest opened the door. Dexter recognized her from talking to her on Saturday morning, when he'd responded to the burglary. He thought her name was Louise, but he wasn't sure. She invited Dexter and Grady in, and they stepped inside, Dexter carrying the envelope he'd found in Ellie Myers' box of personal effects.

"Are you here to see Mr. Pearle?"

"Him and Mr. Fitzner, if he's here, uh, Louise, was it?"

"Yes, I think they're both in the study. Please follow me."

She led them through the house. It was the third time Dexter had been there, and the route through the art treasures was becoming familiar to him, but Grady hadn't seen the home before. The only reason Dexter had asked him to tag along was because Dexter didn't think he'd believe his description unless he saw the place for himself. Grady's expression told Dexter that he appreciated the splendor.

When they arrived at Wallace's study, Louise announced them, and they entered to find Wallace sitting behind his desk reading something. Across the room, seated on a plush leather sofa that looked as if it cost more than all the furniture in Dexter's house, was Edward Fitzner. He was reading the paper. When Wallace glanced up, his welcoming smile and white goatee gave him the kindly look like of a slender Burl Ives—in one of his more pleasant movie roles. Of course he's smiling, Dexter thought. He doesn't know why I'm here yet.

"Ah, Chief Loomis and . . ."

"This is Grady Penz, sir. He's . . . assisting with our investigation."

Wallace studied Grady's med-tech uniform for a moment, evidently deciding that it didn't rate a comment, and then gestured at his companion on the sofa. "I believe you've already met Edward Fitzner, an associate of mine from England." Fitzner nodded. "Please have a seat." Wallace indicated two chairs in front of his desk.

Dexter and Grady accepted the offered seats, and Dexter said, "I'm glad you're here, Mr. Fitzner. It should make this more interesting." Then he turned his attention to Wallace. "I wanted to talk to you about Donald Berglund, sir."

"Of course you do. What about Donald?"

"Well . . ." Dexter paused, considering how to put it. "When I talked to you on Wednesday, about Donald's writing your biography, you told me that in spite of his wanting to include your role as a suspect in Ellie Myers' death, you two had worked things out, and there was no reason you would want to harm him."

"I recall our conversation."

"It should please you to know that I no longer suspect you of murdering Donald Berglund to cover up your role as a suspect in Ellie Myers' death."

Wallace smiled. "Yes, that pleases me indeed." The smile faded. "Unfortunately, it won't bring Donald back to us."

Dexter placed the envelope on the desk in front of him and placed a hand on top of it. "I now suspect that you, and

Mr. Fitzner, here, may have murdered Donald Berglund to prevent your art forgery activities from becoming public."

Wallace's face froze, and his color drained away until, in a matter of seconds, he looked very old. Over on the couch, Fitzner had lowered his newspaper and sat up. After several seconds Wallace finally summoned the words to reply to Dexter. "You must have gotten that information from Donald."

Dexter reached out and traced his fingers along the graceful lines of the brass sextant that was sitting in front of him on the mahogany desk. "That was an unfortunate thing to say."

Confusion now joined the shocked expression on Wallace's face. "Why?"

Dexter pulled out a notepad and pen, ignoring the question. "I take it you aren't denying the forgery?"

There was a moment of silence, during which Wallace looked at Fitzner and must have received some sort of subliminal sign. Slowly Wallace's shoulders sagged, and Dexter could sense his capitulation.

"The allegations of forgery are true," he finally said.

"But *not* the murder," Fitzner added emphatically, getting to his feet. "We didn't have anything to do with that lot."

"Maybe you did, and maybe you didn't," Dexter said. "But one thing is certain—you both had what I would call an airtight motive. I can see why you wouldn't want anybody to know about it."

"You couldn't expect me to rush to announce to the world that I was painting forgeries," Wallace said softly, almost to himself.

"Why don't you two fill me in on how it worked?"

"It represents the one major sin of my youth," Wallace said.

"Have a care, old boy," Fitzner said. "Sin indeed. You're casting me in the role of Lucifer."

Fitzner took a tin of mints from his pocket, opened it,

popped one into his mouth, and then extended it to Dexter and Grady, who both declined.

During this exchange, Wallace seemed to gather his thoughts, and his voice gained strength. "It was 1966, and I was fresh out of Oxford; the ink was still wet on my diploma. Edward and I had become casual acquaintances over the course of several art classes. He was a dreadful art student, had absolutely no talent for it at all." This remark earned him a leer from Fitzner. "But he could be an amusing companion, and he always seemed to have an angle on things. It wasn't until later that I realized Edward had an angle on me. After four years at the university I was weary of existing on my parents' money and eager to become my own man. Edward must have recognized this quality in me. Looking back, I can't imagine that it could have been too difficult. At any rate, he approached me with an unusual business proposal."

"Art forgery?" Dexter asked.

Wallace hesitated and then nodded, staring down at the surface of his desk.

"It began innocently enough, drinks at our favorite pub one evening, and a conversation that veered from cold war politics to women and, inevitably, to art. Edward expressed an admiration for the charcoal copies of the masterworks that he had seen me do in one of the classes. I recall that he compared my ability to capture the correct proportions of the human figure to that of Rubens." Wallace looked at Dexter as if to say, *you see how easy it is?* Then he returned his gaze to his desktop and resumed his story.

"I can attest firsthand to the fact that hubris is an equal-opportunity beguiler, and when an art student hears himself compared to Rubens, it tends to linger with him. He asked me if I thought I could do as well in oils. At that age, the world had not yet had the time to beat the brashness out of me, and I assured him, after several pints of lager, that I could. My memory of the remaining conversation is unclear, but I recall it ending with a plan. A monstrous business arrangement whereby I would return to America and crank out copies of masterworks, while Edward traveled the Continent, ferreting gullible buyers out of the cracks and crevices of the European art scene."

Wallace lifted his gaze. "You would be amazed at what outrageous forgeries a mendacious man, if he is talented enough, can sell to wealthy buyers, and Edward is both. Of course, the sales were fueled in part by the avarice of buyers eager for what they thought were unrealistic bargains. In one instance Edward gleefully wrote to tell me that he had actually managed to convince a buyer that the *Portrait of the Marquise D'Orvilliers* by Jacques Louis David, which hung in the Louvre, was a fake, and he had just sold him the authentic one."

"That was a nice bit of work on my part," Fitzner added.

"How long did this go on?" Dexter asked.

"Well, let's see. I remained in England through 1967 and returned to America and the unwelcome comfort of my family early in the summer of sixty-eight; I recall that the papers were still full of the news of Robert Kennedy's assassination. I applied myself diligently, and within a year I had completed and shipped three paintings to Edward in London. Sequestered behind the protective walls of my parents' estate on Long Island, England seemed an entire world away. I sustained my self-esteem through the illusion that I was merely painting, nothing more. What could be criminal in that? Before long a check arrived by post, and my carefully constructed fantasy of innocence crashed down around me. But at the same time I became convinced that Edward's crazy scheme could actually work, and I could be independent of my parents. I produced more paintings and continued to collect checks. The subjects were always carefully selected beforehand by Edward, who seemed to have a knack for identifying masterpieces that would be saleable. Things proceeded in this fashion for four years, until 1971, when I finally burned out on the whole tawdry affair."

Dexter was writing quickly and flipping pages. "You ended it, not Fitzner?"

Wallace nodded. "I ended it, though it was an amicable parting. By that time Edward had accumulated a backlog of many forgeries. I told him to keep them, explaining that I was going to take my chances in the art world with my own name. I already had several of my own originals placed in galleries around New York and was beginning to build a reputation."

"Didn't you object to the end of the gravy train?" Dexter asked Fitzner.

"We'd had a good run," he replied. "I wished him well."

"But you went to prison," Dexter prompted.

Fitzner coughed and nodded slowly. "I continued to sell off the remaining paintings, a few each year. You might say I stayed a bit too long at the party—I was finally arrested in 1981."

Wallace picked up the narration again. "He managed to contact me through a discreet third party to inform me of his dilemma. By that time I was doing quite well financially, and I was able to provide money to assist with his legal defense. I followed his trial with dread, expecting him to surrender to the pressure from the prosecutor to lighten his sentence by identifying his unknown partner. They had easily deduced that he wasn't the actual forger. I could hardly have blamed him, but he never named me. Instead, he served the full sentence and was released in 1983. I began sending him checks almost immediately."

"Was he blackmailing you?" Dexter asked.

"He never asked for a penny," Wallace said, looking at Fitzner.

"I have to ask the obvious question," Dexter said. "Why?"

"Why did I do it?" Wallace asked.

"You had everything handed to you," Dexter said. "An Oxford education, rare natural talent."

"I wish I could express to you how often I have asked myself that same question," Wallace said. "It was partly for the money. Although distinguished, my parents were comfortable but never fantastically wealthy. But a large part of it was the thrill."

"The thrill?"

"Of being clever enough to fool the art world. In my youth I'm afraid I did not lack for arrogance."

"And you managed to keep your part in the whole thing secret all this time?"

"Thanks to Edward's loyalty, secrecy required only my own silence—that is, until Donald Berglund somehow stumbled onto it. By the way, speaking of Donald, what did you mean earlier when you said, 'That was an unfortunate thing to say'?"

"I was referring to the fact," Dexter explained, "that if Berglund knew about your forgery activities, that would provide you with a solid motive to murder him."

Wallace stared at him for a second. "That's preposterous."

"But only," Dexter continued, "if you knew that Berglund knew, which you just told me you did. That was an unfortunate thing for you to say."

"But I only learned of Donald's knowledge last Saturday when he came to see me. He died on Monday. Do you really believe I could have engineered his murder in so short a time?"

"I only have your word that you didn't know until Saturday."

"It's pretty tough to prove you don't know something," Grady pointed out. His first words since walking in seemed to catch Wallace off guard.

Fitzner coughed and seemed to have trouble clearing his throat. Explaining that he was going to the loo, he went into Wallace's personal bathroom located off the study.

"Tell me something," Dexter said after the bathroom door had closed. "If you didn't murder Berglund, do you know for certain that Fitzner didn't?"

"I can't imagine that Edward is capable of anything like that."

"He came all the way over here from England for something. What was it?"

Wallace looked a little uneasy.

"The best advice I can give you, Mr. Pearle, is to tell the truth."

Wallace cleared his throat, and in the quiet interval they heard water running in the bathroom and more coughing. "Edward told me that he was coming here to 'deal with the problem of Mr. Berglund.' "

"And he arrived on Sunday?"

Wallace nodded.

"He shows up Sunday, and Berglund is murdered on Monday, and this doesn't seem suspicious to you?"

"I was under the impression, from my conversation with Sheriff Tilsen, that the FBI thought that Donald had perished in a gangland slaying."

"That's one line of thought, and it's popular, I'll give you that, but I do have one other question. Do you know how Donald Berglund found out about your art forgeries?"

Wallace thought for a moment and then shook his head. "I didn't ask him. He was a clever man. I guess I assumed that he did some sort of investigation."

"In fact he did, and it all came in a nice neat bundle, courtesy of Ellie Myers." Dexter picked the envelope up from the desk and let it drop. "You remember Ellie Myers, don't you, Mr. Pearle? The flirty, underqualified clarinet player?"

"What has this to do with—"

"Think about it," Dexter said. "If Ellie Myers dug all of this up and knew you were a forger back in eighty-four, that would have given you a motive to kill her too. So we have two people—both knew about your forgery activities, and both are dead."

Wallace's shoulders slumped.

"And both by similar means—poison."

"Chief Loomis, I did not kill Ellie Myers. Until this very moment I didn't even realize that she had found out about Edward Fitzner and all that."

"If you're innocent," Dexter said, "then—"

They were interrupted by a sudden loud thud coming from the bathroom. Dexter and Grady exchanged glances, and Grady was out of his chair before Dexter could say a word.

Grady knocked on the door. "Mr. Fitzner? Are you okay in there?" He gave it two seconds without a reply and tried to open the door. It opened about three inches and stopped. Grady looked at Dexter. "Give me a hand."

Together they leaned on the door and managed to push it open far enough for Grady to get his head inside.

"Call 911. He's on the floor, blocking the door. Lean into it."

Another hard push and Grady was able to slip inside and pull Fitzner's inert body from the path of the door. Wallace was on the phone calling for help when they carried Fitzner to the couch.

"What happened?" Dexter asked.

"Looks like a heart attack," Grady explained, starting CPR. "He's not breathing."

Although Grady never stopped working on him until the ambulance arrived seven minutes later, he was unsuccessful in trying to jump-start his heart, and when they wheeled him out, Edward Fitzner was dead.

Chapter Thirty-five

After seeing the ambulance off, Dexter dropped Grady back at his office, where Grady had left his car. While he was driving back to the sheriff's department, he considered how beneficial Fitzner's fatal heart attack might have been for Wallace Pearle. If the police hadn't discovered Ellie Myers' evidence of Wallace's forgery, Fitzner would have been the only witness still alive. And until only moments ago Wallace hadn't known that the evidence of his forgery had surfaced. Of course, there was always the chance that the heart attack was really a heart attack and purely coincidental, but Dexter thought that "convenient" might be a better description.

Although Dexter now suspected Wallace Pearle more than ever of murdering both Ellie Myers and Donald Berglund, there was one other idea eating at him. He couldn't shake the thought that there might be some significance attached to the person named Sara Ulmer. Her name had turned up in both Donald's notes and in Ellie Myers' appointment book. Was she somehow important? Had Donald's interest in her gotten him killed?

The Curran County Government Center was laid out on

two floors; courtrooms and the clerk's office were on the first floor, and the sheriff's office was in the basement along with the jail. Down there the beige hallways were darker and cooler, so the air-conditioning didn't have to work as hard to keep out the summer heat. Dexter waved at the desk officer behind the bulletproof glass, and she buzzed him in. Across the room, Ann Summer and Zack Rose were sitting at a desk, staring at an intimidating pile of paperwork.

Zack glanced up and spotted him first. "Hey, Chief, after your little talk with the sheriff yesterday, I didn't think we'd be seeing you around here so soon."

"What's all this?" Dexter asked.

"Memos, e-mails, phone and financial records for Garden State Refuse Disposal Corporation," Ann explained. "Hatch wants us to see if we can tie Manzara to Berglund's murder through his connection with the Two Bears tribe."

"In the movies," Dexter pointed out, "mobsters are always stupid enough to put incriminating evidence down on paper. Are they that stupid in real life?"

"I think Hatch has seen too many movies," Zack said, opening another black ledger book. "Oh, by the way, Chief, we got lab results back on that clarinet."

"Already?"

Zack nodded. "The reed was soaked in poison."

"And if it's any consolation," Ann added, "the Sheriff was really irritated that after twenty years, you were the one who finally figured it out."

Dexter thought about almost putting the clarinet into his own mouth. "Yeah, I'm the clever one, all right."

"So what brings you in here today?" Zack asked. "You miss us?"

Dexter held up the manila envelope he was carrying. "Something turned up. I thought the sheriff should see it."

Zack stopped reading and looked up at Dexter. "New evidence?"

Dexter nodded. "Possible motive."

"Pointing to?"

"Wallace Pearle and Edward Fitzner."

"The painter?" Zack shook his head. "Yeah, right." And he turned his attention back to his ledger.

"Who's Edward Fitzner?" Ann asked.

"More to the point, who *was* Edward Fitzner," Dexter said. "I'll explain. Apparently Donald Berglund was going through Ellie Myers' old effects when he discovered evidence of art forgery in Pearle's past."

"*Wallace Pearle* is an art forger?" Ann's voice conveyed her skepticism.

"He used to be. Edward Fitzner was his partner. Ellie Myers put together a circumstantial case that'd make a district attorney proud. I just left his estate, where they both admitted it—just before Fitzner dropped dead of an apparent heart attack."

"Apparent?" Ann said.

"Wait a minute, Chief," Zack said. "He died just now, right in front of you?"

Dexter nodded. "About twenty minutes ago. Grady and the paramedics did what they could, but he didn't make it."

Zack leaned back in his chair. "So the painter's got a motive."

"A bottled and bonded motive."

"Well, if the painter did it, it couldn't have been the mob," Zack said, turning to Ann. "So why are we wading through Garden State Refuse Disposal's garbage—pun intended."

"That's a question for Agent Hatch," Dexter pointed out. "I have a different question for you. Annie, how would somebody go about researching a person if you only had her name?"

"What name?" Ann asked.

"Sara Ulmer. I found it in Donald Berglund's files."

"Significance?" Zack asked.

Dexter shrugged. "I think Donald might have been following it up for some reason when he was murdered. And the same name also turned up in Ellie Myers' appointment book."

"Not that cold case again." Zack gave Ann a pained look. "Would you please tell Chief Loomis that this isn't a television show?"

Ann turned her green eyes on Dexter. "Chief Loomis, this isn't a television show."

"Got it," Dexter said, nudging the pile of papers. "But if it was, I bet it'd be called *Lost*. So, Annie, can you give me some advice?"

"I'd be glad to," Ann said, smiling at Zack. "Statewide or nationwide?"

Dexter considered this. "Wisconsin for starters."

"You should start by casting a wide net; I'd recommend DMV records. Almost everybody drives a car, and the records go back quite a ways. In fact, I have a friend in Madison who can do a database search like that in minutes. Write down the name for me, and I'll give her a call."

Dexter printed the name on a slip of paper, handed it to Ann, and thanked her.

"Not so fast—there's a condition."

"A condition?"

Ann smiled. "I want you to tell me about your father, Victor."

"What do you want to know about him for?"

"Because he's where you came from."

Dexter stared at Ann while he thought about that.

"Is there a problem?" she asked.

"No, that's just a scary thought. Okay, deal. But first I have to tell the Sheriff of Nottingham that one of his biggest campaign contributors just took a late lead in the 'who killed Donald Berglund handicap.' My job isn't completely without perks."

Sheriff Tilsen was seated behind his desk indulging in an

afternoon jelly doughnut when Dexter walked in. Tilsen set the doughnut down and told Dexter that Dennis Stowell had passed a polygraph that morning and had been officially cleared in the Berglund investigation. He picked the dough-nut back up and announced that they were looking harder than ever at the mob angle. When Dexter laid the envelope on his desk and explained what was in it, Tilsen dropped the doughnut and got jelly all over his pants. He lunged for a box of Kleenex, and his hand brushed his coffee cup, empty-ing the contents across his desk. Dexter managed to snatch the envelope off the desk just in time.

While the sheriff mopped up his desk and cleaned off his pants, Dexter explained that the missing piece of chicken from Berglund's KFC bucket might mean that the killer was in the car with Donald Berglund on the night he died. Maybe he even went through the KFC drive-thru with him. Sheriff Tilsen pointed out that Dexter wasn't even supposed to be working on the case and then grudgingly agreed to circulate a photo of Wallace Pearle to the employees on duty Monday night, to see if anybody remembered seeing him in the car. Not wanting to push his luck with Tilsen, Dexter handed him the envelope, thanked him for his time, and tactfully pointed out that it might be a good idea if they had Donald Berglund's car checked for prints—just in case the killer had been inside. The sheriff made an annoyed sound that seemed to indicate grudging agreement, and Dexter left, returning to the area where Ann and Zack were working.

When Ann saw him approaching, she got up to intercept him and steer him toward the break room. Once inside, she armed them both with cups of coffee and sat down at a small Formica table across from Dexter. "Okay, spill," she commanded.

Dexter took a sip of coffee and a deep breath, trying to de-cide where to start.

"My parents were divorced—let's see—I guess twelve years ago."

"Twelve years ago?"

Dexter nodded. "By the time it happened, I was twenty-nine and had already been a highway engineer for Curran County for six years." Dexter watched Ann process this information. "The answer to your question, by the way, is yes."

"What was my question?"

"Their divorce blindsided me. After thirty years together, the split came as a surprise to everybody they knew. When a marriage that old crumbles, it tends to catch a lot of people off guard."

"Must have hit you pretty heavy."

Dexter shrugged, sorting out old feelings. "Emotionally, I don't think so, not really. When it ended, it was a surprise, but there wasn't any big explosion, no 'last straw.' It was more like an iceberg melting; one day they were a couple, and then they weren't. I was old enough by then to recognize that there wasn't any big villain or real victim, just two people growing apart."

"So how does Victor go from divorced husband to the witness protection program?"

Dexter smiled. "That would be the question, wouldn't it? All the time I was growing up, my dad was constantly on the road, working, and when he was home, he never talked about his job. If I asked a question about it, he'd shrug it off and say something like, 'Sales are boring.' What did I know? I believed him. Then, eight years ago, he was arrested for burglarizing a home in Prior Lake. That's a wealthy suburb south of Minneapolis."

"Dexter, are you telling me that your father was a *burglar*?"

Dexter nodded. "He got lucky. With no previous arrests and an attorney who knew his way around the back alleys of city hall, he managed to get a suspended sentence. But even though he didn't actually go to jail, the cat was pretty much out of the bag. I mean, you don't burglarize homes at the age of sixty without being a career criminal. I finally understood why he'd always been gone so much—the son-of-a-gun was leading a double life."

"I can't imagine how your mother must have felt."

"At first my mother was floored. She told me that in thirty years, she'd never suspected—not once. When she got over the initial shock, she paid his bail; they'd been divorced for four years by that time, but he was still family. Mom and I even had a good laugh when I pointed out that whatever Dad had been up to for thirty years, he must have been pretty good at it."

"So Daddy was a rolling stone."

"You have no idea. A year later, seven years ago, he vanished into thin air. I didn't say it to my mother at the time, but I feared the worst. He'd apparently been keeping company with criminals for years, and I suspected he'd finally crossed the wrong guy. It took me a couple of months and a lot of digging, but I finally found him. He'd crossed the wrong guy, all right—I was right about that—but he'd gotten away with it. In exchange for his testimony against a Kansas City mobster, Victor had entered a federal witness protection program. That's all the Feds would say. They wouldn't tell me where he was or give me his new identity."

"And you never saw him again?"

"Once. Five years ago my mother started having blackouts. Her doctor found a tumor in her brain. It was particularly aggressive, and four months later she died." Dexter was aware that when Ann was eleven, her mother had also died of cancer, and the look on her face suggested that she understood all too well how Dexter felt. "We had her funeral at the Lutheran church she used to attend. When it was over, I was walking to my car when a bearded man dressed as a groundskeeper came walking toward me. I could tell when he was still several yards away that it was my father."

"Wow."

"His disguise was pretty good," Dexter explained, "but I knew that the church was too small to afford a full-time, uniformed groundskeeper. We only talked for about three minutes. He said he was sorry she'd died. He was also sorry for being MIA during my childhood, and he was sorry he couldn't stick around then. What I remember is he was mostly just sorry." There was silence for a few seconds while Ann digested what Dexter had told her. Finally Dexter added, "That was pretty much it, until last night when my uncle mentioned him."

Suddenly Ann's cell phone went off. She identified herself and then listened for half a minute before writing down an address on a napkin. She thanked the caller and closed her phone.

"Got a hit," she announced. "There's a DMV record for a Sara Ulmer who applied for a driver's license in 1981 in Douglas County." She slid the napkin over to Dexter.

Dexter looked at the address. "917 6th Street, in Superior? That's interesting."

"Why?"

"Eugene Otto told me that Donald went up to Superior last week to do some kind of research."

"Research on what?"

"He didn't know, but I'm wondering if maybe it had to do with this Sara Ulmer person. Well," he said, putting the napkin into his shirt pocket, "I guess I have somewhere to start."

Chapter Thirty-six

Dexter entered the town of Superior from the south, on Highway 35 as it turned into Tower Avenue, one of the main streets in town. To the northwest he could see the high bridge that led to Duluth, Minnesota. In the old days, the iron ore and taconite mines had kept the lake freighters full and the Duluth/Superior ports active. When the sailors hit port, they went to Duluth to eat and dance, and to Superior to visit the "houses," as they were politely called. The cops were willing to look the other way and let the girls work, so the system flourished. It was the direction in which Superior chose to grow. When the mining and shipping dried up, Duluth managed to transform itself into a thriving tourist town, but things had not gone as well for Superior. For every artsy antique shop and fancy eatery in Duluth, there was an abandoned building, a vacant lot, and two bars in Superior.

The Douglas County Government Center was located at 1313 Belknap Street near the center of downtown Superior. As Dexter entered the building, he recalled that 1313 had been Donald Duck's license plate number, and he realized that maintaining that useless bit of trivia over the years had probably cost him several state capitals. The interior of the government building was completely open, with the offices encircling a large central atrium that extended the length of the building and the full three stories. Everything was marble—the floors, walls, and ceiling, the columns, and the convoluted series of massive staircases. The Clerk of Courts was on the third floor; the courtrooms were on the second floor. Dexter headed straight for the first floor, where the Douglas County Sheriff's Department and jail were.

After he identified himself and explained what he was after, the deputy behind the glass buzzed him through the door and used the desk phone to call another deputy up to the front. Two minutes later a short, attractive brunet appeared. She led him back through three locked doors and a maze of hallways, deep into the Douglas County jail. When they arrived at what looked like a file room, he explained again that he was researching a person named Sara Ulmer and wanted to run a check for any possible arrests. He omitted the fact that he had absolutely no idea why she might have been arrested.

"The place to start is the computer," she explained, positioning herself in front of an out-of-date–looking beige monitor. She tapped on the keys for about five seconds, waited for a few more, and then announced that she'd found the name. She typed in something else and then stood back so Dexter could see the screen. What he saw was nothing; the screen was almost blank.

"There was an arrest," the deputy explained, "in 1975. But apparently she was a juvie, so there's nothing here."

"No record at all?"

"There's a record; it's just not on the computer. You're gonna need some paperwork to get at juvenile files."

That didn't sound like a lot of laughs. Dexter considered the likelihood that this whole line of inquiry was going to yield zilch but then decided, *what the heck—I drove all the way up here.* "Does it at least say what she was arrested for?"

The deputy shook her head. "She was under eighteen."

"Well, where do they keep the files?"

"Records that old are kept in remote storage, and juvie records are locked up. I can't even get the key without paperwork."

"Remote storage. You mean, like, a warehouse somewhere?"

She smiled up at Dexter and wrinkled her nose like an indulgent daughter. "Actually, it's just down the hall, in the equipment storage room."

"You're a deputy, right?"

She nodded.

"What's your name?"

She smiled. "Addison."

Dexter gave her his most congenial smile. "Well, Deputy Addison, why don't we have a look?"

She scribbled something down on a piece of paper and handed it to him. "This is the year of the arrest, and the Binder number for that year, so we can locate the file in storage—after you come back with the Order to Release."

Dexter accepted the paper. "Don't tell me, a judge?"

She nodded. "I think the intake judge today is Julius Cleary. His office is on the second floor. Don't worry. He's ancient, but he gets it. He'll sign a release for you right away—unless he's in session."

"And if he's in session?"

She tilted her head and smiled. "You can always come back down here and wait with me."

Dexter matched her gaze for a few interesting seconds, allowing himself a brief fantasy, but her hazel eyes were no serious match for Ann's green ones. He thanked her, pocketed the slip of paper, and politely asked to be let out of jail.

The judge's office—or chambers, as Dexter guessed it was called—was in the northeast corner of the second floor.

Though he was indeed in his office as Dexter entered, Judge Cleary seemed very much preoccupied with something behind his desk, down near the floor. There was a roll of silver duct tape lying on the desktop along with one of the judge's shoes. Dexter cleared his throat and launched into his introduction. Judge Cleary's fidgeting came to a sudden halt, and he sat up, motionless, like a deer caught in headlights. Without really understanding it himself, Dexter proceeded to present his explanation as to why he wanted access to the more than thirty-year-old juvenile arrest records of Sara Ulmer.

As soon as the judge had the general drift, he held out his hand. "Give me the paper."

"I don't have—I haven't filled out a release form yet."

The judge glared at Dexter as he rose to his feet. He rounded his desk, one foot shoed, one foot bare, and hobbled to a tall, beige, metal cabinet in a corner of his office. He threw open the doors and rummaged around for a minute, while he mumbled something about having to do everything himself, finally emerging with a sheet of paper. He returned to his desk, sat down, signed the bottom of the release form, and thrust it toward Dexter.

"Fill it out on your own time."

"Don't you want to hear the details?"

"Speedy justice—it's guaranteed in the Constitution. Got a problem with that?" He glanced at the clock on the wall. "I've got court in fifteen minutes and two more warts to duct tape. Good luck with your case"—he searched out Dexter's name badge—"Officer Loomis."

Dexter thanked him and returned to the first floor, where he presented the Order to Release to the desk officer. She made a call, and a couple of minutes later Deputy Addison walked into the entry area. Dexter handed the release to her, and she explained through the glass partition that procedure didn't allow him to access the files directly, so she would provide him with a copy. She disappeared again, leaving him standing in the hallway. Ten minutes later she reappeared and handed Dexter a single sheet of paper.

"Thin file," he said, weighing the page on the palm of his hand.

"It's just the booking sheet. That's all there was."

"Well, thank you, Deputy Addison."

She switched on her smile and aimed it at Dexter. "Anytime, Officer," she said, holding his gaze for just a second longer than necessary.

Lamenting the fact that it was apparently his curse to go through life leaving broken hearts strewn in his wake, Dexter sat down on a marble bench along a wall in the atrium to study the report. The booking sheet was dated June 11, 1975, and contained some basic personal information: the suspect's name, Sara Ulmer; her address, 1811 Oaks Avenue, in Superior; and her date of birth, March 10, 1960. It also listed her mother, Francine Ulmer, as nearest living relative, same address. Dexter stopped when he got to the charge—suspicion of murder. Murder? In 1975 Sara Ulmer would have been only fifteen years old. Who did she kill? Maybe nobody, Dexter realized. This was only an arrest; maybe she was eventually cleared of the charge. But most puzzling of all was, how did Sara Ulmer's name end up in Donald Berglund's notes? Dexter wanted to find out the results of the arrest, but juvenile court records would undoubtedly require another visit to Judge Cleary, and he would be in court by now and unavailable. Dexter decided to pay a visit to the local library.

The Superior Public Library, which also served as the Douglas County Public Library, had moved into an old Super One grocery store in 1992. The building, which was located at 1530 Tower Avenue, had been refurbished and actually looked quite good. Large windows had been installed across the front, and the brick had been tuck-pointed.

The librarian attending the front desk, a pleasant, elderly lady, informed Dexter that newspapers older than one year were kept on microfiche. Superior's current newspaper was the *Daily Telegram,* but in 1975, it had been the *Evening Telegram,* a daily that ran from Monday through Saturday. Dexter settled down in front of a large, boxy, microfiche-viewing machine in a small room and inserted a spooled tape of the *Evening Telegram* that covered the period of the arrest. He went to June 12, 1975, the day following the arrest, and found the newspaper's account on the front page. *If it bleeds, it leads,* Dexter thought. Sara Ulmer's name was omitted from the article, but it had to be her. How many juveniles were charged with murder on a typical day?

According to the article, the victim was a man named Joseph Ulmer, and he was survived by his wife and daughter. Dexter stopped there and stared at the name. Joseph Ulmer! Had Sara murdered her own father? The piece went on to explain that Ulmer, who had been poisoned, actually died on June 3 and that the district attorney was still deciding whether or not to try the suspect as an adult. Apparently it had taken the authorities a few days to figure out that it was murder. Then Dexter saw something that stopped him cold—the poison used had been belladonna. Could Sara Ulmer have been responsible for Ellie Myers' death too? Was that what Donald Berglund had been investigating? Was that what got him killed?

Dexter hit a button that printed the page and then removed the tape and replaced it with one covering a period a couple of months later. He turned the handle of the machine, scanning the paper's front section for news of the trial's outcome. It took quite a while, but on the third tape, on October 20, he finally found an article at the bottom of the front page. It explained that a female juvenile had been convicted of second-degree murder in a sealed trial and was remanded to the Southern Oaks School for Girls in Union Grove, nothing more

He also made a copy of that page and then inserted the original tape. He went to June 4, searching for the original article reporting Joseph Ulmer's death. He found the story on page four of the front section. It said that Joseph Ulmer had died the previous evening from what was believed to be food poisoning. It said that the source of the poison had not been determined, but the police were examining the Ulmer kitchen in case it was food that the family had purchased recently, and others were in danger. The article said that the deceased was survived by his wife, Francine, and his daughter, Sara. No problem using her name there, Dexter thought; she wasn't a suspect yet. The only other thing the article offered was a family photo—the Ulmers in happier times. It showed a man with thick black muttonchop whiskers and a clean chin, a woman smiling next to him, and a young girl, perhaps twelve, standing in front. Dexter made copies of the article and photo. The article listed Francine Ulmer's address as 1811 Oaks Avenue. If she was still there, Dexter decided that he would like to have a talk with Sara's mother.

Chapter Thirty-seven

Dexter turned off the ignition and sat behind the wheel of his Jeep for several minutes, studying the house, wondering if this was really a good idea. He wondered if Francine Ulmer would actually have anything to contribute, and if she even lived here now. 1811 Oaks Avenue was a small weathered, wooden house painted green with dirty white trim. It sat behind a neglected wood-and-wire fence, with empty clotheslines bisecting the weed-infested backyard, which looked out onto a set of train tracks fifty yards to the west. The grime that settled gently from the stacks of the passing locomotives was evident on every shingle of the house. Dexter noticed a face peeking out around the edge of the front room curtains, watching him. He finally got out of his car and walked past the broken front gate up to the door and knocked.

A slender woman in a faded blue print dress opened the door almost before he had finished knocking. She looked to be perhaps seventy, and she peered up at Dexter through tortoiseshell-framed glasses.

"I'm sorry to bother you, ma'am, but are you Mrs. Francine Ulmer?"

"Yes." Her voice was soft and tentative.

"My name is Dexter Loomis, I'm the police chief of Higgins Point, a small town a couple of hours south of here."

"Yes?"

"Could you tell me please, is Sara Ulmer your daughter?"

She slowly raised a hand to her mouth. "Oh, my God. Is she all right?"

The expression on the woman's face and her unexpected question touched off a minor panic in Dexter. "As far as I know, she is. What I mean is, I can't say; I'm just trying to establish her identity."

"Her identity?" Dexter could feel the tension drain from Mrs. Ulmer as she lowered her hand from her mouth to the doorknob. "She's my daughter, but I haven't seen her in years."

"Would it be all right if I came in for a few minutes, to talk?"

"I suppose."

Francine Ulmer stepped aside to allow Dexter to pass and then closed the door behind him. After they were seated in the small front room, Dexter asked when and where she'd last seen her daughter. Mrs. Ulmer recounted her trip in 1984, down to the Pearle estate in Higgins Point, where she'd been told her daughter was staying.

"When I got there, a lady told me there wasn't any Sara there. Turned out she was using some other name. I wasn't surprised at that."

Dexter leaned forward. "Do you remember what name she was using?"

Mrs. Ulmer paused. "I don't recall—too long ago. Been more than twenty years, but I remember she was living in one of them cottages out behind a real big house." She looked more closely at Dexter. "Why you askin' now?"

Dexter struggled for an answer. How do you tell a woman that you suspect her daughter is a serial killer? The answer is, you don't—you dodge the question. "I, uh, I've been over to the courthouse checking records, and I came across your daughter's arrest in 1975."

"So you know about that."

"The newspaper said she poisoned her father."

Mrs. Ulmer's gaze drifted around the tiny room, avoiding Dexter. When she spoke, her voice was like a whisper in the confessional: "I didn't believe her."

"I'm sorry?" Dexter said, leaning forward.

"I said, I didn't believe my daughter. When they asked me in court if he done what she claimed, I told 'em no."

"Who done wha—uh, who did what?"

"Abused her."

Dexter suddenly realized what she was saying. "Her father?"

Mrs. Ulmer nodded, looking at the floor.

"And you don't think he did it?"

Now she looked directly at Dexter. "I didn't think so for a long time. Sara went into that Southern Oaks place in seventy-five. When she come out in eighty-one, she wasn't the same person. I still didn't think he done it, but that didn't matter anymore; she didn't want nothin' to do with me."

"You said 'for a long time.' Does that mean that you believe her now?"

"That's why I went down to Higgins Point to see her in eighty-four. Took almost ten years for me to finally own up to what that son-of-a-bitch was doin' to her. I told her I believed her, and I was sorry. Told her I wanted her to come home. She said no thanks." Mrs. Ulmer shook her head. "Can't really blame her, can ya? If I wanted to be her mother, I had my chance up there on the witness stand in seventy-five."

"So you haven't seen your daughter since 1984?"

"Nope."

"And you can't remember what name she was going by?"

She shook her head. "Sorry, the name didn't mean nothin'

to me." Then she repeated her question. "How come you're askin' me this now?"

He searched for an upside to telling Mrs. Ulmer what he suspected her daughter of doing and found none. "Just following up on some leads," he explained. "And you have no idea where she is today?"

Mrs. Ulmer shook her head again. "Leads on what?"

"Someone died at the Pearle estate back when Sara was there. Beyond that, I don't know any more than you do."

It occurred to Dexter that maybe the sheriff's files could lead him to Sara Ulmer's current location. He stood up and thanked Mrs. Ulmer for her time. He walked out to his Jeep, and when he drove away, she was still standing in the doorway.

Chapter Thirty-eight

Sitting in his Jeep in front of the Douglas County Sheriff's office, Dexter leafed through the photocopies of the various news articles he'd collected. Together they provided the skeleton of a homicide, but because of the age of the perpetrator, it was lacking the detail necessary to flesh out the story. Mrs. Ulmer had provided some detail, but as Dexter studied the blurry face of the young girl in the photo, he wondered what had really been going on at 1811 Oaks Avenue to drive her to such an extreme act. Did the man standing behind her in the photo abuse her, as she claimed in court? After talking to the mother, it seemed likely, but a jury had found her guilty anyway. Maybe she was mentally ill, or even a sociopath. But if that were the case, wouldn't she have been sent to a hospital instead of Southern Oaks? The obvious next step was find out what had happened to Sara Ulmer after her incarceration.

Ten minutes later Deputy Addison once again led Dexter through the same maze of hallways to the same file room as before. He explained that he wanted to find out what had become of Sara Ulmer since her 1975 arrest—where was she today?

"After more than thirty years? Good luck."

"Her mother places her in Higgins Point in 1984. But that's all I have."

"Terrific, only twenty-one years ago."

"There's nothing I can do?"

Deputy Addison sighed. "She was tried as a minor, so they would have let her go when she hit twenty-one," she explained. "I suppose we could start by finding out who her parole officer was. She was fifteen when she went in, in 1975, so she would have been released in 1981 at the latest. We can look up the parole reports."

"Am I going to have to get another signature from Judge Cleary?"

"Good point." The deputy went to a file drawer next to her desk and pulled out a slip of paper. When she laid it on the desk, Dexter saw that it was his original release form.

"Do you have the same pen you used when you filled this out?" she asked.

"Sure." Dexter took the pen from his pocket and offered it to her, but she declined and instead indicated the line on the form that asked for a description of the information to be released.

"Where you printed *arrest files*," she explained, "just add *and parole records* after it."

Dexter felt a little nervous. "Are you sure?"

Deputy Addison scowled. "Did Cleary bother to read it the first time?"

"I see what you mean."

Dexter did as she asked, and Deputy Addison returned the form to the file cabinet and said she'd be right back. A few minutes later she handed Dexter a copy of the file that had been kept by Sara Ulmer's parole officer. It indicated her address, 917 6th Street in Superior; her employer, McDonald's; and brief monthly notations of her parole meetings—up to a point. According to the record she was very good at keeping her appointments, but the visits stopped abruptly in August of 1983. All there was in the file by way of explanation was a note by the case officer stating that Sara Ulmer had disappeared and was in violation of her parole.

"She ran," Dexter said, flipping the packet of papers closed. "But the only record that the Wisconsin DMV had of her was the license application in 1981—nothing later."

"She either headed out of state," Deputy Addison explained, "or changed her name. Probably both."

"If she changed her name, there'd be a record, right?"

She shook her head. "If she changed it to violate parole, she would have purchased a phony ID and done it illegally."

Dexter thought for a minute. Sara had gone to prison for poisoning her father in 1975, and Mrs. Ulmer placed her daughter at the Pearle estate in 1984, where Ellie Myers had also been murdered. The fact that the same poison had been used in both murders was too great a coincidence. And Sara Ulmer's name appearing in Berglund's notes could possibly provide her with a motive in his death as well, if she was still around and knew he was investigating her. The only women at the Pearle estate who had been around in '84 and were still there were Wallace's wife, Roberta, and her friend Louise Dahlman. Frankly, the quiet, mousy Louise didn't strike Dexter as the serial killer type, but he could easily work up his enthusiasm for Roberta Pearle. He recalled her imperious manner when she'd lectured him on the importance of her husband's legacy in the art world. Paris Hilton, she had told him, is famous; my husband is eminent. Dexter actually could believe that she was willing to preserve her husband's eminence by any means necessary—including murder.

"Where's the DMV office?"

Fifteen minutes later Dexter walked into the Douglas County Department of Motor Vehicles at 4th and Ogden. The modern, one-story building looked tall in an area dominated by vacant lots. Dexter's request was simple: run a computer check on Roberta Kaplan, Mrs. Pearle's maiden name. Inside of five minutes he was handed two sheets of paper covering her vehicle history in Wisconsin. According to the records, Roberta Kaplan first applied for a driver's license in 1983 at the age of twenty-one. He couldn't find any record of Roberta Kaplan prior to 1983, and her DMV records also showed a change of address in 1984, to Higgins Point. The address she moved from was 917 6th Street in Superior.

Chapter Thirty-nine

Dexter stopped for a bite to eat on the way back from Superior, and it was almost 9:00 P.M. when he finally walked into his office. He called Ann on her cell phone and caught her just as she and Zack were finishing the Friday fish fry at Janet's. He asked her to come to his office and bring Zack. He was prepared to explain why, but to his surprise she didn't ask, just said they were on their way. Dexter sat down and was spreading the results of his day's research across his desk to look it over one more time when he noticed a sheet of paper sitting in his fax machine. It was from the sheriff's department. He read it and tossed it onto the desk with the rest of the papers. Just then Grady called to report that he was having a beer with Dexter's uncle at Dick's Bar. Did Dexter want to join them? Dexter declined but told him if he wanted to see something interesting, he should stop by the office and bring Delmar. Fifteen minutes later, Dexter's office was packed. Ann and Zack, having arrived first, had claimed the only two chairs other than Dexter's, leaving Grady and Delmar to lean against the counter.

Zack gestured at the array of papers in front of Dexter. "Got something to show us, Sherlock?" Zack had temporar-

ily abandoned his usual chewing gum in favor of a toothpick, which he was maneuvering in an attempt to dislodge
the stubborn remnants of breaded cod from his teeth. "We
may have a little news for you too," he said.

"Dexter, is all that material from Superior?" Ann asked.

"What would you say," Dexter asked the group in general,
"if I told you I may have solved two murders simultaneously?"

Everyone in the office glanced at everyone else for a few
seconds.

"Is he talking about Donald Berglund and the casino manager?" Zack asked.

"I don't think so," Ann said.

"Not too late for the rest of Happy Hour at Dick's," Grady
said, voicing his skepticism.

Ann raised a restraining hand. "Hold it, now. I think we
should at least hear him out."

The room fell silent, and they all looked at Dexter.

"I found the name Sara Ulmer in Donald Berglund's
notes," he began. "Donald's files didn't have any information on her, at least none I could find, just the name. I didn't
know if she would turn out to be important or not, but I decided to check her out. I mentioned her to Annie this morning, and she helped me with a starting point, Superior."

"So that's where you been all day," Grady said.

"What'd you find out?" Delmar asked.

"I found out that Sara Ulmer murdered her own father in
1975, at the age of fifteen. Her defense was that he'd been
abusing her, but the jury didn't buy it, and they sent her to
Southern Oaks School for Girls in Union Grove, Wisconsin."

"Southern Oaks, what kind of place is that?" Delmar asked.

"Female juvenile correctional," Ann explained. "The
name's misleading; they take them all, up to and including
homicide."

"Since they didn't try her as an adult," Dexter continued,
"they had to release her when she turned twenty-one. That

was 1981. She ducked out on her parole around August of 1983, and I believe she assumed another identity."

They all stared at Dexter, until Zack finally asked, "What's this got to do with anything?"

"I believe the identity she assumed was that of Roberta Kaplan."

"Never heard of her," Zack said.

"She's currently known as Mrs. Roberta Pearle," Dexter explained.

"Oh," Zack said, "that Roberta."

Ann's expression betrayed legitimate shock. "How sure are you?"

Dexter explained how the DMV records showed no trace of Roberta Kaplan prior to 1983. And then, when she showed up in the system, she had the same address, 917 6th Street in Superior, as Sara Ulmer, who had disappeared around that time. "Roberta showed up at Wallace Pearle's estate in 1984, where she enrolled as an art student. A few months later Ellie Myers was murdered."

"Maybe she was just in the wrong place at the wrong time," Grady offered.

"Remember how Ellie Myers died?" Dexter asked him.

"Belladonna," Grady answered.

"Sara Ulmer used belladonna on her father."

Ann leaned forward and cleared her throat. "But why would Roberta Kaplan want to kill Ellie Myers? What's her motive?"

Dexter shrugged. "Maybe Ellie Myers found out the truth about her, or maybe Roberta just wanted her out of the way; she did end up marrying Wallace a year later. Anyway, I think she might have murdered Donald Berglund too."

Ann and Zack looked at each other. "Because he uncovered her past?" Ann asked.

Dexter nodded. "Her name was in his file, and he was researching something in Superior. Maybe she thought he was going to uncover her murder of Ellie Myers. At the very least you have to assume he might have eventually exposed her past."

"Wasn't that Berglund guy poisoned, too?" Delmar asked.

"He was," Zack said. "But even if you can prove that Roberta Pearle is really Sara Ulmer, you can't prove she's guilty of anything other than jumping parole—what?—twenty-some years ago."

Dexter picked up the fax sheet that had been waiting for him when he walked in and laid it in front of Zack. "Late-breaking news just in."

Ann and Zack both leaned forward, joined by Grady and Delmar, rubbernecking over their shoulders.

"Let me give you the Cliff Notes version," Dexter said. "Sara Ulmer's prints, which were on file with the state from her time at Southern Oaks, were found not only in Donald Berglund's Volvo but actually on the KFC box that contained the poisoned chicken."

Delmar reached past Ann and picked up a photocopy of a photograph lying on Dexter's desk. "What's this?"

"That's the newspaper photo of Sara Ulmer's family," Dexter explained.

"So the little girl in this picture is the one you're talking about?" Delmar asked. "The serial killer?"

"If you include her father, I think Sara Ulmer, alias Roberta Kaplan, murdered three people," Dexter announced. "And I'm starting to be suspicious of Fitzner's heart attack."

Zack looked at Ann. "Go ahead. I'll let you tell him."

"A couple of hours ago the lab report came back positive for a toxic substance," Ann explained. "Fitzner didn't have a heart attack. He was poisoned."

"Just like the others," Zack said.

"See what you started, Dex?" Grady added.

"Way to go, nephew—a four-bagger," Delmar said.

"Four murders with similar means," Ann said. "That's worse odds than the lottery, but what about motive? Why would Roberta Pearle want to murder the Englishman?"

"There is a motive," Dexter said. "Pearle's wife is a fanatic about her husband's precious legacy. I got the impression that she'd gladly crush anyone who threatened it. If Edward Fitzner was the only person who knew that Wallace had once been involved in art forgery, and she eliminated him, Wallace's reputation would be secure."

Zack shook his head. "But Fitzner wasn't the only person who knew."

"Donald Berglund knew," Dexter pointed out, "and he's dead. And Grady and I only found Berglund's notes yesterday morning. There's no reason to expect Roberta to know that we knew, at least not before it was too late for Fitzner."

"Too late?" Zack asked.

"If the poison was put in something ahead of time," Dexter explained.

"Then Fitzner died needlessly," Ann said.

"And if I'm right about her being Sara Ulmer," Dexter said, "then we know she was in Berglund's car and handled the murder weapon."

"Murder weapon?" Grady asked.

"The chicken," Zack explained, "would be the murder weapon."

"So we check her prints, and when they match, we have more than circumstantial evidence."

Ann nodded.

"I'm going to go have a chat with her first thing in the morning," Dexter announced. "Annie, want to tag along?"

Ann smiled. "What should I wear?"

Chapter Forty

December 1984

The queasy sensation in Ellie Myers' stomach was not going away. It had come on shortly after she and Wallace began the first piece and had only intensified. They were now in the middle of the last piece, and she was definitely coming down with some kind of bug. There was a brief break in her part, which allowed her to rest and prepare for the next section. She glanced up from her sheet music at Wallace, who was throwing his usual emotional vigor into his playing; he tended to let his head roll around slightly, as if he were transported by the music. But he couldn't have been too transported, because Ellie caught an unmistakable look pass between him and Roberta. *My God,* she thought, *he's actually flirting with the bitch while he's playing a duet with me in front of half a dozen people.*

Ellie's bags were packed up in her room, ready to throw into her car immediately upon ending the session. She'd placed the sapphire necklace, in its box, on top of his socks in Wallace's top dresser drawer, where he would be sure to find it. Her plan was to bring her things to her parents' house and stay with them for a while, long enough to jettison Wallace from her system. It shouldn't take long. Wallace still had no idea she was even leaving, let alone doing it tonight. Her plan was to tell him on the way out of the house with her last load. She hadn't come up with a really good kiss-off line yet, though she was sure she would be inspired when the time came.

Ellie felt a bit dizzy and had started to sweat. It was getting so bad that the clarinet felt slippery in her hand. Whatever bug she had caught wasn't like any flu she was accustomed to. As she brought her clarinet up to her mouth, she glanced at her portrait above the fireplace, illuminated by a spotlight. Happier times for sure, she thought. She wet her reed, noting once again the odd taste. *Everything tastes funny when you're sick,* she reasoned.

She managed to make it to the end of the last piece but barely made it up the stairs to the bathroom before throwing up. Afterward, in her room, she was a little surprised that she didn't feel any sense of relief, as she normally would after vomiting when sick. She placed her clarinet in its case and into the cardboard box containing her personal effects and thought briefly about the envelope lying at the bottom of the box. It contained evidence of Wallace's forgery activities, but Ellie still hadn't been able to confront him with her knowledge. At this point she was inclined to let the whole thing go and just enjoy knowing that, in the whole world, she alone knew the truth about Wallace Pearle, the great painter.

She managed to carry her cardboard box down to her car, put it in the trunk, and get back up without seeing Wallace, so he still didn't know she was leaving. When she got back to her room, the worsening pains in her stomach convinced her to lie down for a bit before attempting the drive to her parents' house. The sweats she had experienced earlier had turned into chills, so she switched off the light and got under the covers to take a short nap. When she felt better, she would take the rest of her bags down and tell Wallace what he could do with his job.

Chapter Forty-one

Saturday

Ann and Dexter got out of his Jeep and walked quickly through the early-morning drizzle to the protection of the ivy-draped overhang that sheltered the Pearles' front porch. Dexter rang the bell, and a minute later Roberta Pearle opened the front door. She stood in the doorway, staring at Dexter, and finally said, "Good morning, Sheriff."

"Good morning, Mrs. Pearle. I'm not the sheriff. The sheriff's the guy in the uniform, remember? I'm the police chief."

She looked Dexter over, taking in his blue jeans and khaki shirt. "That's right, he's the one with the uniform." She continued to block the doorway, saying nothing more.

"Uh, Mrs. Pearle, may we come in?" Dexter finally asked.

As she stared at him, Dexter swore he could almost feel the heat of a laser beam searing into him. She finally stepped aside and walked away from the door, allowing Ann and Dexter to step into the foyer. Dexter unconsciously wiped his feet on the rug in front of the door.

Roberta turned and stood before them, her arms crossed.

"Wallace is in his study. You'll excuse me if I don't escort you." She thought about it for a minute and apparently felt the need to add, "You've destroyed my husband's career. I can't imagine what more you could possibly expect to accomplish here."

Dexter decided that there probably wasn't any use in pointing out that he'd had nothing to do with leaking the story of her husband's forgeries to the press. "Actually, we're here to talk to you, Mrs. Pearle."

"Me?" Roberta seemed genuinely surprised. "After the way you've treated us, why would I wish to talk to you?"

Dexter wondered if this was where he was supposed to threaten to "take her downtown," but Ann cut off any debate by saying, "Why don't we all sit down somewhere."

Roberta hesitated and then led them into the great room. They seated themselves on a plush, overstuffed leather couch and chairs, facing one another across a massively heavy-looking glass coffee table. Once settled in, Roberta immediately returned to the subject that was clearly uppermost in her mind.

"I wonder if you can appreciate the irreparable damage to my husband's reputation that you've caused."

"With Donald Berglund and Edward Fitzner's deaths for the press to focus on," Dexter pointed out, "your husband probably won't even make the papers."

"It's only eight-thirty, and we're already getting phone calls this morning from some bottom-feeding reporter who calls himself Kahler. One of you police must have told him."

Dexter shook his head and smiled. "Nope. Frank Kahler uses a police scanner."

Roberta fixed him with a withering look. "Although you may find this whole sorry episode amusing"—she looked again at Dexter's jeans and khaki shirt—"*Chief* Loomis, I can assure you, it is not. What it is, is nothing less than an attack on the legacy my husband has spent a lifetime building."

"I see your point," Dexter said. "I suppose getting exposed as an art forger isn't going to do his legacy any good at all. But if he actually did it, I don't see how you really have a lot of high moral ground to stand on." Dexter thought Roberta was going to explode. "I'm sorry about your husband's career problem, but that's not why we're here, Mrs. Pearle. Or should I say Sara?"

"Who?"

Dexter tried to gauge her sincerity. "Sara Ulmer," he repeated.

"Who is Sara Ulmer?"

"You are," Dexter said.

Roberta looked back and forth between them. "I am? Is this some sort of joke?"

"How old are you?" Dexter asked.

Roberta, completely thrown by the non sequitur, took a moment to regain her bearings. "I'm forty-seven," she finally said.

"So in 1983, you would have been—what?—twenty-three."

"I suppose, yes."

"But we couldn't find any record of you prior to 1983. It's as if you sprang into existence fully grown."

Roberta stared at Dexter as though she had no idea what language he was speaking. When it became clear to Dexter that she wasn't going to respond, he said, "I know your story, Sara. I know about your father, and the . . . abuse. I know that you poisoned him in 1975 and went to prison for it. I can't imagine how desperate you had to be to do something like that, but it's only natural to want to suppress such a painful memory."

"Murder my father? Are you insane? And why do you keep calling me that?"

"Because that's your name, Sara," Dexter said.

"No, my name is Roberta Pearle."

Dexter consulted his notepad. "DMV records show that in

1983 you were living at 917 6th Street, in Superior, when you applied for a license in the name of Roberta Kaplan."

"Why would you examine my driving record?"

"Is that true?"

"Roberta Kaplan was my maiden name, yes."

"And the address?"

Roberta shook her head. "I honestly can't remember what my address was in 1983, but I did live in Superior."

"That's also the last known address for Sara Ulmer before she ducked out on her parole and disappeared in 1983. The addresses match because until you changed your name in 1983, you were Sara Ulmer."

"But I didn't 'duck out' on any parole, and I'm not Sara Ulmer."

"We're not here about the parole violation," Dexter said. "We're here because we believe you've murdered two more people since leaving prison."

"Possibly three," Ann added, "if Mr. Fitzner was one of yours."

Roberta's mouth was working slowly, but no sound was coming out. Dexter thought that being confronted with her lies might be sending her into some kind of shock.

"The poison you used on your father in 1975 matches the type you used on Ellie Myers in 1984," Dexter said. "And we have your fingerprints in the car that Donald Berglund was driving the night he died, and also on the KFC box that held the poisoned chicken." Dexter leaned forward in his chair and spoke softly at Roberta's downturned head. "Why don't you just admit it? You'll feel better. I spoke with your mother yesterday—she still loves you. She told me she believes you were telling the truth about your father. She wants you to come home, Sara."

Roberta raised her head slowly. "You couldn't have spoken to my mother," she said. "She died in 1991, of a stroke."

Dexter looked at Ann, who returned his confused look.

"I came into this country illegally, in 1983," Roberta explained.

"Illegally?" Dexter asked. "From where?"

"Canada."

"Where in Canada?" Ann asked.

"A town called Kenora, in Ontario. And my father wasn't abusing me—he was just a jerk."

Dexter hesitated and then wrote this information down. "How did you get your new identity?"

"What new identity?"

"You mean Roberta Kaplan was your real name?"

Roberta nodded.

"Well, then, it'll be easy enough to check out. And in the meantime we're going to bring you in and take your prints, to see if they match the ones found in Berglund's car. If they do, it won't make much difference what you call yourself."

Roberta stood up. "If that will prove to you that I'm telling the truth, I'll go with you." She started to move around the table, then paused. "And then you'll believe me?"

"As long as the prints don't match," Dexter said.

Chapter Forty-two

Dexter picked up his desk phone and dialed slowly, looking at Ann. She took a sip of the coffee he had provided for her and then set the cup on top of the desktop collage of documents that made up Sara Ulmer's paper trail. Ann was sitting where Grady usually sat, facing Dexter across his desk, while they waited for the lab to tell them that Roberta Pearle's prints matched Sara Ulmer's.

"Hello, is this Connie? Yeah, it's Dexter. Can I talk to the sheriff?"

Dexter held his hand over the phone, expecting to say something to Ann while the call was transferred to Tilsen's office, but he couldn't think of anything to say.

"Yeah, Bob? It's Dex. What? Right, she was brought in for fingerprints a little bit ago. Calm down—we let her go home. We're waiting for the results—that's not why I'm calling."

Dexter paused while Tilsen went on a small tirade about "rousting" a pillar of society like Roberta Pearle. He eventually ran out of steam and asked Dexter why he was calling.

"I want you to issue an APB on my uncle, Delmar Loomis."

Dexter put his hand over the mouthpiece again. "I think he's laughing."

"No, I'm serious, Bob. Burglary. Specifically, the Pearle burglary. He was gone when I woke up this morning. Evidence? For now let's just say a nephew knows these things, okay? All right, thanks. I'll be in touch. Bye."

"He said he was sure he'd seen Delmar somewhere before."

"Dexter, how do you know he did it?" Ann asked.

"I'll tell you later. Right now I want to keep my eye on the ball," he said, indicating the pile of papers on the desk between them. "I'm starting to wonder. Mrs. Pearle seemed genuinely sincere, and without the prints, it's all circumstantial. What if I've made a big mistake?"

"If she's really crazy enough to murder all those people," Ann pointed out, "she probably would come off as sincere. And except for the prints, which we don't actually have yet," she added, "you're right, it's totally circumstantial—like most murder cases. All we can do is try to pile on the evidence until it outweighs any reasonable doubt. But if we can prove she actually handled the KFC box, that would be the ball game."

Dexter finally voiced what had been bothering him the most since talking with Roberta Pearle. "We don't have an airtight motive, do we?"

"We've got the motive you provided; she killed Berglund because he was investigating Ellie Myers' death and got too close to the truth."

"I know that's what I said," Dexter agreed, "but that only makes sense if she also murdered Ellie Myers, because *that's* the secret she would have been trying to protect."

"That's true."

"And aside from the use of belladonna in both murders, there's nothing that implicates Sara Ulmer in Ellie Myers' death."

"Like you said, Dexter, it's circumstantial."

Suddenly the phone rang, and for just a second Dexter imagined that they'd somehow managed to pick up his uncle already.

"Chief Loomis, Higgins Point police. Uncle Delmar!" Dexter glanced at Ann, who sat up straight.

"Hey, Del. Am I ever glad you called. I feel like a complete idiot. Knowing what my dad did for a living, how could I not realize that you did it too? Hell, you two were probably partners. Dexter listened for a minute and then put his hand over the phone. "He says, 'No partners. You got a partner, you got a problem.' " Ann smiled.

"You're going to have to come to my office and turn yourself in. What? What photo? Oh, the photo of the Ulmer family, sure."

Dexter fished around on his desk until he found the photocopy of the photograph of the Ulmer family that he'd gotten in Superior. "What about it? Right, the little girl in the picture is Sara Ulmer. We think she's a serial killer."

Dexter put his hand over the phone again and said, "I don't know what he's talking about."

"What? Yeah, we're pretty sure that Roberta Pearle is Sara. Why? You were here last night—you know why." Dexter listened for a minute, while his world crumbled around him. "Are you sure? Of course I believe you know your way around a strange house—at least I do now. And you're sure it was in her dresser? Okay. Hey, Del, you have to come in. There's an APB out on you. Del? Uncle Delmar?"

Dexter set the phone down. "He hung up. Oh, well. I tried to talk him into coming in."

"Or warned him to stay away," Ann pointed out.

Dexter cleared his throat. "Uh, I suppose that's right."

"What was that all about?" Ann asked.

Dexter took a deep breath. "Del told me that while he was burglarizing the Pearle estate, he saw that same Ulmer family photo, but the original, in the bottom drawer of a dresser—and it wasn't Roberta's dresser."

Ann thought for a minute. "Louise Dahlman?"

Dexter nodded slowly.

"Is he sure?"

"That's what I asked, and I got a lecture on how, after a lifetime in the business, he knows his way around a strange house."

Suddenly Dexter's fax machine rang. They waited silently while it rang a second time before the customary high-pitched tone indicated it was receiving a transmission. Dexter walked over and picked up the single page the machine kicked out. It contained the results of the fingerprint analysis they had requested: Roberta Pearle was not a match for Sara Ulmer. He handed it to Ann.

"How did I manage to come up with the same address for Roberta Kaplan and Sara Ulmer?" Dexter asked.

"Roberta Pearle and Louise Dahlman are friends. They both came to the Pearle estate at the same time," Ann pointed out. "They must have been roommates back in Superior."

"We have to go pick up Louise Dahlman," Dexter said.

Chapter Forty-three

W hen Ann and Dexter arrived back at the Pearle estate, Wallace answered the door, waving them in from the rain with sharp, jerky movements of his left hand.

"Quickly, she's in the kitchen."

"Who's in the kitchen?" Dexter asked.

"Louise, of course. She's in there with Roberta. That's why I called you."

Dexter and Ann looked at each other. "Nobody called us," Ann explained.

"But I phoned the police." Wallace paused to think for a second. His voice held the tenuous quaver of barely controlled panic. "That's right, I only just set the phone down. You couldn't have gotten here that quickly." He began leading them out of the foyer toward the kitchen in the rear of the house. "Then why are you here?"

"We're here," Dexter said to his departing back, "because the results of the fingerprint analysis came back, and we know your wife was telling the truth. I'm sorry about the way I handled it, by the way."

Wallace paused and turned around, fixing Dexter with an

icy stare. "By leaking my indiscretion to the public, you have destroyed me, Chief Loomis."

"You're still the same man," Dexter pointed out. "The only damage is to your reputation."

"I am my reputation. Roberta was right about that."

"We're here to see Louise Dahlman," Ann said, trying to get them back on track. "You said she was in the kitchen."

"That's right." Wallace turned and hurried toward the kitchen, seeming to regain the thread of the emergency at hand. "And she's gotten hold of my gun."

"Gun?" Dexter said.

"From my office," Wallace explained. "I keep a revolver in the desk. I didn't realize she knew about it."

"Is she threatening Roberta with it?" Ann asked.

"As far as I know, she's only threatening herself—so far."

"How long have they been in there?" Dexter asked.

"Only a few minutes. Roberta told Louise that the police were checking the fingerprints from Donald Berglund's car against hers. When she learned that, she became extremely agitated. She disappeared for a few minutes, and then Roberta saw her walk into the kitchen carrying my gun. I was on the phone with the police when Roberta went in to talk to her."

They'd arrived at the kitchen door, which was closed. Dexter turned to Ann and whispered, "I'm going in."

"That's not a good idea, Dexter," Ann replied quietly. "You should wait for backup."

"You're my backup. When the others get here, just make sure they don't do anything rash, okay?"

Ann nodded and then grabbed Dexter's arm. "At least take my Glock in with you."

Dexter considered it and then shook his head. "She's only threatening herself. I'm not going to give her the opportunity for death by cop." He gently pushed the kitchen door open and stepped inside, letting it close behind him.

The kitchen was lit by the pale morning sun except for a single light above the table on the other side of the center counter, where Roberta Pearle was seated with Louise Dahlman. When Dexter entered, they both looked up at him. Louise was drinking coffee and had a tiny crooked smile on her face, and Roberta's expression was one that Dexter would describe as dazed disbelief. The gun was lying on the table a few inches from Louise's right hand.

Louise calmly watched as Dexter walked slowly across the kitchen and around the counter. Without waiting for an invitation, he sat down and joined the two ladies at the table. He pulled a small pad of paper and a pen out of his pocket, then took a long breath. He looked at the gun and then directly at Louise.

"Hello, Sara." When she heard her real name, some faint emotion seemed to flicker across her eyes. "How about if I take care of that for you?"

Sara's hand moved to the gun, not to pick it up, but protectively. "No," she said softly.

Dexter decided to drop it for now. "I know how you fed belladonna to your father," he said, "and I have a general idea why he may have deserved it. I know about the years you spent at Southern Oaks and how you jumped parole in August of eighty-three. It's fairly clear that you assumed the identity of Louise Dahlman sometime before you came to Higgins Point."

During Dexter's brief narration, Sara brought her coffee to her lips and took a slow sip, watching Dexter over the top of the cup. "The way you say it, quick like that, it sounds like nothing, like a vacation or something."

"I'm sorry. I didn't mean—"

"I thought my father was bad news until they put me in that 'school.' Things happened in that place." She paused. "If I hadn't met Roberta when I got out, I don't know what I would have done."

"Did she help you?"

Sara looked at Roberta. "She's the only person who was ever there for me. Who ever cared about me. Who ever liked me."

Roberta reached over and took Sara's hand in hers.

"I'd do anything for Roberta," Sara said.

"Why don't you tell me about Ellie Myers?"

Sara set her cup back on the table. "You should ask Roberta about her."

Roberta looked at Dexter, and he noticed that her eyes were shiny with tears.

"She—" When Roberta looked at Sara, she couldn't get the rest of it out.

"I poisoned her," Sara said simply.

Wishing he'd brought a tape recorder with him, Dexter said, "Just like that? You poisoned her?"

Sara nodded.

"Why should I ask Roberta about it?"

"Because I did it for her." Sara said this as though it should have been obvious to anybody but a simpleton.

"I'm afraid I don't—"

"Ellie Myers had no idea how great an artist Wallace really was," Sara explained.

When she offered nothing more, Dexter said, "Do you really think that's a reason to murder somebody?"

"She didn't have a clue as to what he was all about; she simply did not deserve him. Wallace needed someone to nurture his talent, to watch over his legacy. He needed someone who could understand and appreciate him—like Roberta."

Roberta dropped her head into her hands.

"Are you saying that you murdered her to get her out of the way, so Roberta could have Wallace Pearle to herself?"

Sara cleared her throat and took another sip of coffee. "Roberta wanted him to understand where he stood in the grand scheme, to know he ranked with the great artists. Ellie Myers would have ruined Wallace. She would have ruined all our lives."

Roberta was sobbing quietly now. She raised her red, tear-stained face to Dexter and shook her head slowly.

"That's too bad for Ellie Myers," Dexter said.

"I was sorry to have to do that. I didn't enjoy it."

"I'll be sure to pass your sentiment on to her folks."

This comment brought no reaction from Sara.

"Did Roberta help you kill her?" Dexter doubted it, but he thought he'd ask anyway.

"No!" Sara said sharply. "Roberta had nothing to do with it—with anything. I changed my name before we met."

Dexter glanced at Roberta. "So she never knew you as Sara Ulmer?"

"No."

"Did you tell her about poisoning Ellie Myers—after?"

Sara shook her head. "Not until today."

Dexter jotted this down. "You murdered Ellie to get her out of the way, as a favor to Roberta. So I guess you didn't know Ellie was planning to leave Wallace anyway."

Sara gave Dexter a surprised look.

"It's true. Ellie Myers was leaving Wallace. Her parents told me she'd arranged to move out on the night she died. She was going to play one last duet with him, but you made sure it really was her last."

"I don't expect you to understand."

"Unfortunately, I think I'm beginning to understand all too well. You believed you were doing Roberta a favor—that it was worth a human life to preserve your comfortable, easy lives."

Sara took another sip of coffee.

"How about two human lives? You killed Donald Berglund too, didn't you? Your prints are all over the KFC box we found in his car."

Sara set her cup down as a look of pain crossed her face. She put her head down for a moment, and as soon as she did, Dexter stood up, reached across the table, and grabbed the gun. Sara looked up suddenly and watched Dexter open the gun's cylinder and dump the six bullets into the palm of his hand. He put them into his pocket.

"I found your name in his notes," Dexter said. "Did you murder him because he found out who you really are?"

Sara shook her head as though she were dealing with a slow child. "It's not about me. It never was. I did it for Roberta. To keep Wallace's forgeries from being discovered."

Dexter thought her eyes looked a little strange, a little distant. "Oh, that's right, I forgot—the legacy thing. See, Ellie's death, and Donald Berglund's, were a little personal for me. Ellie was once my babysitter and Donald seemed like a nice guy. I'm just curious, what excuse did you give him to get into his car the night you murdered him?"

Sara was looking down at the table. She took several shallow breaths. "I'm associated with Roberta, who's Wallace's business manager as well as his wife, remember? I told Donald that I had a message for him from Wallace about a compromise on the book they were discussing." When she looked up, Dexter noticed that her face had gone pale.

"Sometimes a sacrifice is necessary for the greater good," she added.

Dexter shook his head. "That'd be a noble thought—if you hadn't let two other people make the sacrifices for you."

"Three other people."

Dexter looked at Sara more closely and for the first time thought he noticed a delicate sheen of sweat forming on her face. "Three people? Oh, that's right—Edward Fitzncr, Wallace's accomplice in the forgeries. I suppose you murdered him because he could have threatened Wallace's legacy too."

Sara nodded.

"How did you do it?"

Sara hesitated and then said, "His Altoids."

Dexter thought back to the mints Fitzner had offered to Grady and him. "The Altoids?"

Sara nodded again. "I soaked them in poison. I wasn't sure it would work—I guess it did."

Dexter shook his head. "By the time he died this morning, we'd already found Berglund's notes about the forgery, so it didn't make any difference—except to him, of course. And by the way," Dexter added, "I almost ate one of his mints myself."

Sara doubled over, and Dexter suddenly realized why she'd been coughing—she'd poisoned herself. He grabbed her cup. It was empty. "What was in here?"

Her breath was coming in ragged gasps, and she was sweating freely. She began coughing and then gasped and doubled over again. Roberta jumped out of her chair and stood frozen with her back against a kitchen wall. Dexter also jumped up, sending his chair toppling over backward. He came around the table and grabbed Sara, cursing himself for playing detective instead of paying attention.

Sara's body was wet with sweat, and she was jerking involuntarily, trying to curl up into a ball.

"Get in here!" Dexter yelled. "She poisoned herself. Call an ambulance."

At the sound of Dexter's voice the kitchen door burst open, and several sheriff's deputies rushed in. Two of them, their uniforms still wet from the rain, helped Dexter carry Sara's doubled-over form out of the kitchen to the couch in the front room.

Roberta followed slowly, repeating softly, "Why would she do that?"

Dexter knelt next to the couch and put his face close to Sara's, speaking loudly. "What did you take? What's the antidote?"

Sara rolled onto her side on the couch and doubled into

the fetal position. The spasms were coming almost constantly now. The blood she was choking up spattered the
area of the couch in front of her.

Dexter racked his brain to try to remember what you were
supposed to do in the event of a poisoning. Induce vomiting
was all he could come up with. That didn't seem to apply in
this instance, however, because Sara was already vomiting—
blood, in a steady flow now. Roberta, having apparently recovered somewhat, came hurrying out of the kitchen
carrying a damp cloth, which she placed on Sara's forehead.
Sara seemed to be struggling to say something. Dexter put
his ear close. Her voice was weak, but he could just make out
her words, forcing themselves out past the bloody froth on
her lips.

"Too late. It's too late."

Then Roberta took Sara's hand and moved Dexter aside,
cradling Sara's head in her other arm. "Oh, my God, hold
on, Sara," she said. "An ambulance is coming."

Sara's entire body was clenched rigidly against the pain,
and her breathing was almost imperceptible now. This lasted
for perhaps a minute, and then suddenly there was a release,
and Sara went limp. Dexter noticed that the blood had
stopped flowing from her mouth.

Roberta looked up at Dexter through her tears, and he
shook his head slowly. Roberta touched Sara's hair and began to cry. Then she looked at Dexter again. "She said something. What was it?"

Dexter's brain froze. What should he tell her?

"I saw her trying to talk. Please tell me what she said,"
Roberta pleaded.

"She said . . ." Dexter hesitated, thinking. "She said she
wanted you to forgive her."

Chapter Forty-four

Sunday

Ann stood next to Dexter in his living room, staring at the blank spot on the wall above the couch, where his watercolor used to hang.

"He took it with him," Ann said.

"You were there when I gave it to him," Dexter pointed out. "It was his to take."

"The search came up empty. If they haven't found him yet," Ann said, "I have a hunch they're not going to."

Dexter nodded in agreement. "Maybe *they* won't, but Valerie McBride stopped by this morning on her way out of town. She's decided to take my uncle's disappearance personally. She said something about 'hunting him down,' and judging by the way she was acting, I don't give him much of a chance."

There was a moment of silence, and then Ann said, "I wonder if the count stops at four."

Dexter considered this. "She said 'three other people.' Counting her father, that's four."

"Think she was telling the truth?"

"At that point she didn't have any reason to lie—not anymore. I believe her when she said she did it for Roberta."

Dexter put an arm around Ann's shoulder. "Asta misses you." Ann looked up at him, and he could see the doubt surfacing in her eyes, but she didn't pull away. "I miss you too," he added.

"Dexter, I—"

"Annie, I'm sorry for the way I acted last summer. I don't have any excuse except to say that sometimes it takes a while for a person to figure out what he wants."

"And now you know what you want?"

Dexter had no trouble maintaining a steady gaze into Ann's green eyes. "I believe I do. Are you going to give me a chance to prove it?"

Ann finally smiled. "How can I refuse? You've got my curiosity up now."

Dexter turned Ann toward him, leaned down, and kissed her. He wrapped her in his arms, and when he buried his face in her neck, the scent of her hair carried him away. Ann's hands were warm on his back. They stood like that for several minutes, their curves blending softly, feeling each other breathe, until finally, reluctantly, Dexter released her. They smiled at each other, and then suddenly Ann's eyes grew large.

"Oh, by the way, Dexter, you should enjoy hearing this. The Feds took Manzara into custody last night. Hatch got somebody to talk in the Danvers killing, and they're going ahead with a murder indictment."

"Wow," Dexter said. "Who spilled?"

"His bodyguard, a guy named Pete Gumbusky. Apparently he contacted the sheriff and told him he wanted to go into the witness protection program. Can you believe it?"

Dexter grinned. "Now, that's a smart career move." Then he snapped his fingers. "Before I forget . . ." He walked to the front hall closet, reached up to the shelf, and took down a rolled up canvas.

"What's that?" Ann asked.

Dexter walked into the dining room and unrolled the canvas, spreading it out on the table. "That is *Girl on a Window Seat.*"

"That's the painting that was stolen from the Pearle estate," Ann said, and then realized what she'd just said. "That's the painting *your uncle* stole from the Pearle estate."

"Correct."

"But how did you get it?"

"I removed it from the back of the watercolor I gave to Delmar," Dexter explained. "He'd hidden it between my painting and the backing board."

They both studied the painting for a minute, while Ann sorted this out. "But how did you know it was there?"

"I got suspicious when my uncle kept raving about my watercolor and then asked to buy it. I mean, come on. I'm a rank amateur. The painting didn't rate the praise."

Ann looked at him. "Dexter, I think your paintings are great."

"You might be a little biased. Anyway, I decided to check, so I opened up the back, and there it was."

They both looked at the painting again, and as Dexter gazed at Ellie Myers' beautiful face framed with golden braids, he thought of her parents and the cold comfort the closure of her murder case had brought them.

"So that's Ellie Myers," Ann said.

"My old babysitter."

"When did you figure this out, about the painting?"

Dexter picked up the phone and dialed a number from a slip of paper he'd had in his pocket.

"After dinner on Thursday night. I waited until Del was asleep, then I got up and took the frame apart. I removed the canvas, but when I got up on Friday, Del was gone. Hello, Mr. Pearle? This is Chief Loomis. I'm sorry to bother you, but I wanted to tell you that we recovered your painting."

There was a short pause. "That's right, *Girl on a Window Seat*. If it's okay with you, I can swing by and drop it off at your convenience. Would you—"

Dexter listened for a minute, growing increasingly perplexed.

"Are you sure? Maybe you should think about—"

Dexter listened for a few more seconds.

"All right, if you're sure. This is gonna require a little paperwork, but I'll be in touch. Good-bye."

He hung up the phone and shrugged. "He says he doesn't want it back. He told me to keep it."

"Keep the painting? Seriously?"

"That's what he said."

They both looked at it again, a little more closely this time.

"How much did you say it was worth?" Ann asked.

Dexter cleared his throat. "Roberta said a quarter of a million dollars."

"Do you think the value will drop now that the mystery surrounding Ellie Myers' death has been solved?"

Dexter shrugged. "Who knows? It could go up. Doesn't really matter, though. I'm going to give it to her parents, and I don't think they're going to want to sell it."

"That seems appropriate," Ann said. "Her parents finally get the closure they've wanted for twenty years." Ann took Dexter's hand in hers. "And I get what I want, my very own police chief." She smiled at Dexter. "Isn't there anything you want?"

"Come to think of it, there is," Dexter said, gently drawing Ann's face toward his. "I want to see my uncle's face when he opens up that watercolor."